12.3.02

To Sarah

for fun, from Anne Marie

THE GOVERNOR-GENERAL'S LADY

The GOVERNOR-GENERAL'S LADY

a novel by

Jean Heyn

FITHIAN PRESS
Santa Barbara
1988

Cover illustration by Susan Billipp

To the memory of Dr. Christian Heyn,
who settled on St. Croix nearly one hundred years ago,
thus drawing the attention of the family to this island
for which we have an enduring affection.

LIBRARY OF CONGRESS
Cataloging-in-Publication Data

Heyn, Jean
The governor-general's lady / Jean Heyn.
p. cm.
ISBN 0-936784-68-7
1. Heegaard, Anna—Fiction.
2. Scholten, Peter von—Fiction.
3. Virgin Islands of the United States—History—Fiction.
I. Title.
PS3558.E86G68 1988
813'.54—dc 19   88-21257 CIP

Published by
FITHIAN PRESS
a division of John Daniel and Company
Post Office Box 21922
Santa Barbara, California 93121

Acknowledgment

MOST OF THE MAJOR characters in this novel based on the life of Anna Heegaard, mistress of Governor-General Peter Von Scholten, actually lived at the end of the eighteenth century and the first half of the nineteenth. However, the slave, No-no, is a fictious character. Adam Gottlieb, better known as Buddhoe, the leader of the slave rebellion, was very real. Many of the events in the novel are pure conjecture on my part.

I am indebted to the late Eva Lawaetz, librarian in Christiansted, who encouraged me to write about Anna Heegaard. It was she who supplied me with a list of the descendents of Charlotte Amalie Bernard which included mention of the white men with whom Anna lived. Anker Heegaard, descendent of Anna's father, and his wife Unce, have been supportive. Also I depended heavily on Florence Lewisohn's excellent history, *St. Croix under Seven Flags*.

Most especially I wish to thank my daughter, Susan Billipp, for the time and effort she invested and the artistic skill she has shown in designing the book's cover.

Chapter 1

FOR HANNAH the letter came as a welcome diversion. She had called an emergency meeting of her Board of Trustees for eight o'clock that morning to discuss the school's financial crisis. The meeting had not gone well, and by the time she returned to her office her usual optimism had deserted her. In this year of 1912, when the academic world was largely dominated by males, it was not easy for girls of modest means to go on to higher education.

She had sat down wearily at her desk. She noticed that her morning mail had been delivered, but her mind was still on the meeting. She'd have to go begging to several wealthy philanthropists in the city whom she knew were sympathetic. She knew that her father, pastor of a Moravian church in the city, would do his best to help. She was determined not to raise the tuition. It was hard enough for the girls' parents as it was.

She glanced again at her mail. Seeing that the letter on top was from her father, she opened it at once. Inside she found a note from him and a legal communication of some sort. Her father explained: *This was addressed to your mother. Apparently the sender did not realize that she passed away last year. As her sole heir this belongs to you. God bless, and love always. Dad.*

Hannah examined the legal letter and saw that the heading was that of an attorney located in the town of Christiansted on St. Croix in the West Indies. Her mother's father was a West Indian by birth, but he had died long before she was born and she knew little of his island. She was aware that her mother occasionally received word from distant cousins still living there.

She read the letter her father had enclosed. The attorney wrote to inform her mother that on the death of one Laurentius Sobotker she had become partial heir to a townhouse in Christiansted on St. Croix.

The deceased, being without issue, has left his estate to be equally divided between eight cousins, and you are one of these. The property is of no great value, the islands having come upon hard times and the house being in bad repair. The only heir now resident upon the island, Benoni Bensen, feels that the wisest course for all concerned would be to sell the property for whatever it will bring. If you agree with this line of reasoning sign in the space provided . . .

Hannah gazed out of her window across the campus. The dogwood was in bloom, airy puffs of pink and white blossoms. What is it like in the West Indies this time of year? she wondered. Not dogwood, to be sure. What would be in bloom? Poinsettias, perhaps, or hibiscus? She glanced again at the letter. Suddenly, she felt a longing to see this island where her mother's people had lived. Summer vacation was only a few weeks away. The school would be closed for two months. She could take a month's vacation, travel to the West Indies, and still have a month to work on fund raising before school opened in September. It would do her good to have a break, a complete change from administering a school in trouble. There must be practical ways to reach St. Croix. After all, trade with the West Indies had been going on for years. She rose from her desk and took her atlas down from its high shelf.

Three weeks and four days later Hannah stood on the deck of an ancient schooner watching the shoreline of the island of St. Croix grow ever wider on the horizon. She had taken a freighter from Philadelphia to St. Thomas in the Danish Virgin Islands. Here she was able to arrange passage on an old sailing ship heading for St. Croix. While on the island she would stay with her cousin, Benoni Bensen. She treasured his letter of invitation, so formal, so polite in somewhat stilted English, yet warm and welcoming. Yes, she felt that he and his wife Susanna were truly looking forward to her visit. Benoni (she wondered if friends called him Ben) had written that he would take time from his job as supervisor at the Central sugar factory to meet her if she would send a wire stating the time of her arrival.

Hannah found the sail from St. Thomas exhilerating. The wind was strong, rippling the intense blue of the sea into lacey whitecaps. The schooner was well heeled, her leeward scuppers taking on solid water. Standing by the forward mast Hannah steadied herself against it to keep her footing.

Now she could distinguish the low masonry buildings in the town of Christiansted nestling in the arms of gently curving, cushiony hills. She saw a massive red brick fort with the Danish flag flying from its ramparts sleeping in the sun, a clock tower poking up among a cluster of low corrugated iron roofs and the large red roof of what she took to be Government House. Guarding the harbor stood a tiny green island, or key. To its right stretched a long reef with wild surf pounding over it.

The schooner sailed close to the key, avoiding the shallow green water of a bay on the port, then came about. The order was given to lower sails. The schooner slid easily on its momentum over the calm water of the harbor to lay alongside the wharf where she was made fast.

Tied stern to, lay a number of inter-island sloops, heavy-hulled with stubby masts and elongated booms to accommodate big sails in light winds. Their open cockpits were loaded with stalks of bananas, sweet potatoes, cabbages, eggplant, breadfruit, crates of live chickens, and tethered goats. Their transoms were used as bargaining areas from which their owners sold their produce.

The boat people were dressed in workclothes, the men in broad-brimmed straw hats and the women with colorful turbans on their heads. They stayed in their boats, chattering and laughing with one another. Children scampered about, leaping from one boat to another with no apparent thought of slipping or fear of the water.

Soon a small gangplank was secured for the schooner's passengers. A good-looking, dark-skinned young man with a thick head of curly black hair, was waving his broad-brimmed hat. He wore a white tropical suit stretched tightly over his muscular shoulders. Hannah realized at once that he must be Cousin Benoni. She waved her handkerchief, and he moved quickly to the end of the gangplank, where he held out a hand to help her as she stepped onto the wharf.

"Welcome, welcome Cousin Hannah," he said. "I mos' pleased t' make your acquaintance. Susanna, also. Come. Island sun not good for northern skin. I have a rig nearby."

Patting her moist forehead with her handkerchief, Hannah

said, "It's good of you to meet me, Cousin. I know you're a working man, and it can't be easy to get time off from your job."

"Not so hard. Islanders understan' importance of family." He smiled at her shyly. "Mos' specially long-los' kinfolk."

He beckoned to a teenage boy who was looking at them curiously. The boy approached, and Benoni put a coin in his hand.

"You fetch lady's trunk?"

The boy nodded.

With a smile of approval Hannah tucked her arm in Benoni's. As he handed her up into his buggy, he said, "It's a way we have to go. Our small house out Centerline Road close by the Central Factory near Bethlehem."

"Very sensible to live near your work. Tell me, Benoni, this property we have an interest in, is it nearby?"

"We pas' the old house goin' out o' town. I point it out to you."

"Good. I'm really curious to see it. The other cousins who share in it live where?"

"Sophia and Pepe, they live in Puerto Rico. Inga, she live in Denmark. James and Arnold, in New Orleans. No one of them visit island for many year."

They drove out of town on King Street, past the Custom House, the West Indian Warehouse, Government House. The buildings were thick walled and solid, mostly painted a buttery yellow that had faded with age. In places the plaster had worn away revealing the brick beneath, which gave the walls a soft rosy glow. Sturdy hurricane shutters painted dark green flanked most of the windows. Along the street-side of the buildings stretched arched colonnades that provided shade from the sun and protection from the torrential rains that came in autumn. It seemed a sleepy town. The few carts, wagons and buggies in the street, even an occasional car, drove at a leisurely pace, the drivers often stopping to visit with folk on the sidewalks.

They had gone two or three blocks when Benoni slowed the horse and pointed to a house squeezed tight between two larger dwellings. "There it be—our inheritance. It not much t'talk 'bout, as you can see mos' plain."

It was rather a sad little house. Several of the shutters hung loose, the paint was crumbling and shingles were askew on the roof.

"Mr. Sobotker spend much time off d'island. More times than not, house empty. He business man with concerns far from St.

Croix. He die in New York."

"The house looks as though it needs lots of repairs."

"For sure. Best t'sell."

They continued on their way passing the Anglican Cathedral and the historic Moravian church, then they took a road northwest skirting the sea. Working people walked by the side of the road, cane cutters carrying machetes and women with baskets of fruit or vegetables on their heads. All at once Hannah was looking down on Turquoise Bay, a silky sheet of vivid blue-green water bordered by a dark reef frosted with foam.

"Long Reef," Benoni said. "A fine place for fishermon but tragical for small ship not knowing safe way."

"That I can easily believe," Hannah said looking at the sinister stretch of dark coral beyond the placid water.

"The ship you come on, the old *Vigilant*, she has long history. She built, they say, in Baltimore, near a hundred years ago. She been slaver."

Hannah looked at him skeptically. "Slaver?"

" 'Tis true. She brought men and women clear 'cross from Africa long time pas'. Likewise she privateer. Once she get 'way from Spanish pirates sailin' in and out of reefs where they couldn't follow. She sink in hurricane in harbor some years back but come up again. She mighty fine old ship, hard to make die."

"Remarkable! Your island, Benoni, is so beautiful! Never in my wildest imaginings had I visualized sea water of such a color. You truly live in a tropical paradise."

"It good to hear you say so, Cousin—you from fine city like Philadelphia. Some day I like to see big city."

"Good. Then you can stay with me."

They passed several fields of waving green sugar cane where both men and women worked, hoeing the rows. On hilltops Hannah saw the stone bases, geometrical cones, that still remained, all that was left of the sugar mills that for many years formed an essential part of the island's economy.

Following her gaze, Benoni said, "The sails rotted long since. And the iron parts, mostly they sold for scrap."

"But how amazing that the bases remain to this day! Built by . . ."

"Built a hundred, a hundred fifty years pas' by slaves."

They drove close to one mill, and Hannah marvelled at the

skill evident in its building, the close fit of the stones and the perfect shape. A herd of goats was grazing around its base. The kids leapt playfully from the raised stone floor through its arched openings onto the hard baked ground outside, butting each other and jumping about.

At Bassin Triangle they turned up Contentment Road, the horse straining to pull the buggy up the steep grade between the hills. They passed Beeston Hill.

Then Benoni pointed to an overgrown property on their right. "Up that way is Bulow's Minde."

Hannah saw a rutted lane largely covered by thornbush leading up a steep hill. "Bulow's Minde. What a strange exotic name! Tell me about it."

"It the mos' beautiful estate on d'island, the Greathouse built by Governor von Scholten and Anna Heegaard. Anna Heegaard our kin, 'round 'bout way. You know of her?"

"No. I never heard of her. We kin, Benoni? Incredible."

"Christine Cappel our great-great-grandma. She half-sister to Anna Heegaard. Anna Heegaard mos' famous lady on our island. Grandfather Benoni, he know Anna Heegaard from young boy. He visit her toward the end of her life at Bulow's Minde. He still lives. He tell you her story. We visit him one day."

"I should like that, but can't we stop and see the property . . . Bulow's Minde you called it, now. It sounds enchanting."

"You understan' it only a ruin. An' it hard going up the hill . . . 'specially for fine lady in long skirts."

" Ruin or not I'd like to see it, Benoni. As for my skirts I can manage them well enough. Look. I have heavy travelling shoes fit for hiking."

"Susanna do look for us for dinner but she patient lady. An' dinner, he not run off by heself," he chuckled. "I tie the horse."

Hannah tucked her skirts up and followed Benoni up the hill. A couple of times she stumbled. A couple of times she felt a jab of pain in her hand from the thorns she pushed aside. But at last they reached a clear place at the top of the hill and were rewarded by a refreshing breeze, a breathtaking view, and the sight of a magnificent ruin.

It was larger by far than Hannah had expected, and even in its dilapidated state it had a grace and dignity she was unprepared for. The late afternoon sun warmed the old walls of coral blocks, making them glow. Dainty ferns grew out of crevices. Scarlet and yellow blossoms on wildly running vines festooned the walls, while little green lizards waited motionlessly in sunny spots for any unsuspecting flies.

The original shape of the building was still apparent, though the roof had fallen in and some of the walls had crumbled. One could see that the main section, which still had remnants of the "welcoming arms" staircase leading to the main gallery, had large wings on either side. Best preserved were what had once been the chapel and the watchtower with its flight of steps leading around it to the top.

"The old house take many a big blow," Benoni said. "Heavy rain do it work. Likewise the people take wooden parts, doors, boards from floor and shutters. See blackened stones yonder? Slow fire burn there for many day."

"No matter, Benoni, it's still beautiful," Hannah said, strangely moved.

"Come. I show you one thing more. The grave of Anna Heegaard not at Bulow's Minde, but on next property. It this way."

Hannah followed Benoni along a different path than the way they had come from the road.

Soon, about halfway down the hill, they came to a small, overgrown plot that had clearly once been a family graveyard. There Benoni pointed out a fine marble slab. On it was this legend:

IN MEMORY OF
Anna Elizabeth Heegaard
Born—25th January 1790
Died—1st January 1859
Peace be with your ashes.

Hannah stood silently, thinking of the woman whose remains lay beneath . . . strange as it seemed, a kinswoman.

After a moment Benoni moved restlessly, and she realized she was trying his patience. "Thank you for showing me this. Now, we must go quickly. We mustn't keep Susanna waiting any longer. I hope she isn't cross with us . . ."

"Susanna never cross," Benoni said loyally. "She understan' your feeling."

The small house by the side of the road where Benoni and

Susanna lived was simple but spacious and airy. There was nothing at the windows to keep out the breeze, only screens and louvres that could be adjusted in case of rain.

Susanna welcomed Hannah with a bashful smile. She was a slim pretty girl with short, cropped black hair and lustrous black skin that glowed with health and good humor. She wore a crimson hibiscus behind her ear.

"Make our house you' house, Cousin," she said in a soft musical voice. "You are mos' welcome." With pride in her large dark eyes she pushed forward a boy of about six who had been hiding behind her skirts. "He be another Benoni. How many that be in one line, Ben?" she asked. "Five or six?"

"Jus' five, and that be with the one in Denmark. Love, Cousin Hannah would like a wash, I'm thinkin'. I'll fetch her trunk from the rig so she can change into lighter clothes."

Hannah was impatient to visit her cousin's grandfather and hear Anna Heegaard's story. But the Bensens were not to be hurried. There was always tomorrow . . . and the day after that. Hannah soon learned about "Cruzan time." Islanders lived by a different clock than the one in bustling Philadelphia.

The days slipped by with lazy afternoons spent in the Bensens' small garden learning about tropical plants and indigenous birds. She enjoyed the banana quits, or sugar birds, lively little black and yellow birds with long curved bills that hopped around the yard. Susanna hung half a coconut shell filled with sugar in a flamboyant tree, and they swarmed around it squabbling for space.

Hannah made the acquaintance of the small lizards she saw sunning themselves everywhere. She was less favorably impressed by the enormous cockroaches that sometimes scuttled across the floor when she lit the kerosene lantern by her bed in her room at night. One night she was momentarily terrified by the braying of a nearby donkey.

She took walks in the countryside. Neighbors came to visit. On market day she rode with Susanna into Christiansted. Susanna took honey from her hives to sell and ripe, yellow-gold mangoes from the huge tree that shaded her house.

Hannah took this opportunity to walk past the old house once more. She had to agree with Benoni, "Bes' t'sell." She called on the attorney whose letter had brought her to the island and signed the papers which gave permission. She called on the pastor of the Moravian church, spoke of her father and of her work with the school. She did some sightseeing . . . marvelled at the ballroom in Government House, ducked her head to enter the old dungeon in the fort, and visited the historic clock tower church.

The next day, a Sunday, Cousin Benoni said it was time to visit his grandfather. Grandfather lived by himself in a house in the rain forest on the western end of the island. He was expecting them. Rum punches were poured into tall glasses, and the family settled down on the gallery that ran around the house to hear his story. He told of the part Anna Heegaard had played in the history of the island. Then he spoke of visiting the Greathouse when he was a boy, of the works of art, the fine silverware and furnishings, the charming garden where bloomed yellow Ginger Thomas, crimson Pride of Barbados with butterfly petals, and pink-blossomed lemon guava.

When he stopped speaking, Hannah sat silently for several minutes thinking of Anna Heegaard, the charming mistress of Governor Peter von Scholten, and the years they lived together on a grand scale at Bulow's Minde, entertaining notables from the island and abroad. She was deeply impressed. What an extraordinary story! And told exceptionally well! She could see the life and times of her distant kinswoman slowly unfold before her mind's eye. She felt drawn to her more strongly than could be accounted for by the tenuous blood line that existed between them.

Grandfather Benoni was speaking again, this time in a hushed voice. Hannah leaned forward to listen. "There is said t'be a ghost, a white-clad figure movin' with grace 'round the ruin of Bulow's Minde. She been seen on moonlit nights. Amanda, she the first t'see it."

"A ghost? Truly a ghost?" Hannah looked skeptical.

"Aye. Anna's ghost been seen by islanders and visitors alike. Many say so."

"How fascinating!" After a moment's thought she turned to Benoni. "Benoni, I must visit Bulow's Minde again now that I've heard Anna's story . . . and this time it must be in the moonlight."

17

Benoni laughed. "You expectin' t' see a ghost, mebbe? Big city lady like you believe such foolishness?" Mocking her he teased, "Me crazy cousin from Philadelphia want t'see ghost at Bulow's Minde. That some funny!"

"Mebbe so. Mebbe not," Grandfather Benoni said nodding his head sagely.

"I don't know what I expect to see, Benoni," Hannah said softly. "But I do know I'd like very much to see Bulow's Minde again, and in the moonlight. Will you take me there?"

"The moon come full next week, and if it pleasure you, we return to Bulow's Minde," he agreed rather reluctantly.

Midweek the moon rose over the eastern hills of the island, huge and golden. By the time she and Benoni reached Bulow's Minde the moon was sailing high in the sky and had turned from gold to white. Benoni had brought a lantern, and by its light they found the path shadowed by overhanging trees and brush. Climbing up, it seemed to Hannah the thornbush purposely reached out to grab at her skirts and shawl. But the top of the hill was clear of brush and bathed in moonlight.

Hannah said, "Look, Benoni! We can see almost as well as day."

Benoni glanced around nervously. "I not mon to b'lieve in zombies, jumbies an' all such trash. Still, visitin' this old place in nighttime make me feel kinda creepy. You see the ruin, how it look. Now we go?"

"Let me look around just a little bit. I want to walk through the old walls and visit the chapel."

"Very well, but don' be long," he said grudgingly. "I stay here by lantern. Be careful. Creeper catch at you' foot and stone steps crumble."

"Thank you, Benoni. I'll just be a minute."

Hannah picked her way through rosebushes mostly gone to bramble but still fragrant with a few stubborn blooms. She made her way carefully between the crumbling walls and entered the chapel. Moonlight streamed through the old windows making geometric shadows on the floor. She climbed the curving stair that led to the top of the watchtower and gazed over the moonswept landscape. In the distance she could see the harbor, where a few lights twinkled on boats at anchor. Then she looked back toward the gallery and thought how lovely the arches stretching along it were, their curves accentuated by the deep shadows cast by the moonlight. It was easy to imagine her ancestress standing there waiting, perhaps, for her governor-general to arrive.

A whispering breeze rustled the acacia trees, and the fragrance of old roses and night blooming jasmine reached her nostrils. The air had turned suddenly cooler. She shivered and pulled her shawl more closely around her shoulders. Suddenly, she heard a pebble that had been loosened on the staircase rattle down the steps and fall to the ground. She stared at the spot, the spot from which the slight noise had come.

No ghostly apparition materialized before her eyes, but she felt a presence, a presence that could not be denied. Anna's spirit, Anna's ghost, whatever—something of Anna was nearby. And she seemed to want something of her, her kinswoman. Perhaps to have her story made known? Yes, it must be done. Anna's ghost, visible or invisible, demanded it of her. She would put it down as Grandfather Benoni had told it, only filling in the gaps—Anna's young years, her dreams, her romances—imagining how it might have been. She would begin tomorrow.

Chapter 2

No CHILE o' mine will leave d'yard this day!" Susanna said firmly as she stood up, arms akimbo, facing her three daughters, who sat across the eating table. She had large, luminous black eyes, a softly rounded face with curved sensuous lips, and a small chin. But now she was making her face severe, her chin thrust forward aggressively.

"How come, Mama?" As the eldest, Anna asked the question for the three of them.

"Never you mine. It sufficient you know t'ings take place in town this day unfit fo' eye o' innocent children. There'll be rough persons 'bout. No time fo' me gels t'be roamin' d'streets. You mine what I say or . . ." Her eyes moved to a corner of the shed kitchen where a light tamarind switch, which was sometimes used to redden the bottom of a disobedient child, stood.

The girls followed her gaze with some apprehension. "Yes, Mama," the two younger ones said in unison, nodding their heads obediently.

Anna kept quiet. Her eyes were fixed on her mother's face, trying to guess what was going on in town that she was not supposed to see.

Anna's skin was lighter than her mother's because of the white blood, more than half, that flowed through her veins. She had high cheekbones and forehead, deep-set eyes, and a determined chin. Her face was framed by straight black hair that fell to her shoulders. She was tall for her twelve years, tall and slender.

Susanna took the wooden bowls that had held the breakfast mush to the stone sink. A pitcher filled with water drained from the roof stood ready for the washing up.

"There be beddin' t'air, an' sweepin' t'do," she continued, admonishing her children. "When d'chores be done, you can play how you want. But you'll stay by d'house till de abomination whereof I speak be over an' done with."

Anna's curiosity grew. "What abom . . . bomination, Mama?"

"No more talk-talk, Anna. Wash d' bowls. Then he'p me rid up inside."

Leaving Anna to her task, Susanna went inside the house, one of the small houses on Hill Street in Christiansted where most of the free-colored among the population lived. She was followed by Christine and Sophia.

Anna took her time about washing the bowls. After they were clean she arranged them with care on the table where the sun would dry them. All the while sounds came to her ears from the town that further excited her curiosity—men shouting, womens' high-pitched excited voices, and occasional raucous laughter. She heard traffic, more than usual, horses' hoofs, and the grating of wheels on the street that ran by their house heading down toward town. Suddenly, she stood still with the last wooden bowl in her hand. Someone was blowing the conch shell, a signal to the townspeople that something of importance was about to take place. It's deep baying was followed by the ragged beat of drums. What was going on? She had to know.

She put the bowl down and moved cautiously out into the yard. She looked back toward the house to see if anyone was watching. Seeing she was unobserved she made a dash for the acacia bushes that grew against a stone wall at the back of the yard and, heedless of their scratching, slipped in among them. She glanced back to be sure she was still unobserved, then raised herself to peer over the wall. Coming toward her along the lane were two swaggering blond sailors, each with a black girl on his arm. Early as it was, the men had clearly had more than the day's allotment of rum. She ducked her head to let them pass. When she was sure they had gone she tucked up her skirts, pulled herself up onto the wall and, looking both ways to make sure the coast was clear, let herself down on the other side. She then turned toward the town, following the men and girls.

When she reached the main street she fell in with the crowd. It was made up of men, women, and children, black, white, and all shades in between. Some were free-colored, some resident Danish, English, or Scotch-Irish. Some were visitors from overseas. All were talking excitedly and heading for the town wharf where the West Indian warehouse stood. No one took any notice of Anna.

The warehouse was a two-storied masonry building in Danish colonial style. Within the spacious courtyard a stone staircase lead to the second story, where offices and quarters for government employees were located. The space below was used for storing cargo, human and otherwise. A high wall with wrought iron gates enclosed the courtyard.

Outside the courtyard Anna saw a cluster of carriages belonging to the island's planters. The planters, their tanned faces shaded by broad-brimmed hats, sat in their carriages waiting patiently for the action to begin. They called back and forth and told jokes to make the time pass.

Some of them had brought their ladies with them. The ladies, dressed in their best for the occasion, held parasols over their heads to protect them from the hot tropical sun and waved palm leaf fans or held handkerchiefs in front of their noses. Anna soon knew why. The sea breeze brought a nauseous stench to her nostrils. Looking across the harbor the saw the source. The schooner *Vigilant*, variously inter-island freighter, privateer, or slaver, was anchored in Gallows Bay. Anna's nose left no doubt in her mind to which use the ship had been put on this occasion. And now she knew what it was, the "abomination" of which her mother spoke! She was repulsed. Yet her curiosity prevented her from running away. The gates of the courtyard were swung open, and she was drawn in by the crowd.

Inside a platform had been set up. On it stood a large block of dark mahogany. At sight of it Anna swallowed hard to keep down a sickish feeling for she had heard about, "de block." The sun beat down on her bare head, and she felt drops of sweat trickling down her back.

All at once, the men and boys who had climbed onto the walls around the courtyard to have a better view, stirred and craned their necks toward King Street, the town's main thoroughfare. Anna heard the rat-a-tat-tat of drums, and a moment later two drummer boys appeared at the gates, followed by Mr. Cregh, the auctioneer, who was mounted on a jug-headed nag. He rode rudely into the courtyard. People were pushed aside to make room for him and his bodyguards, two militiamen who marched beside him. Another militiaman marched behind carrying a pole from which hung a Danish flag.

Mr. Cregh was a brutish man with coarse features and ill-fitting clothes. He wore spurs and carried a heavy riding crop. Dismounting, he climbed onto the platform. A sturdy black stationed by the door to the warehouse raised the conch shell to his lips and blew a mighty blast. The crowd grew silent.

"Hear ye, hear ye, ye good people of St. Croix in His Majesty's West Indies," Mr. Cregh called out. "Today, in this year of our Lord eighteen hundred and two, we needs must sell a passle of blacks fresh brought from Guinea. As you know, His Majesty and parliament in their wisdom," he paused, and there were jeers and grimaces among the crowd, "have decreed there'll be an end to the slave trade this year. Good people, no more Africans legally imported! Think on it and make the most of this opportunity to add to your work gang before it's too late.

"In addition to the Africans we will put on the block a number of local slaves, well trained and docile, who must be sold by their masters for reasons not reflecting on their characters. We conduct this sale in the name of His Majesty, King Christian. God Bless the King!"

The crowd cheered lustily. Mr. Cregh nodded to the man by the door of the warehouse. He opened the door, and out into the courtyard blinking in the bright sunlight stumbled twenty or more nearly naked blacks—men, women, and children. The men wore shackles on their legs. Some had their hands bound behind them as a further precaution. The women were chained together in groups. Children clung to their mothers. Anna could plainly see the terror in most of the faces. Their eyes rolled, their lips were drawn back from their teeth and several were trembling so that they could scarcely walk. Twice she saw the flick of a lash and heard an agonized cry, the punishment for holding back. The sickish feeling she had felt before rose in her throat, tasting sour. She dropped her eyes but held her ground. She was determined to see what was to be seen, to know what was going on, and to learn from it.

The first male slave mounted the block. He had the grayish tinge of ashes and was thin to the point of emaciation. His head lolled to one side as though too heavy for his thin neck.

A planter called out, "That un' sick, mon. He'll not make it through the week!"

Cregh's riding crop struck the slave's bare legs, and the black gave a piteous wail.

"Stand up straight, man! Let 'em see you've some spirit," Cregh hissed.

The slave cringed and muttered something under his breath, hanging his head still lower. Cregh struck him again. He hid his head in his arms. Cregh's face turned red with vexation. He raised his crop to strike the black across his bowed shoulders when a woman's call, clear and piercing in one of the many Bantu languages, reached the wretched man. Comprehension dawned and he immediately raised his head, looking dully at his tormentor. Cregh let his crop fall to his side.

In spite of the man's poor conditon the bidding was brisk. The planters were desperate to buy slaves with the end of the slave trade in sight. He was finally knocked down to a government clerk for 125 rigsdaler.

The next man prodded forward was huge with shoulders like an ox and muscles bulging in his arms and thighs. His wrists were chained behind him. He looked wildly around as though searching for an avenue of escape. Nearing the platform he threw himself against one of the guards and, shackled though he was, would have knocked the man down except that Mr. Cregh jumped from his platform and struck him brutally across the back of his neck with the butt of his crop. The man fell face forward. Anna closed her eyes. When she found the courage to look again, the man was standing on the block panting and heaving, enraged eyes rolling in his head. Guards on either side held onto him. Blood dripped from the side of his head.

"Here's a strong un' for you!" the auctioneer cried triumphantly. "He'll make a fine field hand under the bomba's whip. Look at that chest, those arms . . . !"

"Dear me! I wouldn't sleep peaceful with the likes of him around!" Anna heard a painted and powdered woman in lace and worn satin exclaim.

"Mayhap you'd like t'sleep *with* him, Betty. He looks quite the stud," her male companion said with a lecherous leer. She slapped his face, but without conviction.

The bidding began. Though he'd been beaten the big man stood straight and defiant, teeth bared, jaw set, and eyes blazing. Two planters bid heatedly against each other. As the price rose both moved forward until they were standing directly in front of the auctioneer. They grew red-faced with anger, shaking their fists at one another and glaring. At last the man was sold to Mr. McKay of Estate Anna's Hope for 350 rigsdaler.

The remaining Africans were disposed of rather quickly. Then the local slaves were lead to the platform. By and large their skins were lighter, showing a mix of white blood. Anna knew some of them by name or at least had seen them around town. They were simply but modestly dressed in coarse linen suits or gowns. The women wore colored kerchiefs around their heads. They were not bound, but guards with blunderbusses stood ready in case anyone should be foolish enough to try to run away. There was a stoicism about the older ones who had gone through all this before and knew they had no choice but to endure. Many of the younger ones, especially the girls, looked badly frightened.

The first in line, a boy not many years older than Anna, stood out from the rest because of his proud bearing and his scornful surveillance of the crowd. He was as tall as any of the men and, though slim, was beginning to show the smooth muscles of early manhood. Studying his face Anna felt he was somehow familiar, someone she ought to know. The guards took hold of the boy to urge him toward the block. He shook them off impatiently, strode to the block unattended and stood tall and straight. A small boy perched on the wall called out, "Hi-ya, No-no!"

The young slave ignored the youngster, his eyes remaining fixed straight ahead.

No-no! At the sound of the strange nickname Anna's heart leapt. She remembered him now. Long ago, when she was perhaps four or five, he had been her playmate in the big garden behind Auditor Eigtved's house. He was the merriest, most inventive, altogether delightful playmate she had ever known. Her eyes stung with tears seeing his present humiliation.

Mr. Cregh was speaking, his voice satin smooth. "These people are island born. They have known good masters and mistresses and been well trained. The bids should come high." He pointed to No-no with his riding crop. "Here stands Obadiah Gottlieb, commonly known as No-no. His mama, big Emma, finest cook on the island, has been taken to St. Thomas to serve the gov'nor. He's a smart 'un, smart enough t'be a major-domo, gang boss in your sugar works, or manager of your stables. Many of you know him by sight. He's been livin' with his mama at Orange Grove for the last seven years, where he helped with the horses. Before that he and his mama were with Auditor Eigtved. Let's hear your bids, good people. I want 200 rigsdaler to start. I'll find it where, where, where?" His eyes darted around the crowd.

Mr. Burke, the manager of Estate Little Princesse, mounted the platform to get a closer look at the boy. He put his hand out to feel the muscles in his arm. No-no drew back haughtily.

"Stand still, boy!" Mr. Cregh ordered, tapping him smartly on the back of his legs with his crop. "Open your mouth and show Mr. Burke your fine teeth."

No-no's mouth remained tightly closed.

"Stubborn, eh? Well, that's not entire t'yer discredit. A boy, like a colt, should have some spirit. But, seein' as how I want Mr. Burke t'see yer teeth . . . hold him," he said to one of the guards.

The guard held No-no while Mr. Cregh put his hand over No-no's nose, forcing him to open his mouth.

Anna had had all she could stand. Her heart was pounding with revulsion. A lightheadedness made her feel as though she might faint; and the sick feeling was again mounting in her throat so strong, this time, she feared she might vomit. She turned her back on the ugly scene to make her escape. "L'me pass! L'me pass!" she cried in a high thin voice tinged with hysteria.

She forced her way between close-pressed bodies to come out at last onto the street where she ran as fast as she could in the direction of Hill Street and home. When she came to the corner she stopped. Across the street stood the old Lutheran church, the church her family habitually attended. The door stood open and the interior, cool and secluded, looked inviting. She entered swiftly.

Looking around the dim interior Anna saw that she was alone. She slipped into one of the pews and knelt, leaning her forehead against the seat back in front. It took several minutes for the nausea to pass. When it had, she lifted her eyes to look at the altar. It had been carved by an artist in wood. It was of fine-grained mahogany with columns either side supporting a heavy arch on which a cherub's head and wings were lovingly carved. Below the arch hung a life-size oil painting of Jesus. Tall unlit candles set in heavy gold candlesticks stood on the altar.

Anna fixed her eyes on the painting and walked slowly forward. She stood in front of the altar clasping her hands. "Lord Jesus," she prayed, "give them free. An' let it be soon. Show me how t'he'p, t'he'p anyway I can, anyway at all."

Having made this solemn prayer she felt a need to do something dramatic to prove the seriousness of her purpose. She knew where the flint and tinderbox were kept. She found what she needed, struck a spark and lit one of the candles. As she held it she let some of the hot wax drip onto the tender skin inside her wrist. A gasp escaped her as the pain made itself felt; but she held the candle steady and let the wax drip, drip like white blood. She let the wax burn, three large drops, one for No-no, one for herself, and one for the Lord Jesus whom she trusted to show her the way. She blew out the candle, returned it to its holder and crept out of the church.

The wax still clung to her wrist as she headed once more for home. Halfway, it grew cool and brittle. She brushed it off, noting with satisfaction that the skin beneath was an angry red. She hoped it had burned deep.

As Anna came close to the house she saw Grandmother, Charlotte Amalie Bernard, who lived next door, sitting on the narrow front porch. Though Amalie Bernard was not yet fifty, the hardships she'd endured had etched fine lines in her nut-brown face. She had high cheekbones and a beak-like nose. Her head was wrapped in a white headcloth that hid her crinkly, graying hair. Her eyes, black with yellow lights in them, shone with inner strength and vitality.

Anna mounted the steps with dragging feet. Amalie Bernard looked at her sternly but said nothing. Susanna, who'd been watching for Anna, burst from the house, eyes flashing with anger. She grabbed Anna's arm and raised the tamarind switch she held. Before the blow could fall Amalie Bernard pulled Anna toward her out of harm's way.

"No whippin', Susanna. Look at she face. 'Pears t'me she growed up considerable since this mornin'."

"But she do run off when I bid her stay," Susanna protested.

"She do need punish, punish fo' no heedin' you' words, but no whippin'."

"What then?" Susanna asked sullenly.

"I think you send her to she room. Give time fo' long thought, a li'l bread an' water t'las d'day."

"You too easy, Mama. But by now, me arm lose it pow."
Bringing her face close to Anna's she said crossly, "Go to you'
room, gel. I try t'save you some misery but you' head too strong
fo' you' own good. In future do what I say."

Anna hung her head. "Yes, Mama."

In the large room under the eaves she shared with Christine
and Sophia, Anna threw herself down on her cot. For a while
she stared at the ceiling. Then she went to a dresser and
opened the drawer that was hers alone and felt under her
underclothes. Her fingers touched a small hard object. Taking
it out she let it lay in the palm of her hand and studied it. It
was a shard of pottery, blue and white. She swallowed to rid
herself of a lump growing in her throat and put the shard back,
closed the drawer and lay down on her cot again.

As the day dragged slowly by she thought of many things.
Finally she imagined herself leading an uprising against all
white oppressors. She would ride a fine horse and wear
flowing white robes. On her head would be a turban of scarlet
and gold and she would carry a golden cross. No-no, garbed in
red and purple and brandishing a flashing sword, would ride
by her side. Together they would lead the exulting workers on
the road to freedom. Then, as the bitter reality of her
limitations swept over her, she wept soflty.

The sun set, and the room was suddenly dark. Christine and
Sophia came up the steep stairs. Christine carried a candle.
She put the candleholder down on the dresser and sat on the
edge of Anna's cot.

"Tell us 'bout it, Anna," she demanded. "You saw d'slave
auction. Hans an' Peter see you there."

"It bad!" Anna said. "It make me hurt deep inside. I don' wan'
t'talk 'bout it." She turned her face to the wall.

Disgruntled by her uncommunicativeness, Anna's sisters
undressed silently, snuffed out the candle, and climbed into the
double bed they shared. They were soon asleep, breathing
regularly and deep. But Anna lay awake a while longer.
Outside she heard the clip, clip of a carriage horse's hoofs and
the swish of wheels on the ballast brick pavement in front of
the house. After the carriage had passed she heard the rap of
a gentleman's cane and the smart click of his heeled boots.
Then came the song of a pair of drunken sailors. The wind
sighed in the branches of the huge tamarind tree in their back
yard. It was accompanied by the peep-peeping of tree frogs.

All at once the faint moonlight at the window was snuffed out by a cloud sailing across the moon's face. It began to rain, the rain making a sad soft sound on the wooden shingles close over Anna's head. At last she slept. She dreamed of No-no and the garden they played in long ago.

Chapter 3

No-NO, how come you called No-no?" four-year-old Anna asked. She giggled. "That funny name."

The children were having a mid-morning sugar bun in Auditor Eigtved's kitchen, where No-no's mother reigned supreme. She removed the plate of sugar buns just as No-no was about to reach for another. "You hep you'self to anudder an' you have belly ache fo'sure. Now wipe de suger frostin' off you' mouf."

In those days No-no was as lively as a banana quit, the little yellow and black bird that hopped around everyone's yards. He had snapping black eyes and an impish grin, impaired only by a missing front tooth.

Anna persisted. "No-no, how come . . ."

"That fo' me t'know an' you t'fine out," he answered sassily.

"You got no call t'sass li'l Anna," his mother said. To Anna she said, with the air of a conspirator, "I tell you why. He called No-no 'cause he such a bad chile! De mos' t'ing he hear all he born days is no, no touch d'pies—no, no tease d'cat—no, no stray out o' d'yard." Chuckling, she cuffed her son's small, woolly head.

Anna liked the kitchen. It was a warm and friendly place and smelled of cinnamon, sugar, and vanilla. Emma treated Anna like one of her own, and Anna responded with equal affection.

Seeing that the children had reached the finger-licking stage, Emma picked up her broom and swished it menacingly as though to sweep them out of her kitchen along with the crumbs. "Get 'long with you now. There's work t'be done, bread t'set, an lobstah t'stew fo' company comin' this night."

Auditor Eigtved's elegant townhouse stood high on a hill overlooking Gallows Bay. Built of yellow ballast brick, the strong morning light gave it a golden glow. A colonnade of Danish arches ran around the ground floor, which was used for

30

servants and storage. Eigtved had his quarters on the second floor. Here he could take advantage of the breeze and the view.

The garden where the children played was laid out in the rear. It had a vegetable patch where okra, tanya, sweet potatoes, and chickpeas grew. There was a masonry basin filled with salt water in which turtle and lobster were kept alive until wanted for the table. Hibiscus and oleander were set along the old garden wall of crumbling coral rock, and swags of bougainvillea, orange, pink, and magenta, had artfully draped themselves over it. In one corner of the garden stood Emma's brick oven covered with extra mortar to better hold the heat. In the opposite corner a giant silkcotton tree reared its massive trunk, its roots spread in elephantine folds beginning four feet or more above the ground.

No-no raced from the kitchen door toward the silkcotton tree. "Want t'see me treasure?" he called over his shoulder to Anna.

"Uh-huh." She was trotting after him fast as her short legs would allow. Before she could catch up, he mysteriously disappeared.

"No-no," she cried plaintively. "Where you be?" There was no answer.

She circled the tree peering into the depths between the root folds. All at once she heard a gurgle of merriment and saw him. He was sitting cross-legged in one of the deep cavities between the roots grinning up at her.

"No-no, what you . . ."

"Ssh! This secret place. Make no noise."

Her eyes wide with expectation, she crawled in beside him. No-no cautiously raised his head to peer over the root fold. Satisfied that no one was spying on them he reached into a hollow place under the tree trunk and pulled out a rusty tin biscuit box. Slowly and carefully he worked at loosening the lid. Anna held her breath in anticipation. At last the lid popped off, and Anna gasped with pleasure. Inside the box lay a hoard of pretty blue and white bits and pieces of china.

"Oo-h, No-no," she sighed. "It bea-u-ti-ful!"

Pleased with the impression he'd made he scooped up the shards and let them dribble lovingly through his fingers. " 'Tis chainy-china, good as big folks' money! You can trade with anudder kid fo' all kind o' stuff, fish hook, string, knife even."

Shyly Anna put out her hand to touch the china bits.

No-no said generously, "You can have a piece. Which one you want?"

Anna took a long time choosing, picking up pieces and putting them down. Finally she settled on a shard with tiny blue flowers on it. The bit of border that remained from the plate it had once been was a darker blue.

Anna remembered other things about the time they spent at Auditor-General Eigtved's; remembered, or was told things she would have had no way of knowing about at the time. She remembered that many nights after she was put to bed she would hear carriages coming and going in the driveway. Often from the drawing room of the house came the scraping of fiddles and the tinkle of a spinet. Torches burned late to light the way of visitors. She was aware that grandmother, Amalie Bernard, was Eigtved's "special friend." As often happened in those wifeless colonial establishments, a favored slave played the role of hostess —and mistress.

Besides being an extravagant host, Eigtved was a compulsive gambler. He took bets anyone was willing to offer—cards, cockfights, horses. One afternoon he came home from his government office earlier than usual and went directly to his room. He could be heard pacing back and forth distractedly. When a maid was sent to bid him come to dinner he refused to emerge, so Amalie Bernard went for him herself.

Some years later Anna learned what happened that night. When her grandmother insisted he open the door and saw Eigtved she was shocked. From the overconfident man that had left the house that morning he had turned into a scared rabbit. His face was drawn and pale, his red hair rumpled, and his eyes wild.

"What am I t'do, Amalie?" he moaned. "Whatever can I do?"

"First t'ing, stop you' moanin', set down and tell me what happen."

Eigtved slumped into a chair. In broken phrases well punctuated by oaths he told her of his troubles. To pay his gambling debts he had accepted a sum of money to overlook certain "irregularities" in the accounts of the major-general, head of the Danish Militia and the town fire department. The conniving between Eigtved and this officer had been discovered by a junior clerk hoping for advancement. Early that morning the major-general had been courtmartialed and sent to jail.

"I'll be next, Amalie. I'll go to jail in the morning. Stedman will tell all, of that I'm certan. Blast his hide! Tomorrow I'll become the king's guest for an unspecified time . . . unless you, Amalie, have a better idea."

Amalie Bernard knew that Eigtved was something of a scamp. But he had been kind to her and her family, and she was fond of him. "If in de mornin' they goin' put you in jail, why then you leave d'island this night."

"But how? I don't doubt the bastards are watching the house. If I set a foot outside . . ."

"You put on me dress and shawl. Island sloop be leavin' for Tortola. We go down to de wharf togedder, two women servants. The cap'n, me friend. He let you on board."

Amalie Bernard's scheme worked well. By morning ex-General-Auditor Eigtved was safe in Tortola, British territory, out of reach of the Danish government.

His hasty departure brought about drastic change in Amalie Bernard's life. To pay his debts his creditors sold his house and personal property which, of course, included his slaves. Once more Amalie Bernard found herself on the auction block. But her daughter, Susanna, was spared this indignity because as a small child she had been given her freedom by her aristocratic French father, Lucas, Baron de Breton's eldest son.

Amalie Bernard was purchased by a retired sea captain, Hans Cappel. However, his real interest was not in the middle-aged slave woman but in her comely daughter, eighteen-year-old Susanna. Both women and little Anna moved into Captain Cappel's modest home on Hill Street. A few months later, being a generous and compassionate man, he gave Amalie Bernard her freedom.

"So," Amalie Bernard would conclude when she told the story, "I lose me shawl and dress, but gain me freedom. The Lord move in mysterious way."

Before the year was out Anna had a Cappel half sister named Christine. Sophia was born two years later. As the house grew more crowded Amalie Bernard moved next door to live with her other daughter, Lucia, mother of Anna's cousins, Hans and Peter Petersen. Susanna took the name of Cappel as her own and kept it for the rest of her life. Though she and the Captain were devoted to each other, there was no thought of marriage.

At that time a marriage contract between a Dane and one of African descent was illegal.

Anna was now almost eight years old. The rainy season had passed. Christmas had come and gone. On New Year's Day Captain Cappel shocked his family by telling them he'd be sailing for Denmark within the week. He had been offered command of the frigate *Frederica.* He was eager once more to command a ship and he had family in Denmark he'd not seen in years. Susanna wept bitterly when she heard the news, but to no avail. The captain was determined to go.

On the morning scheduled for his departure he took a document from the strong box where he kept his valuables and handed it to Susanna. " 'Tis the deed to the house made over to Christine and Sophia. It's understood, my dear, that you and Anna will live with our daughters as long as you choose. Christopher Hansen is your legal guardian. He prepared the deed and had it witnessed. Put it in a safe place, Susanna, just in case—"

"Oh, Hans!" Susanna cried, tears welling up in her eyes again.

"There, there, my girl. No time for tears. I'll be back 'fore Easter. You'll see."

The family accompanied him to the wharf followed by a servant pushing a wheelbarrow that held his sea chest. They walked in silence. Even the little girls were subdued.

Anna kept peeking at her mother's face beneath her broad-brimmed bonnet and was shocked to see her look so sad. She understood that kind "Papa" Cappel was leaving them, but she couldn't imagine what "far across the sea" meant, or how long "three long months" really was. Months were bigger than weeks, she knew, but how much bigger? And what would a "winter storm" be like? Was it like the heavy rains they sometimes had in the fall?

They reached the wharf, and Captain Cappel, shading his eyes with his hand against the sun, scanned the harbor. "There she be," he said. "There's the *Frederica* now."

Anna's eyes turned in the direction he pointed. Anchored in the channel between the small island known as Protestant Key and the fort she saw a dark-hulled, many-masted ship with great gold letters stretched across its stern. Men were hurrying about its deck like ants on an anthill. Some had climbed the rigging and were loosening sails.

34

Christine was holding onto Anna's hand, but suddenly broke away to run after a stray kitten. Anna ran after her to the edge of the wharf where sloops from other islands—British, Dutch, and French—were tied. Their open cockpits were crowded with brown-skinned children and a wide variety of produce. The kitten jumped onto one of the boats and nuzzled up against her mother, a large yellow tiger cat. The boat children laughed at Christine's woebegone look and made faces. Anna put an arm around her shoulders and lead her back to the others.

A ship's officer in a uniform similar to the captain's, but with two gold stripes on his sleeve instead of three, stood by an ox-drawn wagon giving orders. Blacks, stripped to the waist, their skins glistening with sweat in spite of a cool breeze, rolled heavy barrels from the rear of the wagon onto the wharf. Sailors loaded the barrels onto a lighter.

The officer, a pen and pad of paper in his hand, approached the driver of the wagon and said, "I make it twelve of sugar and seven o' rum. D'you agree, Mr. Burns?"

The driver nodded in agreement. The officer turned away and for the first time saw Captain Cappel, who was striding toward him followed by his family.

"Good day, Mr. Clausen," Captain Cappel said. "All proceedin' on schedule?"

"Aye, aye, sir. All go's well."

"Very good. Carry on. We'll sail as soon as the cargo's aboard and properly stowed. Those lingerin' Christmas winds will fill our sails, once we've cleared the Key."

"That they will, sir."

A gig stood out from the *Frederica* and came swiftly to the wharf. The coxswain stood in the stern giving orders to the sailors. He laid the boat against the wharf, port oars presented smartly.

"Your gig, sir," the officer said.

"Yes, well . . . thank you, Mr. Clausen." He motioned for the boat to stand by and turned to Susanna. They had already said their private farewells. Now they spoke of a safe voyage and biding safe at home. She urged him to dress warmly, for the change of climate would be severe and most certainly his blood had thinned after his years in the tropics. He assured her that he'd follow her advice and be back in good time for Easter.

"Take good care of yourself, my girl," he said. He kissed her cheek, gave baby Sophia a pat and hugged the other girls. A sailor stood by the gig waiting for him to board. He settled himself in the stern and, after a final wave to his family, turned his face toward the sea.

Susanna turned sadly away and started for home, holding Christine's hand. She was thinking about pirates and winter storms, speculating about and a bit jealous, too, of the family he was sailing to see. At best she knew she had lonely months ahead. Anna guessed by her mother's face something of what she was feeling and walked close by her other side.

As they approached the Custom House they heard a clatter of horses' hoofs and a carriage pulled up to its entrance. A small black boy jumped down to hold the horses, while the driver climbed down from his seat and went around to assist his passengers, a woman and two children.

Suddenly, Susanna put a hand on Anna's shoulder to hold her back. She was staring at the children, a boy and a girl. "See that gel? She be darker than you, Anna," she muttered, "an' she with nothin' but white blood in she veins."

"Who they? An' why you care, Mama?" Anna was puzzled.

Susanna didn't answer at once. Her attention had shifted to the man coming out of the door to greet the occupants of the carriage. He was tall and thin, dressed as an accountant, with a shock of unruly black hair, long nose and thin lips. He offered the woman his hand, and she stepped from the carriage. Then he took the little girl in his arms and set her on the ground.

"See that mon?" Susanna asked Anna. "That mon, Anna, be you' natural papa. He Jacob Heegaard."

Confounded by this startling information, Anna stared at the group by the Custom House door. "Then de boy an' de gel be my—"

"That's right. They be you' sister an' brother . . . half that is. Don' stare, Anna! He no worth you' notice. No more is de white woman, he wife. Come 'long."

With head held high and eyes straight ahead, Susanna marched past the Custom House, then headed up Hill Street toward home. Anna felt confused and envious. How was it that these other children had their father's personal attention while she, his daughter also, would not be worth his notice if they met on the street? They rode in a fine carriage pulled by a matched team while she . . . it was strange. She didn't understand it at all.

That night in the four-poster, the fine mahogany bed the captain had given her, Susanna was achingly aware of its emptiness. This bed. So big! So lonely! Dear God, send him soon back to me, she prayed. She blew out her candle at last and made herself as comfortable as possible on the high pillows. But she couldn't sleep. The breeze from the window caressed her face, her bare arms and breasts under her thin nightgown. It brought disturbing scents of sweet lime from the garden. All at once she heard a soft footstep outside her door. Raising her head she saw by the pale light of a half moon shining in her window a slight figure garbed in white.

"Who there?" she asked.

"It me, Mama," a small voice said. "Let me in with you?"

"Come then, Anna. The bed over-large this night."

Anna snuggled down by her mother's side. "Mama, you love he, that mon you say me papa? How come he marry that white woman? She no' so pretty as you."

"Such questions, Anna? An' you so young! How I say it so you understan'? You see, I stupid young gel, strong in d'head. Me mama tell me bad t'ings white mon do, but I pay her no heed. A friend, free-colored like me, say, 'Why you no work fo' white mon? It good t'get out from under you' mama's skirts, do wha' you like. Also, you get gift, even money sometime.' She tell me 'bout Jacob Heegaard, clerk at de Customs House. He'd let it be known he needed a gel t'red up an' do he washin'. I work fo' you' papa t'ree months 'fore he come t'me bed. He say sweet t'ings an' make big promise. When he first take me I hurt—an' I scared. Many night I cry after he gone. But then I know you on de way, an' I happy thinkin' havin' he chile be nex' t'ing t'wife.

"When me time come he say I should go t'me mama, so she can look after me. It was hard, d'birth, so young I be an' small. I long t'die 'fore it over. You' oma stand by me de whole time holdin' me hand, prayin' an' givin' me hope. Next day he come to see you'. You' skin every bit as white as he, an' you're pretty baby, oh so pretty! He say you t'have he name an' be baptized in de church, proper. I want t'go home with he, but he say no. I'm t'stay with me mama till I be strong again. He leave some money. Next t'ing I hear he marry that white woman, that Dorcas Lillie Rogers. She papa own all o' Herman Hill. You' papa never come near me no more."

"How come, Mama? How come he no care?" Anna felt hurt

and more confused than ever.

"That white womon, she don' wan' him messin' with colored, and she rich. I poor womon-born slave."

Anna was quiet, thinking about what her mother had said. It all seemed so unfair! Then she murmured, "Oh, Mama, I hope Papa Cappel come home soon!"

"So do I, Anna. So do I."

Susanna gently stroked Anna's hair. Soothed by her caresses and the comforting warmth of her body, at last Anna drifted off to sleep, her head on her mother's arm.

Several months later Anna went down to Gallows Bay to buy fish. Cap'n Greg was weighing a grouper for her on the spring scale that hung at the back of his fish cart. While she was waiting she glanced seaward and noticed a new arrival at anchor in the harbor. The ship was a large merchantman, square-rigged, flying the Danish flag. Anna plucked at the fisherman's sleeve. "Cap'n Greg, what ship that be?"

"Dat de *Roepstorff* out from Copenhagen, chile. I bespoke her when out by me lobster traps." He studied the scale. "Now this here grouper weigh . . ."

He looked for Anna, but she was nowhere to be seen. At the word, "Copenhagen" she had raced up the hill to tell her mother. Perhaps, there would be word of the *Frederica*.

Many of the townsfolk, Susanna and Anna among them, waited on the wharf for the captain and his crew to come ashore. He delivered despatches to the government officials on hand to greet him, then shared what shipping news he had with the people. He brought news of the brig *Erica*. She had arrived safely in Copenhagen and sold her cargo at a profit. The *Vigilant* had outmaneuvered Spanish pirates and got clean away. She was now safe in St. Thomas.

The crowd cheered lustily at this good news.

His other news brought tears to some. The *Frederica* was listed in Copenhagen as lost at sea. Norwegian fishermen attested to the report that she went down with all hands off the Norwegian coast in a violent winter storm on the night of February fifth.

At first Susanna refused to believe what her ears were hearing. There could be some mistake, a mistake in the ship's identity perhaps. Or maybe there *were* a few survivors. How could they be sure *no one* had made it to shore. She had seen the small boats, lifeboats, the *Frederica* carried. Perhaps survivors were still adrift. But then she thought despairing, Hans would be the sort to stay till the last and go down with his ship. She waited until the crowd had dispersed so that she could speak with the captain of the *Roepstorff* in private.

"For sure t'was the *Frederica* of which you spoke, sir?" she asked with tears in her eyes.

"For sure, my girl. No doubt about it. You had family aboard?"

Susanna nodded her head. She didn't trust herself to speak. She walked home in a daze, stunned by her misfortune. Anna clung to her hand, fighting the lump in her own throat. Susanna wept the whole night through.

The next day Christopher Hansen, her guardian called to offer his sympathy. "If there is ought I can do . . . ?"

Susanna stared at him dry-eyed, her tears all spent. "No, Herr Hansen, nothin' . . . nothin' at all."

"Well, pray let me know. . ." His attention had been caught by Anna, who stood in the doorway, her dark eyes large and soulful in her pale face.

"I let you know," Susanna said softly.

The young attorney left without delay. But as he closed the door behind him, it crossed his mind that Anna was an unusually appealing child.

As the days wore on Susanna came to accept her fate. She had learned early that the lives of Cruzian women were often touched by tragedy and that there was nothing to do but stoically endure. When the court settled Captain Cappel's estate it acknowledged the deed making Christine and Sophia owners of the house. Christopher Hansen was confimed as Susanna's guardian. From that time on he became a regular caller at the Cappel house on Hill Street.

Chapter 4

ANNA ELIZABETH ULRIEKE HEEGAARD was confirmed on the 8th day of July, 1804. The confirmation service was held in the same church in which she'd sought refuge from the horrors of the slave auction two years earlier. Since then the slave trade had been abolished. That didn't mean it had stopped altogether. Slaves were still smuggled into secluded coves or dumped from slavers into small boats, brought ashore at night and sold at higher prices than ever because the supply was dwindling.

As she remained kneeling with the others at the altar rail, after taking her first communion, she heard the pastor say, "Lord, let these young people go forth into the world to do Thy will. Let them spread Your light among the heathen, feed the hungry, comfort the sick, and lighten the burden of the oppressed."

That was it, she thought, to lighten the burden of the oppressed, to lift the yoke of slavery from the necks of her mother's people. She glanced at her wrist and saw that the three tiny scars were still visible. Rising, she walked down the aisle to the pew where her family sat, her mother, grandmother, Christine and Sophia. Her mother held baby Johannes, Anna's half brother, sired by Skipper Peter Abraham Wittrog, another seafaring man who had succumbed to Susanna's charms. Anna squeezed into the pew beside Christine.

It was time for the closing hymn. Everyone stood to sing. Rich voices sang in harmony, using the words and music of an old Dutch hymn. Altar boys extinguished the candles, and everyone filed out of the dim interior of the church to blink in the bright sunlight. Overhead the clock in the clock tower struck twelve.

The family stood on the street corner smiling and nodding to friends and relatives, receiving greetings and congratulations. The women wore broad-brimmed straw hats over bright-colored headcloths to protect their faces from the sun. Because of the heat the long sleeves of their white dresses clung to their arms and their skirts hung limply to their ankles. Anna's long black hair was tied back off her face by a rose-colored scarf.

When only the family remained on the corner her grandmother gave her a hug. "God bless you, young Anna!" she said.

Pride shone in her mother's eyes. "Us proud of you this day, Anna. No young person in d'class so tall, so good-lookin', give answer so clear."

Anna glowed. It was pleasant to hear words of love and praise.

"D'you feel different inside, Anna?" Christine asked.

"You look d'same," little Sophia observed.

"'Course I d'same, dupies," Anna assured them. "Only I feel somehow . . ." She couldn't find the right words to express the feelings the service had inspired. All she could manage was, "I—I feel hungry!"

Amalie Bernard chuckled. "Come then. Lucia'll have d'chicken in d'pot stewed by now, de kallaloo an' fungi made. I don' doubt she lookin' down de street for a sight of us this minute."

"It good of Lucia t'fix dinner fo' us this day," Susanna said. "Come 'long, gels. It hard up de hill an' gettin' hotter every minute."

"I carry Johannes, Mama," Anna said. "Put he on me back. He like t'ride so."

Susanna settled Johannes on Anna's back, and Anna clapsed her hands beneath his bottom to hold him securely. He grabbed two fistfuls of her hair.

"Ouch!" Anna cried. "Mama, make he let go me hair!"

Susanna disengaged Johannes' chubby fingers and placed his hands on Anna's shoulders. "So, Johannes," she said. "Hold on so."

Anna trotted up the hill like a good "horsey," and Johannes laughed at her antics. At the top she paused to catch her breath and let the others catch up. She looked out over the shingled and tiled roofs that stepped steeply down the hillside towards Gallows Bay. The water shimmered in the sun, pale green in the shallows, aquamarine and peacock blue beyond. Several frigates stood at anchor, their sails furled. The slight breeze bore harbor smells to her nose, fish and rotting seaweed, tar and the sweetish smell of molasses seeping from barrels of sugar waiting to be onloaded.

The family continued past the fine houses with a sea view to the row of small shingled ones in their own neighborhood. Aunt Lucia's narrow porch was hung with woodrose and trumpet vine, the deep-throated blossoms the color of good Danish butter. She stood waiting for them and took Johannes from Anna's back. A bulge beneath her apron showed that she would have a baby of her own before the fall rains came. It would be the child of merchant, Jacob Keylow. Thomas Petersen, Hans and Peter's father, had died the year before.

"So how was it?" she asked, cuddling Johannes in her arms. "A long service I'm thinkin', or did you stan' 'round with tongue clackin' like pods on thibet tree?"

"Such a idee, Lucia!" Susanna protested. "You know better then that."

"I know you great for talk-talk. Well, now you' here, come in out o' de sun. Evert'ing ready, and de boys got water down de chin from lookin' at de food!"

They passed through the house to the outdoor kitchen where a black kettle suspended over glowing charcoal gave off the mouthwatering odor of chicken stewed with herbs. As a special treat in Anna's honor, Lucia had baked small white sugar cakes frosted with brown sugar and coconut. A large jug of maubie, spiced and sweetened, stood ready to slake the thirst.

After Amalie Bernard had offered a blessing, the food was attacked with forks, knives, and fingers. The conversation was lively. Only Anna was quiet. Her thoughts were on the church service and what it had meant to her.

When everyone had had all they could eat, the family parted. The boys were off to the parade grounds to watch the Danish solders drill. Susannna took Johannes home for his nap. Amalie Bernard settled herself in her favorite chair on the porch where she could see all that was going on up and down the street. Meanwhile her hands busied themselves with her knitting. She was knitting a fine scarlet and black wool cap for Hans. It was to be as fine as that of any boy on the island.

Anna found a stool and placed it beside her grandmother. "Oma, when you join d'church, it make you stronger an' better?"

Amalie Bernard thought for a moment. "When I you' age,Anna, I live on plantation far from de town. There be no services for slaves. It work, work from sunup t'sundown. But sometimes Moravian missionaries teach us. I no older then you when I learn t'turn to de Lord in time o' trouble. He me strength an' me comfort. A black woman's life brim full o' sorrow. More time then not, it taste bitter in de mouth. Placin' me burden on de Lord, that an' doin' wha'soever I can t'ease de pain of others, lighten me load."

"How was it, Oma, t'be slave?" Anna lowered her eyes. She felt guilty bringing back bad memories.

"Misery, chile, pure misery! You' body b'long to another. Always you at another's beck an' call. An' I be kind-treated compared t'some. I house slave an' didn't do back-breakin' work o' womon in cane fields. First t'ing in de mornin' it me job t'gather up de slops an' scrub out de pots good with wood ash. Then I spread up d'bed, careful not t'leave wrinkle fo' me mistress back. I dust d'furniture an' sweep d'floors. Evenin's I he'p in d'kitchen, servin' d'food at d'master's table an' helpin' t'clean up after d'meal. If you young an' pretty de master, or he son, apt t'come t'you' bed in d'night wantin' he way with you. No courtin'. No sweet talk. Just take you where you lie, in an' out, in an' out— an' leave you quick, hurtin' an' weepin' in you' pillow."

For a long moment after her grandmother had ceased speaking the only sound was that of the clicking needles. Anna was considering her words. Then with some anger she asked, "Oma, how is it de Lord allow some t'be slave an' some t'be free?"

Amalie Bernard rested her hands in her lap trying for a reasonable answer. "That hard question, Anna. Seems t'me de Lord don' will it that way. De Lord give mon free t'be good—or bad. The wickedness come from mon's evil heart. If mon turn he back on de Lord, d'Lord let him go he sinful way. But you, Anna, in you' time, you mebbe see better ways. Already there be sign. De stoppin' o' d'slave trade be one. Missionaries he'p. Pastor Mueller, he he'p. It may be, as free-colored, you can he'p."

Anna's eyes lit up. "How, Oma? How can I he'p? How can one gel—or even womon growed—he'p? I got no say 'bout gov'ment rules."

43

"As t'ings be on this island," Amalie Bernard said weighing her words, "de bes' t'ing you can do is try for affection o' mon in high place, mon what do have say 'bout de rules. Through he, you make change. You good-lookin', Anna, an' you have d'wits t'learn fine manner an' smart talk. You got blood o' aristocrat in you' vein. Baron Breton was French noblemon, come to this island t'get out from under de popish church. Keep you' head an' you' eye on de main t'ing, an' you' go far. Don' give you'self to de first dumbclop what come down de path. Wait till mon with some say-so ask for you' favors."

"Oma, I will. Truly I will."

Amalie Bernard laid her hand on Anna's head. Anna looked up into her eyes. Amalie Bernard smiled. "You good gel, Anna. I t'ink you do what you say."

That same afternoon Christopher Hansen came calling on Susanna. Hansen was a tall thin man, somewhat round-shouldered. His eyes were an opaque gray and his sandy-colored hair was beginning to thin at the temples. A limp red moustache covered his upper lip and hung down on either side of his mouth. He wore a conservative black suit, appropriate for his profession and the Sabbath day.

Susanna graciously ushered him into the house. "Will you have coffee, Herr Hansen? Sit in that chair an' it please you. You fine it most comfortable."

"Coffee would indeed be welcome, my dear Susanna," he said. He sat down and crossed his long thin legs. "I was impressed with the confirmation service and Anna's part in it. Allow me to commend you for arranging to have her confirmed."

"It be Anna's own wish. She have serious thought, that gel. Herr Hansen, you pardon me whilst I fetch de coffee?"

When she returned Anna was with her, carrying sugar cakes on a fine blue and white china plate. She placed the plate carefully on a table by Christopher Hansen's chair. To her surprise he rose to greet her, holding out his hand. Hesitantly, she offered hers, and he pressed it warmly. "Allow me to congratulate you on your confimation, Anna. I have a small gift." He reached into the pocket in the tail of his coat and drew out a little box. "For you, a token of my esteem and reminder of this day."

Anna felt her cheeks grow warm. It was the first time a man had offered her a present. She raised her eyes shyly to his but found his unreadable. She held the box in her hand, uncertain what to do next. Christine and Sophia had run in from the yard bursting with curiosity.

"You may open it," Christopher Hansen said.

She slowly lifted the lid. Inside lay a small gold cross attached to a shimmering golden chain. The richness of the gold and the fine workmanship on the cross did not escape her. She stared at it, speechless.

"What you say, Anna?" her mother prompted her.

Flushing a still deeper red she stammered, "Thank you, thank you, Herr Hansen. Thank you ver' much. It most bea-u-tiful."

"I'm glad it pleases you." He was admiring, not for the first time, her fine dark eyes.

"Put it on! Put it on!" chorused her sisters.

"I fetch d'mirror," Christine said. She ran from the room and returned with a small oval mirror in a mahogany frame. She held it so that Anna could see herself. Anna placed the chain around her neck. It showed to advantage over her simple white dress.

"See!" she said turning toward her mother. "It becomes me, Mama. You mos' kind, Herr Hansen!"

"Not at all. But I agree. It suits you well. I hope you'll wear it often."

Anna helped her mother by putting Johannes to bed. Afterward she climbed the stairs to her room. She opened her dresser drawer and felt for the piece of chainy-china No-no had given her long ago. She held it thoughtfully in her hand. It was nothing compared to the cross and golden chain she now wore around her neck; a bit of broken china from a plate. Most likely the broken piece from which it had come was surreptitiously thrown on the trash by some servant afraid to let the master know of his clumsiness. She smiled to think how excited she had been about a bit of china. Still—still it brought back memories of a beautiful garden, a beautiful young boy, a beautiful time in her life. Her throat tightened as she thought of the last time she'd seen No-no standing on the auction block. She wished she knew what had become of him. Had he been sold to the manager of Estate Little Princesse? She hadn't been able to endure the auction long enough to find out. She had asked some around town. But no one seemed to know. However, town people seldom knew what went on in the country; and Little Princesse, though it was only a few miles down the beach, was definitely in the country. With a sigh she put the chainy-china back, took the gold chain from her neck, laid it beside the chainy-china, and closed the drawer.

Going to the window she saw that the light was golden over the plump, cushiony hills behind the town. Heavy rain clouds, irregularly shaped, looked like dark islands floating in a soft blue sea. A sliver of moon, daytime white, hung above. She watched until the sun slipped behind the hills and was gone. The sky darkened, and the moon turned into a golden crescent. Beside it a diamond twinkled on, the evening's first star.

She lit the candle beside her bed and sat on it thinking about Christopher Hansen. A suspicion had formed in her mind that he had more interest in her than was called for as his ward's daughter. It was flattering to think such thoughts. Yet he was so old, over thirty she guessed. He made her feel uncomfortable when he looked at her directly, made her feel painfully young and gawky. And she could never even guess at what thoughts lay behind those opaque eyes. She knew as a lawyer he had a secure place in the community and that he understood the rules , perhaps even how to change them. Was he the sort of man Oma meant? She wondered how it would feel to have him do that thing to her Oma had spoken of, in and out, in and out. She shivered a little and was glad to hear Christine and Sophia coming up the stairs.

"Aren't you de lucky one," Christine said, "t'get present from fancy mon like Herr Hansen!"

"I don' like he moustache all droopy," Sophia said. "It ticklish lookin'." She giggled.

"You like him, Anna?" Christine asked. "I think he like you plenty."

"I don' rightly know," Anna said. "He makes me feel squiglish inside, an' I never know what thoughts he have in he head."

Sophia yawned and threw herself down on her bed fully dressed. It had been a long day.

"Come then, Sophie," Anna said reprovingly. "Take you' clothes off. You know better then t'lie down in you' best dress. Come here an' I undo de back buttons."

The girls undressed and climbed into their beds. As Anna was dropping off to sleep she heard a rapping on the front door, heard it open, and her mother's soft words of welcome. She knew it was Skipper Wittrog come to call. The skipper no longer went to sea. He was content owning and operating a rum shop. About a year ago he had lived with them for a few months. Then his Danish wife, more courageous than most European women, had come out to the island to join him. Now it was rumored that Mme. Wittrog was grievously ill.

Two weeks later church bells tolled for her funeral. At about the same time another death caused a stir among the islanders. In honor of the deceased, the flag on the fort stood at half-mast. Word had come on a Yankee trader that native son Alexander Hamilton had been killed in a duel. He had made disparaging remarks about one Aaron Burr during a political quarrel, and Burr had demanded "satisfaction." The older islanders remembered the precocious Hamilton working as a boy in Nicholas Cruger's hardware store. It was a great pity, they agreed, that his brilliant career had ended so abruptly, and he so young.

Chapter 5

CHRISTINE SHOOK Anna's shoulder gently. "Wake up!" she whispered in her ear. "It mornin' an' we go down t'see de parade an' de dancin'."

Anna sat up and rubbed the sleep from her eyes. She blinked and saw that the window framed a bright square of sunshine. It was hard to believe it was that late. Then she remembered going with the family to the midnight Christmas Eve service the night before. No wonder she was sleepy! She glanced over at the double bed and saw that Sophia still lay there.

Christine saw her look and said, "Let her be. We go t'gether. It more fun jus' we two. Come on, Anna! Hurry! I hear d'drums."

Anna swung her feet to the floor, stood up and stretched. Christine looked at her with envy. In the three years that had passed since Anna was confirmed she had grown into a well-proportioned young woman. Her full, uplifted breasts gave shape to her straight white nightgown. Her waist was small, her hips nicely curved. The flesh of her upper arms was round and firm. Christine at thirteen was still childishly formed, her breasts newly budded.

"When I get figger like you, Anna, all curvey?" she asked wistfully.

"Don' be anxious. It come. Already I see mon an' boy follow you with they eyes. How 'bout that Scotsmon, that Jamie Miller?"

Christine blushed becomingly. She had tied yellow ribbons in her wavy brown hair and wore a string of tiny pink shells around her neck. "You think he like me, Anna?"

"I certain sure. It plain as d'nose on you face." Anna let her nightgown fall to the floor. She put on a full skirt and a blouse with a low-cut neck loosely gathered over her shoulders. Her bare feet went into leather slippers. Christine watched impatiently while Anna carefully combed her hair, parted it in the middle and formed it into loose coils over her ears.

She was about to close her dresser drawer when the gold chain Christopher Hansen had given her caught her eye. He had become a persistent suitor this last year, making it plain that he wanted Anna to live with him, run his household and share his bed. She drew the chain out and put it on.

"You mus' like d'mon, you wear he chain," Christine said.

"Truth is, I like d'chain," Anna replied dryly.

"Well, come on then. You move slow as ol' sea turtle!" Christine's green eyes sparkled with excitement. She started for the stairs.

Anna grabbed a straw hat with a floppy brim, plopped it on her head, and followed her. Running down Hill Street, the girls' feet fairly flew, drawn by the sound of pipe and drum.

On the parade grounds in front of the old red fort small booths had been set up and decorated with tinsel and brightly colored paper. For a pfenning one could buy a tot of rum. Sweet cakes sold for two. Anna bought two cakes which served the girls well enough for breakfast.

The people milling about were all dressed in their best. The women wore gaily printed skirts and white bouses, the men wore colored shirts and dark trousers. On the wharf a scratchy band, gaudy in "white folks" cast-off finery, played their assorted homemade instruments. They banged on iron hoops and blew on metal pipes of assorted sizes and flutes made from bamboo. The drums, modeled after those their forebearers had used in Africa, were played with the flat of the drummers' hands in complicated toe-tapping rhythms. A determined fiddler, who made up with energy what he lacked in skill, scraped out a lively tune that bound together all the sounds the other instruments were making.

The entertainment on Christmas Day was traditionally planned by leaders among the slaves for their own pleasure, the only time during the year when they were encouraged to really enjoy themselves. Masters, mistresses, and free-colored were welcome to take part if they liked, but had little to do with the arrangements. A "queen" was chosen, the most talented and beautiful young woman that could be found among the black population. She was dressed in flamboyant satins and gauze, decked with jewels, and crowned with a wreath of flowers. Her escort was a young man chosen for his good looks and popularity, dubbed "Sir Christmas." The queen would do a solo dance, then be joined by six handmaidens for more dancing. At the end of this dance the queen and her handmaidens would choose partners from the crowd. Those chosen chose again until everyone in Christiansted who could shake a leg or swivel his hips would be prancing and twirling around the parade grounds and later cavorting through the streets.

Anna and Christine watched entranced as a girl they knew as Julie, this year's queen, approached the ring of spectators to do her dance. She was indeed beautiful and moved with astonishing grace. Her flashing black eyes, her high color, the toss of her head, all suggested that the blood of some dashing Spaniard flowed through her veins. Her escort was tall and slim-hipped, and held himself proudly. He wore a cloth-of-gold cape over a short scarlet jacket, tight buff-colored breeches, and high-polished boots. A large blue velvet tam with an ostrich plume hid his face from the girls as he led his partner into a ring made by the spectators.

With her hand placed lightly on his arm Queen Julie bowed and smiled to favorites among the crowd. Then she turned toward her escort and curtsied. He doffed his cap and made a sweeping bow, the signal for her to commence her dance. As he stepped back to give her room, Anna caught sight of his face. She gasped. This year's Sir Christmas was her old friend No-no, No-no grown into a mature man!

The eyes of the specatators were fixed on Queen Julie as she swayed and whirled, petticoats flying, to the sensuous rhythm of the drums. Anna's eyes were fixed on No-no. He was glancing casually around, surveying the crowd. She willed him to look her way, and at last he did. For a brief moment their eyes met and held. Then he looked back at Julie. Did he recognize her? Did he remember? Anna could feel the beat of her heart. She clutched Christine's arm. "Christine, that's No-no!"

Christine was confused. "Who you talk 'bout?"

"Sir Christmas, that's who. No-no *is* Sir Christmas!"

"No-no? What sort o' dupie name that be? An' why you care?"

"Think once, Christine. I told you 'bout he. I know he at Eigtved's 'fore you' born."

Christine looked at Sir Christmas curiously. "You talk 'bout that black buck bowin' an' scrapin' to Julie? You know she be whore, Anna?"

"I don' care 'bout she! It No-no I care 'bout. What a bea-u-tiful mon!"

The dance continued, the crowd applauding and whistling in appreciation. Suddenly, above the sound of the festivites, came the incongruous roar of cannon. It seemed incredible, but the sound could not be mistaken for anything else. Stunned, the crowd turned en masse toward the harbor. Mouths fell open with astonishment. On the parade grounds the celebrating slowly ground to a halt. Visible entering Gallows Bay was a British man of war, the Union Jack flying from her mast-head. She was rapidly bearing down on the town.

As the reality of the cannon's threat dawned, women screamed and men cursed. Again the warship's sides blossomed with sinister red roses born of the cannon's mouth. The sight was soon followed by the loud boom of big guns. Fortunately, for the town the cannon balls fell short of their target, hissing but harmless. Still, no one could doubt the warship's hostile intentions.

From the Danish fort a bugle sounded. Soldiers suddenly came to attention. Some still struggling into their uniforms, they rushed to gun emplacements. An officer standing on the ramparts flashed his sword in the sun and gave the order to fire. The Danes returned the British fire, but like the British, the balls spit from the cannons' mouths splashed harmlessly into the sea. The warship was still too far away to make a good target. The solders rammed new shot into their pieces. The British ship kept on coming . . . closer, closer.

Suddenly, to the confusion of soldier and civilian alike, the warship changed course and came up into the wind. The sails shivered and went flat. Sailors leapt to the capstan and ran out the ship's anchor. Along her beam preparations were being made to lower the captain's gig.

Anna was watching fascinated by the drama taking place in the harbor. But all at once she felt a hand on her shoulder. Turning she found herself face to face with No-no. She felt a rush of blood to her cheeks and again the pounding of her heart.

He smiled down at her. "I know you," he said. "I know you from long ago."

"I be . . . Anna," she faltered. "We play together in Eigtved's garden. I follow you 'round like puppy dog." She grinned mischievously. "Mos' like you think me one big bother."

No-no chuckled. "I 'member. You funny li'l skinny t'ing with

51

big black eye in pale face. I give you piece o' chainy-china an' you happy as thrushee."

He cast his eyes over the heads of the milling crowd. Confusion reigned. The timid were rushing for cover. The brave pressed forward, followed closely by the curious. Looking toward Gallows Bay he saw the British captain's gig was on its way to the fort, carrying a white flag and several officers.

"Come," No-no said. "I don' know what happen here, but fo' sure we not be missed. Come. I want t'talk with you."

Anna's heart skipped a beat. Did she dare go off with him? She turned to speak to Christine and saw that she was standing some distance away talking to Jamie Miller. Her eyes met No-no's again. They begged her to say yes. She nodded her assent.

"You go. I follow," he said. "Bes' we not leave together."

Anna edged through the crowd, then picked up her skirts and ran. She headed for the beach north of town. When she reached the sand she stopped and slipped off her shoes to make running easier. She ran along the water's edge, splashing in the water, feeling strangely excited and free as the terns that swooped and dove, then soared again, circling high to look for fish along the reef. Her hat fell off, and her hair came loose. She stopped to pick up her hat, and No-no caught up. When she took off again, he loped easily along by her side. She kept on running until she came to the watergut, a small tidal stream that ran from the town into the sea. She waded across. On the other side she stopped breathless.

"Good you stop," No-no said with a grin. "You have me gaspin' like fish out o' water!"

Anna laughed. She flopped down on the sand and fanned her face with her hat. Her hair hung loose about her shoulders

No-no stretched out beside her, leaning his head on his elbow and looking up at her. "Such a long time!" he said. "Now you womon growed. Come, Anna, tell me all what happen these long years."

Anna dug her toes into the sand, wondering where to start. Speaking hesitantly at first she sketched the events of her life, skipping much that would be meaningless to him. She didn't tell him about the slave auction or her visit to the church afterward. She didn't tell him about Christopher Hansen. "An' you, No-no. What 'bout you?"

As he spoke of his growing up years she studied his face. It was a strong face, the brow well developed above the deep-set eyes. The nose was straight, the chin firm, the mouth full and sensitive. His jacket strained against its buttons, too snug a fit for his chest. The story he told was short. He didn't dwell on the auction, simply stated that he'd been sold.

"An' where you live this time, No-no?"

"By Li'l Princesse, way up d'beach. De Greathouse stan' on a hill. De roof show above cocopalms. I be in charge o' de stables."

"You still slave. You be in trouble runnin' off."

"Not this day. This Chris'mas. All . . . all unfree give liberty this day."

Anna pulled up her knees and hugged them. True. It was Christmas. She'd forgotten. She looked toward town. Nothing could be seen from the beach to indicate what was going on.

She turned back toward No-no. "That gel, that Julie. She you' gel?"

"Julie, huh! She b'long to d'whole island, to any mon what pay she price. I wan' no part o' Julie!"

"But she so pretty! She dance so good!"

"So-o? Anna, you better then pretty. You warm an' sweet like sugar. I wan' we should meet agin. You come to d'beach an' talk with me?"

"I might. How I know you be here?"

"I get message to you. I come t'beach mos' days give horses sea bath. I tie horses an' we talk. I can write! I learn at Orange Grove."

"I can write some," Anna said. "Pastor Mueller teach me."

"Where I leave message?"

Anna thought for several minutes. "Already I tell you where I live. You come to lane behind house. There be a stone wall an' acacia bush. I place loose stone on wall. You put message under. I look each day."

"Good. I fine a way. Now we bes' go back."

He stood up and offered her his hand. At his touch she shivered. His grasp was firm and warm. He pulled her to her feet.

Anna went directly home. Her hair hung down in a tangle. Her skirt was sandy and the hem damp. She took the precaution of approaching the house from the rear. If her mother saw her disarray, there would be questions.

To her relief she found the house empty. She surmised that

her mother and Skipper Wittrog had gone down into the town, taking the younger children with them. It gave Anna a chance to change her clothes.

When they returned Anna learned that Major Krause, commander of the Danish fort, was ferried out to the British warship to confer with Admiral Lord Cochrane. The admiral convinced Major Krause that the British force was so overwhelmingly superior that the Danes wouldn't have a chance. Furthermore he stated that he was determined to take over the island at any cost. Already St. Thomas had fallen into British hands without a fight. When Major Krause relayed this information to Governor Lillienschield, the governor, bowing to reality, agreed to surrender. Thereupon the Danish flag was hauled down from the fort, and the Union Jack raised instead.

"What this mean t'us, Abr'am, to d'family?" Susanna asked. She was sitting beside him on the porch fanning herself. She was tired from standing overlong in the sun to hear what the Governor had to say. Johannes was practicing climbing up and down the steps, and the girls stood nearby listening.

"I dare say, my dear, precious little. Government people will be relieved of their posts. The British may shut up our soldiers or send 'em back to Denmark. Most of our planters are English, Scottish, or Irishers anyway. I doubt they give a damn whether it be English George or Danish Frederik they doff their hats to. That is if it's shippin' sugar and rum as usual. Now, I must be off to the shop. There'll be those who want t'drown their sorrows, and those who'll want to celebrate by drinkin' to our new king, by God!"

Susanna and Anna were willing to go along with his easygoing view. Besides, they had more absorbing concerns on their minds. Christopher Hansen had accosted Susanna on the parade ground and complained about Anna's coolness. Would she plead his case? Would she try to talk some sense into the girl and convince her of the generosity of the offer he'd made her?

Anna paid little attention to her mother's comments. Her mind was full of her encounter with No-no. Would he be able to get a message to her without being caught? Slaves were allowed to leave their plantations only under very special conditions. Would he dare run the risk? Did he care enough to try?

Chapter 6

ONE DRY DUSTY DAY followed another—New Year's, Three Kings' Day. The dust in the yard blew into the kitchen. The branches of the tamarind tree moaned and sighed and dropped some of their leaves. Down at Gallows Bay the fronds of the coconut palms did a capricious dance, while the sea wore whitecaps day and night. "Christmas winds," the natives remarked.

Morning and evening Anna looked in vain for a message from No-no. She longed with all her heart to see him again. She relived every detail of the time she'd spent with him on the beach, remembered everything they did and said. When she thought of the touch of his hand, sensations that were new to her coursed through her body. She longed to have him hold her in his arms, caress her, and press his lips against hers. Gone was her cool calculated decision of three years ago to wait for a man of position in the community, one with influence in the government, before she gave herself. The thought of sharing Christopher Hansen's bed was more repugnant than ever to her now.

One evening Christine caught her emerging from the acacia bushes by the stone wall wearing a doleful face. After much wheedling she pried Anna's secret out of her. She had the advantage of having seen Anna go off with No-no on Christmas Day. Anna swore her to secrecy. She felt sure Christine would honor her promise, for she knew Christine was seeing Jamie Miller on the sly. Not that there was anything wrong with Jamie, but their mother thought Christine too young to be courted by anyone.

Dealing with her mother was more difficult. One day Susanna cornered her. "Anna, why you run out to d'wall mos' mornin'? What you lookin' for anyways? You 'spect some person come by you wanna see?"

Caught off guard Anna's explanation was none too convincing. "Uh, yes, Mama. That friend o' mine. That Bessie Williams. She come by with news o' de town. She know this Britisher, a soldier he is. . ."

"Anna, you have nothin' t'do with British soldier."

"Not me, Mama. Bessie."

"'Pears to me, you' waste you' time talkin' to Bessie. You do better think o' Herr Hansen an' he offer."

"He think enough o' he own self for de both o' us, Mama."

"He want you bad, Anna."

"Well, I don' want him. He droopy. He stan' droopy. He moustache droopy. I wish he let me be!"

It had been so long since Anna had heard from No-no she began to fear he'd forgotten her. She grew nervous and irritable. She found it hard to endure Christopher Hansen's visits. He burdened her with tedious details and problems connected with his law career. The British occupation meant that some Danes were leaving for home, and there were tricky matters concerning transfers of real estate and selling of slaves that were grist for a lawyer's mill.

One evening, after he'd been droning on for some time, she purposely started an argument. "How come you lawyers, so smart 'bout settlin' all manner o' things, do nothin' 'bout bad treatment o' free-colored. Some way they no better off then slaves. There's that letter o' freedom' Mama forced t'carry. It demeanin', an insult, an' a great nuisance besides."

"I'm surprised that you take exception, Anna. You certainly know it was designed to protect, to keep slave holders from taking free-colored as runaway slaves."

"But Mama free since small chile. She carry it all that time. Every person in town know Mama, know she no slave."

"Laws are made for the majority. There can't be exceptions to suit every Tom, Dick, or Harry. If there were, things would be in an awful muddle. Certainly you're not simple-minded enough to think the government has the time or inclination to examine each and every case?"

"Well, mebbe they should make time. And how come, Herr Hansen, free-colored can't be lawyers or doctors? An' when they join up with de militia, even if they smarter then white, they can't be officer? How come?"

"Anna, Anna, let's not quarrel. I agree some of the laws are unfair. But they can't be changed overnight. It must be done by due process."

"Due process, indeed!" Her eyes flashed angily. "Mama get no younger. How long for 'due process'?"

"Anna, come live with me. You'll be same as white in my house. If we have children they'll pass as white. Wouldn't you like to have sons with all the privileges accorded white men?"

"An' would they be shamed by they mama? An' even mo' by they oma? Pray leave me be, Herr Hansen. I no way ready . . ."

"Very well, Anna. I am a patient men. Now, I must bid you good night. I'm overdue at the reception General Harcourt is giving to celebrate King George's birthday, and the general is not so patient a man as I. I'll call again soon."

After she was in bed that night Anna lay awake. Moonlight filtered through the leaves of the big tamarind tree outside her open window and traced dappled shadows on the floor of the room. She heard faint music borne on the breeze, coming from the reception at Government House. She could imagine the king's officers in their splendid red uniforms trimmed with gold braid, the ladies in gleaming silk or satin gowns, high waisted with low-cut bodices and skirts falling in soft folds to their slippered feet. Couples would be twirling around the dance floor in time to the music. A few of the ladies would be wives. A few would be daughters. A few, snubbed by the wives, would be dusky-skinned girls from a family like hers.

The music ceased. Anna grew drowsy. Then she heard the thump of a small stone landing on the floor inside the open window. Instantly awake, she ran to the window and looked out into the moonlit yard. A low voice called her name. The sound of the familiar voice sent shivers racing up and down her spine. She searched the yard and saw a tall straight figure move slightly clear of the shadow cast by the tamarind tree. Her heart leapt within her. Without a moment's hesitation she crept stealthily down the stairs, ran out the back of the house and straight into No-no's arms.

"Oh, No-no! I think I never hear from you more."

"It agony pure and simple not comin'! I try. Many time I try to get away. Each time I be caught. Once I be caught an' whipped. Damn them! Damn them t'hell, de white masters!"

"Sh-h!" Anna laid a finger on his lips. "We no talk o' them."

He drew her closer, holding her in a tight embrace. She felt breathless and suddenly stiffened with alarm. The sensations she was feeling were new and strange, not unpleasant, but strange. She felt a warmth and a throbbing in parts of her body that she had given little thought to before. She wanted to stay in his arms and wanted to break away. She wanted to run but she had to stay. She felt confused.

Aware of her misgivings, he held her more gently. With one hand he brushed the mass of dark hair back from her upturned face and ran his fingers lightly over her smooth cheek. Her face was like an ivory cameo in the moonlight, he thought, her eyes dark pools with the light of beginning love burning in their depths. He stroked her neck and ran his hand down her spine.

The gentleness of his touch was reassuring. She relaxed and closed her eyes. She felt the rapid beat of her heart and his, the warmth of his breath on her cheek. He touched her lips tentatively with his and, when she offered no resistance, he kissed her passionately. Her lips parted, and he explored the space between with his tongue. He continued to caress her, and she returned his kisses. Then his hand moved to her breast and gently cupped it.

Her eyes flew open. "Oh, No-no! You musn't!"

He held her off a little, the better to see her face. "Please, Anna," he implored in a husky voice, "let me show you how I love you. Anna, Anna, you so beautiful, so sof'. I think I love you always . . . since children. At las', this night, we fine each other. Anna, say you love me."

"Oh, I do, but . . ."

"I want you t'be mine, Anna. You an' no other, for ever an' ever."

His mouth covered hers, his lips firm, his breath sweet. She couldn't resist. He kissed her again and again. She felt his body hard against hers and was filled with wild nameless desires. He loosened the cord that held her nightgown around her shoulders. It fell to the ground. For a moment he stood deeply moved as he looked at her young body revealed in the moonlight, the firm rounded breasts, the flat abdomen, the long column of her legs, the dark smudge where they joined. Then he was holding her close again and kissing her, her throat, her breasts.

She felt weak in his arms and slumped against him. He picked her up and carried her deep into the shadow of the tamarind tree where he laid her gently on the ground. His coarse work pants, all that separated them now, were easily disposed of. He lay beside her cradling her in his arms and murmuring words of love, sweet as honey to her ears. She snuggled closer. His hands caressed her, searching, finding. There was no way, now, that she could retreat. She wanted the delicious sensations she was feeling to go on forever.

He rolled her onto her back. His body covered hers. He entered her with a hard thrust. She felt a moment of pain. She heard herself cry out. But the pain quickly eased, and she was carried out of herself on a wave of ecstacy that sent her senses reeling toward the stars.

For an hour or more thay lay in each others arms, filled with a delightful euphoria neither had experienced before. Then Anna shivered. A drop of rain had fallen on her bare thigh. No-no reached for his pants and tried clumsily to cover her.

"I bes' go in," she whispered. "You has a long way back."

"Anna, say again you love me."

"I love you, No-no."

"An' we meet an' love soon again?"

"Soon as can be."

He helped her to her feet. She put on her nightgown. He helped her adjust it. Then he held her for a moment, kissed her tenderly, and was gone. She tiptoed through the house and up the stairs, marvelling at the change that had occurred in a few short hours. Nothing would ever again be the same. From now on seeing No-no, sharing their love, would be more important to her than anything else in the world.

Their meetings were difficult to arrange. The next time was on the beach. She had found a message on the wall telling her when he would be there. In the shelter of the seagrape, within sight of Little Princesse, she waited for him. First she heard the pounding of hoofs. Then he appeared riding bareback on a great black stallion, his body and the horse's enough of the same hue that they appeared to be one, one creature in motion, beautiful against the turquoise water. As the horse came close he galloped at the edge of the water, throwing up showers of sparkling spray. The stallion was followed by three mares and a colt.

No-no leapt off and tied the stallion to a coconut palm. The mares stayed close, cropping beach grass.

With words of love on her lips Anna ran to meet him. No-no

folded her in his arms. After they had made love, she sat with his head in her lap, and they talked. He spoke passionately of the day when black men would be free. "It will come t'pass, Anna. Strong only survive under yoke o' slavery. Each generation more strong, more smart, less forgivin'. One day d'blacks will rise and demand they freedom. They will take control from de white masters. They will fight if need be."

"But, No-no, how there be rebellion without awful violence, awful destruction?"

No-no sat up. "Mebbe violence de only way. Mebbe many die, both black an' white. Bloodshed an' burnin' may be all de white masters understan'. But when smoke from greathouse blow away, de island be island o' free men. It been done. Bordeaux led rebellion on St. John. He hold de island for t'ree month till French navy . . ."

"But, No-no, that will happen again. Warship from one white country or 'nother will bombard an' invade, an' black rebels will hang."

"It chance we mus' take. Mon can no' go on forever in chains. We mus' be willin' t'die for free. In America some mon say, 'Give me liberty or give me death,' an' when he say that, de British let de people go."

"But, No-no, mebbe law can be change, so black mon free without all that killin' an' burnin'. That's what I hope for. Once on a time I vow t'use me life to he'p bring that change." She showed him the inside of her wrist. "There you see? I made tiny scars to remind me. I made them with hot wax from burnin' candle."

No-no raised her wrist to his lips and kissed it. "Oh, Anna, Anna, how I say how I love you?"

The stallion was pawing the sand and whinnying.

"He thirsty, Anna. I bes' go. I come again soon."

Reluctantly he stood up. He pulled her to her feet and kissed her once more. Then he untied the stallion, jumped on his back and headed back the way he had come. The mares followed. Anna stayed where he'd left her until she could no longer hear the thundering of hoofs.

Another Christmas rolled around with the British still occupying the island. With Napoleon supreme in Europe, the British were determined to control the Caribbean. Napoleon had organized a continental blockade, forbidding all trade between the continent and Britain. He condemned as fair prize not only every British ship, but any ship of any nation which had touched the coast of England or her colonies.

For Anna it was a year of emotional turmoil. The ecstatic happiness she knew in No-no's arms often gave way to anxiety and despair. She never knew when or if she'd see him again. She worried about his slipping away from Little Princesse, aware that each time he risked a beating or worse. Yet, when he didn't come, she fretted about not seeing him. She grew thin and hollow-eyed.

Changes were taking place in the family. In the spring of 1808 Christine was wooed and won by merchant Jamie Miller. Her mother thought her too young to know her own mind, but the alliance turned out to be a good one. Jamie and Christine lived together devotedly until his early death. They raised a large family.

In the prosperous years before the British occupation Susanna had bought a small house at Number One Company Street as an investment. Now, with Christine gone and to economize, she and the skipper moved into it, living on the top floor and making the lower one into the "needles and pins" store of Susanna's dreams. Sophia at eleven followed her mother, though she and Christine still held the title to the Hill Street house. Johannes, of course, came along, and room was made for Anna.

After the move Anna was more distraught than ever. She missed the big back yard and the tamarind tree where she and No-no made love. They still met occasionally in the shadows beside the new house, but they knew the danger of discovery was greater. Susanna was sure Anna was under a strain of some sort and began watching her closely.

One day she ushered Christopher Hansen into the upstairs sitting room and shut the door. "Anna has a lover!" she said.

The color drained from his face, making it even paler than usual. "How . . . how d'you know?" he stammered. "Isn't it possible you're mistaken?"

"I see he. I see he plain standin' in de moonlight under she window. She go t'he like a flash."

"In her nightdress?"

"Course, in she nightdress."

With a groan he sank into a chair. "You any idea who he is?"

"Aye, I know for sure. He No-no, de young buck chosen Sir Christmas year 'fore last. That's when they first met. Christine tell me."

"Good God! You mean this has been going on that long? It's a wonder to me you didn't notice anything sooner. I told you to keep an eye on her!"

"I know. I . . . I sleep soun' mos' nights. It grieve me she behave so. I can forbid she see him. If I say, Skipper give her thrashin'."

A cunning look had come into Christopher Hansen's eyes. "No, that won't be necessary. Since we know who the bastard is, I can handle it. Anna never need know of my part in the affair."

"It grieve me for de pain she feel, but it be for she own good. I don' favor she joinin' with such a one."

Anna never saw No-no again. A month went by and another. At last, she could no longer stand not knowing. Speaking to the family of errands to be done she headed for the beach and Little Princesse. She walked rapidly along the shore looking for the chimney from the estate sugar factory that No-no had said could be seen from the beach. She was apprehensive, for she knew deep within, though she was reluctant to look there, that the only news she could expect of him was bad news. The beauty of the seascape before her, the magic of the turquoise water, the lovely curl of wave on reef, the pleasant look of plump green hills in the distance at Judith's Fancy, were lost upon her. She was too preoccupied with her worries to notice such things.

She was tired and footsore by the time she found the path that led from the beach to the estate buildings. She followed it until she came to a branch leading off to the slave quarters.

The men and able-bodied women were at work in the fields, but she found an old crone sitting in an open doorway sucking on a pipe.

"Good marm," Anna said. "I be told there's one here knows much o' obeah, charms for sickness an' death, even potions for love. Me lover—"

"Come inside," the woman said. "We no talk o' such t'ings in de open."

Anna followed her inside a small musty room. The only light came from the door and one tiny window.

The old woman eyed Anna suspiciously, sucking on her pipe. "You' white. White womon need no he'p from ol' Jess."

"Look close, good Oma. I not white."

Jess put down her pipe and peered intently into Anna's face, then took both her hands in hers, turning them over and studying them carefully. Seeming satisfied she let them drop and looked up into Anna's face once more. "You say you' lover. . .?"

Anna slumped down onto a bench against the wall and wept. Jess moved unheeding around the tiny room, straightened the coverlet on a straw mattress, closed a shutter that was banging in the wind. Finally Anna ceased sobbing and sat quiet and spent, leaning against the wall. Jess filled a gourd cup with water and offered it to Anna. Anna drank gratefully.

Pulling a three-legged stool close to Anna, Jess sat down, her withered hands lying like brown leaves in her lap. "Tell me all wha' you can 'bout you' lover, chile. You want love potion, bring he back?"

"I fear no charm or potion he'p." Anna said sadly. "I fear he no come 'cause he cannot come. You tell me true. He No-no, real name Obediah. You know ought o' he?"

A light came into Jess's dim eyes and she nodded her head. "It be easy t'tell de firs' part. Last part no person here 'bouts know. Chile, me words will ease you' pride but no' you' heart."

"Tell me, Jess. I want true. Is he dead?"

"No, he no' dead. He be strong an' kickin' las' time I lay eyes on him. Trader mon buy. Price so big me master can't say no. Where he go I know not . . . mebbe West End, mebbe off-island. Who can say? One t'ing I do say. He was chained to de wagon an' he fight like wild bull!"

Anna returned home drained of all emotion. The feeling of being numb and half alive stayed with her for a long time. She was convinced she'd never again care deeply for anyone. Life seemed to her to be without meaning, without purpose. She did what was expected of her at home. At Skipper Wittrog's request, she assisted him as barmaid in the rum shop in the evenings. Her only pleasure came from her close association with her little brother, Johannes. She liked taking him for walks, telling him stories, and teaching him his letters.

Though angered by Anna's faithlessness, Christopher Hansen was a stubborn Dane not easily diverted from a well-defined goal. He pressed his suit more persuasively than ever. The skipper and Susanna added their pressure to his. Veiled hints that it was time she no longer occupied a place under the family roof were abundant. The skipper assured her he could find another barmaid.

Susanna lectured her on the subject of financial security. "So you don' love he!" she said impatiently. "He good mon. You be safe, well-cared for. No matter what fate bring down de road in he basket, you no poor. Poor de worse t'ing, Anna. Romancin' be nice, but often it go pouf with de wind. Mon die young or fine 'nother womon. Money in de sock, that's wha' counts d'mos'."

Anna was beginning to feel old at nineteen. She knew of hardly any other girls of her age who had not made some sort of arrangement with a man or men, as servant, mistress, or prostitute. She felt unwanted at home but feared making the break. Her romantic dream had turned to ashes and the future looked bleak. In a misery of indecision she went to her grandmother for advice. "What I do, Oma?" she asked, sitting on a footstool by her grandmother's knee.

Amalie Bernard leaned forward and looked deep into Anna's eyes, her own sympathetic. "Go with him, chile. Herr Hansen no' de big powerful mon we talk 'bout once on a time. But you need change. Orderin' white mon's house give you new t'ing to think on. As for de other part . . . you get used to it."

"How can that be, Oma?" she asked dismally thinking of her lovemaking with No-no.

"Take me word. You will. Meantime you learn many t'ing, learn t'talk good like white lady, meet new peoples. Who know who you bump into one day? One mon seldom las' de life o' strong womon like we."

Within the month Anna went to live with Christopher Hansen in his modest house on the Strand. From an upstairs window she could see the beach where she and No-no had met and made love.

Chapter 7

ANNA ROSE EARLY. She was anxious to be out from under the sheets and away. As she went through the door she glanced back at the bed. Hansen was not an inspiring sight. He lay on his back, his jaw slack, breathing heavily. The ends of his moustache quivered as he exhaled. She almost smiled.

It had not been a happy year for Anna. The evenings she spent with Hansen were tedious. He droned on endlessly about his legal practice, his appearances in court where he always played the clever lawyer. Each night in bed it was the same. He was quickly hard and quickly done, with no thought for her pleasure.

But, as Amalie Bernard had said she would, she profited in some ways. She now knew how to keep a gentleman's house. She had learned how to handle servants, oversee the household shopping, and keep the accounts. She saw to it that the meals were properly prepared, the silver polished, the lamps kept bright, and fresh linen always laid on the table. When Hansen entertained she played the part of hostess with skill. Her speech had improved, and she was able to carry on a lively conversation on a variety of subjects with the white men who came to the house as guests. The few men that had wives on the island seldom brought them to Hansen's, so her contacts with white women were few.

Hansen was not stingy. The fine mahogany furniture he allowed her to buy was hers alone. He bought her two slaves to care for her personal needs. One was a woman named Matilda who was a skillful seamstress and made Anna's clothes. She also helped Anna bathe in a large tin tub and with deft fingers arranged her hair becomingly. Her grown son, Jeremiah, drove Anna's gig.

After leaving the bedroom she shared with Christopher Hansen, Anna went down the back stairs to the stone kitchen which was separate from the main house. It was strangely quiet. The cook should have been getting the fire up to cook breakfast. Anna jerked open the door, which was warped by humidity, and a rat ran across the floor just in front of her foot. She gasped with revulsion, then threw a stone at it. It got down a hole in the wall behind the stone sink. The day was off to a bad start.

When Anna pounded on the cook's door to rouse her she was answered by groans. With a "misery in she back" she couldn't possibly get out of bed that day. Anna got hold of Matilda and together they attacked the problem of breakfast, Matilda grumbling all the while about doing the cook's work. Though Anna tried to be quick, Hansen was downstairs wanting his breakfast before it was ready. He was unpleasant about waiting and lectured Anna on the importance of his being at his office on time. "And don't forget," he said as he left the house, "I've invited Major Fergus to dinner. Sorrensen is coming, too. Do try to have an adequate meal—and at a reasonable hour—if that isn't too much to ask."

Anna worked hard to have everything just right for company dinner. She had Jeremiah butcher a turtle and made a fine rich stew of the meat. She prepared dumplings according to an old Danish recipe she'd mastered. She set the table with the best linen and arranged a mound of pink and red hibiscus for a centerpiece. She polished the hurricane lamps and replaced the used candles with fresh.

Hansen came home late and seemed preoccupied. Thinking to lighten his mood Anna drew him into the dining room. "See the table. Does it not look fantastic? See how the goblets and the hurricane lamps sparkle. I wash them myself. The guests will soon be here. I must . . ."

"I see the table is set for four." Hansen was looking at her in a strange way.

"Aye, as you told me. Major Fergus and Herr Sorrensen."

"Well, there's been a change. This afternoon, unexpectedly, Hans Jennings and his wife arrived in town from Denmark. He is a junior member of my father's firm. I had no choice but to invite them to dinner."

"Well, 'tis no big matter. 'Tis short notice, but Matilda and I will change quickly from four to six. I made a fantastic lot of turtle stew!"

She started for the cupboard to take down more china.

"Anna."

She turned.

"Add only one place. I think it would be best all 'round for Matilda to serve you a tray in your room this evening."

"A tray in my room?" Anna was bewildered. "You . . . you don't want me at table?"

"No I don't. Not this evening. Mme Jennings is . . ."

"Is too fine a white lady to eat with colored! Is that it?" The color mounted in her cheeks. "For that matter," she said caustically, "why should I be served in my room? Better I should eat in the kitchen with my own kind."

"See here, Anna, don't be unreasonable. I'm asking you . . . one night out of many . . . a tray in your room. What's so bad about that? Why must you make so much of it, make such a confounded fuss?"

"But what's so special about this Mme Jennings? Why would it offend her to sit at table with me? You said long ago with your friends I'd pass as white."

"And so you do, but . . ."

"A married couple. Is that it? This wife-woman would be offended to sit at table with a wife that's not a wife according to the law. She must be . . ."

"A lot of white women are downright persnickety—too much so to my way of thinking."

"And you think Mme Jennings is per-persnickety?"

"I hardly know the lady. She spent her childhood here, then went to Denmark for her education, where she met Jennings. He was curious about the West Indies, and she wanted to visit her childhood home."

"But in case she's persnickety, just in case . . . you want me out of the way?"

"Anna, it's rather more than you think. Mme Jenning's maiden name was . . . was Heegaard."

For several seconds Anna was too stunned to speak. Then she said, remembering the white child her father had taken in his arms in front of the Custom House long ago, "So she's my half sister . . . only . . . she come from d'right side o' d'bed!"

"My only wish is to save you both embarrassment. She would not like to be reminded her father had a relationship with a black woman before he married her mother, that that relationship resulted in a child. Her husband might see a resemblance or discover your name. Then she'd have some painful explaining to do. It just seems sensible, Anna, not to flaunt your relationship."

Anna's cheeks were flaming red, and angry sparks showed in her eyes. "Well, res' your mine, Herr Hansen. You seen d'las' o' me for this night. Kindly ask Jeremiah t'bring 'round d'gig. I'll not stay where I'm not wanted."

She was still angry when she walked into her mother's house. Susanna was not entirely sympathetic. "You fool, Anna, t'be so uppity! He treat you no more bad then wha' we come to 'spect. You sittin' pretty by Christopher Hansen, own servants, own carriage, fine clothes. You have envy o' mos' de gels in town."

"I feel insulted, Mama, an' demeaned. To invite my sister t'sit at table where I sit by custom and ask me t'leave is intolerable an' . . ."

"My, oh my! Such whoppin' big words!"

"They all mean the same thing. He use me bad."

"Maybe he think by keepin' you out o' de way t'spare you' feelin'. He no he'p what she be, what you be."

"Mama, he not think o' my feelin's. He think of his. Mama, let me stay with you."

"Well then, stay d'night. T'ings always look better come mornin'. If you talk to Herr Hansen nice, mebbe he take you back."

"Mama, I don't want t'go back . . . never, never, never! It not just what happen this night. It a lot of things all rolled into one big bundle weighing heavy on my heart."

The morning brought no change in Anna's feelings. She returned to Strand Street to collect her possessions. Matilda helped her pack. Jeremiah made several trips to Company Street carrying bags and boxes of clothes and the furniture that was Anna's own. When it had all been taken away Anna sat in the sitting room wearing her best black silk. Her hair was neatly combed, parted, and pinned into a prim bun over each ear. Her face was pale and determined. She felt icy calm inside as she sat waiting quietly for Christopher Hansen to come home.

He arrived just before six. "So, Anna, you're back," he said smugly. "I was certain you would be, though I wasn't sure it would be so soon."

"I'm not staying, Herr Hansen. I'm leaving for good." She spoke slowly and carefully. "I only came back to fetch my things and tell you of my decision. Everything that is mine is packed and carried to my mother's."

He stiffened. "Anna, you can't be serious! You'd not be such a fool!"

"I am very serious. I have not been happy with you, Herr Hansen. Last night's . . . offense, is only part of it. My mama has agreed to take me back."

"But you're so well off here! I've given you position in the community. I've given you comforts and servants, things not commonly accorded girls of your background. Why . . . why you should be grateful beyond words!"

She answered softly, "I also have given . . . though I think you scarce noticed."

"Reconsider, Anna. Think of the consequences of what you talk of doing. If you leave, I warrant you'll regret it within a week. You don't really want to go back to the poor sort of life you lived on Company Street. Not really. But once you go, there'll be no changing your mind. If you leave me now, I wash my hands of you. There's many a girl who'd be more appreciative."

"Find her then, Herr Hansen," Anna said with spirit, "because I'm bidding you farewell, and that's for true."

"You mean that?"

"I do."

With a grimace he sank into a chair. The color slowly drained from his face so that the large freckles across his cheeks and the bridge of his nose stood out clearly. "Oh, Anna, I expected better from you," he whined. "How can you treat me so after all the years of kindnesses to you and your family. Without any by-your-leave, you think of taking off like a faithless, wanton . . ."

"Believe me, I sorry to grieve you, but . . ."

"You came to me besmirched by that black buck, that slave with the ridiculous name. Still I forgave you, counting it girlish infatuation. I was patient, hoping in time you'd warm to me. You never did, of course, cool as a chunk of ice. But I continued to lavish affection on you, and this is my reward."

Anna rose slowly to her feet. "You knew of No-no?"

"Of course, you stupid girl!" A malicious glint shone in his eyes. "Who'd you think arranged to have him sold?"

Two quick steps and Anna stood glaring in front of him. She raised her hand and struck him savagely across the face. "You wretched mon! You took mean advantage, he slave, you free. They took him away in chains. I don' know if he live or dead." At the memory tears ran down her cheeks. She covered her face with her hands.

Hansen fingered the stinging red hand print on his cheek, surprised and shocked by her violence. A cold fury burned within him. She raised her tear-stained face and asked with icy calm, "How you know 'bout him?"

Pleased that he could wound her further, he said, "Your mama told me."

Half-blinded by tears, Anna fled from the house. Outside Jeremiah sat in her gig waiting. She climbed in.

Though unsettled by her distress, Jeremiah knew nothing better to do than ask the expected question. "Yo' mama's house, Mistress?"

"No, Jeremiah," she said, stifling a sob, "not yet. Drive me 'round. Drive me out in the country. Any place. I needs time. I needs time t'get pas' hatin' my mama."

Jeremiah did what he was bid. He drove the horse northwest out of town to Golden Rock, and from there up the hill to Peter's Rest, around Strawberry, and down Contentment Road. During the drive Anna tried to understand what her mother had done. She began to see that her intentions had been good, that she had acted in what she believed at the time to be in Anna's best interest. It made a difference.

Finally Jeremiah said, "Mistress, horse gettin' tired."

"It's all right. You can drive me home now."

By the time Anna confronted her mother she was outwardly calm. "Mama, Hansen tell me he arrange t'have No-no sold an' that you, you Mama, told him 'bout us."

Susanna looked pained. "Oh, Anna, I never want you should know. I do what I do, thinkin' it for de bes' . . . bes' for you."

"Mama, you broke my heart."

Susanna began to weep. "I sorry for that, Anna. Mebbe I do wrong."

Anna couldn't bear to see her mother's distress. She held out her arms, and they clung together, both weeping. Finally Susanna raised her head, searching Anna's face for forgiveness.

Anna said gently through her tears, "Mama, it happen long ago. We never speak of it more."

Anna took her old place in the family circle, resuming her role of unattached daughter. The skipper offered Matilda and her son the room above his rum shop in return for help in running it. Matilda was to keep the shop clean, and Jeremiah to help in serving customers.

Two weeks passed and Anna began to fear she was pregnant. It was five days since her due date, and the blood had failed to come. With nothing but hatred in her heart for Hansen the thought of birthing his child was more than she could bear. She spoke to her mother about it. "Mama, what I do. I don't want his child."

"You no choice, Anna. It be our lot. Baby born every day on island not wanted. You bear chile. You come t'love it."

Anna shuddered. "No, Mama, no! Not child of mon I hate!"

"Anna, I say it one mo' time. You no choice, gel."

"Maybe I do. I talk to Oma. She know everything."

Anna found Amalie Bernard in her usual place on Aunt Lucia's porch. Anna sat down on a step near her chair and leaned against the porch rail, feeling weak and nauseous.

"You look poorly, chile. You have trouble?"

"Oh, Oma! I be with child. I don't want it, Oma. I can't bear the thought of havin' child of that mon. There no love, no happiness between us.'

"Come, come Anna. Don' take on so! It no so bad as all that."

Anna sat up straight, her eyes probing her grandmother's. "It is bad, and I won't have it. I come to you, Oma, to find out what t'do. You know so much! Tell me, Oma, tell me how t'rid myself of it. There must be ways. Tell me true."

"I see it done, Anna, on de plantation when times so hard there no food t'go 'round. I see womon mutilate sheself when brutal master make life so cruel de thought o' bringin' baby to such life not t'be borne. But all ways bring great danger, Anna. I beg you, do not think o' such a t'ing! When child come you love it. Nothin' new in black womon bearin' child o' mon she hate."

"That's what Mama say." Seeing she was faring no better with her grandmother, Anna rose, put her arms around her neck and hugged her. "Sometime, Oma, I like t'have child, but t'mon I care 'bout."

Amalie Bernard took Anna's hand and pressed it against her cheek. "Be at peace, me Anna. It God's will you' be with chile. Let Him work within you an' bring you comfort. Now you feel ill but that pass away. When de babe stir in you' womb you forget earthy father an' think only o' heavenly one."

Anna wasn't convinced. That afternoon she went to call on Matilda in the room over the rum shop. It was a small room, scarcely more than an attic, with the stale smell of pipes smoked and beer drunk over the years filtering through the floorboards. There was a broken-down bed and a straw pallet for Jeremiah. A table, two stools, and a bench completed the furnishings. Matilda sat on a stool gazing out of the one small window, a pair of Jeremiah's trousers in need of mending lying across her lap. With so little to do, time hung heavy on her hands.

"Tilly!" Anna was breathless from her quick walk and climbing the steep stairs.

Flustered, Matilda stood up quickly, upsetting the stool. "Missy Anna! I no think t'see you here. Come set you'self. You look all done in." She righted the stool and Anna sat down.

"I've neglected you, Tilly. How you be?"

"Not so good, Mistress. This room hard t'live by. Smell bad. Noisy with laughin' an' swearin' from b'low. Too small for mama an' growed-up son."

Anna glanced around the room. "I can see you speak true. Tilly, I been thinkin' 'bout you an' Jeremiah. I don't need Jeremiah t'drive anymore. I have in mind sellin' the gig. You can't stay here much longer on account of the reasons you said, and in my mother's house there's no place for you."

A worried look came into Matilda's eyes, and she sat down abruptly on the edge of the bed. "You no t'ink t'sell . . . ?"

"Tilly, I think 'bout settin' you and Jeremiah free!"

Matilda's eyes grew wide with wonder. She searched Anna's face to determine if she meant what she was saying. Satisfied, she knelt beside Anna and kissed the hem of her skirt. "Oh, Missy Anna, that's de bes' news these ears ever hear. With free, Jeremiah can get job with pay."

"Aye. I should think so. Get up, Tilly. Free woman no need to kneel. As it happens I need help from you in return."

Matilda scrambled to her feet. "Ah, Missy Anna, anyt'ing! Anyt'ing at all! Jeremiah so happy he scarce walk on de groun'!"

Anna chose her words carefully. "I know you know 'bout all kind o' potions and way t'help people in trouble. My time of the month pass by. It make me nervous. I want the blood to come—soon. Can you help me, Tilly? Is there something I can swallow that will rid me of what I fear's planted in my belly?"

Matilda slowly shook her head. "There's no such t'ing, Missy Anna."

"Tilly, you grew up on a large plantation where womon has t'take care of herself best way she can. If you don't know how t'help, mebbe you know some wise weed womon what does."

Matilda's eyes grew wary. "Oh, no, Missy Anna! Never! No good for fine lady like you! There's some hurt. There's some danger. No, no! I know nothin' 'bout such t'ings!"

"Tilly, you want Jeremiah free, don't you? And I pay some money, a little money to help him get started. Maybe he could set up a stable with horses and rigs for hire. He's good with horses."

The pressure was too much for Matilda. She hesitated but finally said, "Seems like I bemembers some person mid-island do such t'ings."

"Yes, go on."

"Las' t'ing I know this person at King's Hill."

Early next morning Jeremiah drove them out into the country in a farm wagon. Anna wore old clothes and a straw hat that came well down over her face. She didn't want to be recognized. When they arrived at King's Hill Matilda took Anna to a hut set apart from the rows of shared-wall slave quarters. In answer to Matilda's knock a big yellow-skinned woman of uncertain age came to the door. She had muscular arms and a neck as thick as a man's. Anna wondered how she'd escaped work in the fields. Then she saw that the woman limped, dragging a twisted foot just visible beneath the hem of her bedraggled skirt.

Matilda talked fast in a dialect so broad Anna could scarcely understand what was said. But she understood the shaking of the woman's head, the fearful expression that came into her eyes. Anna opened her purse so that the woman could see the gold coins inside. The fear in the woman's eyes turned to craftiness, and she motioned the women to enter.

Anna sat down on the only chair. Looking around the small, untidy, windowless room she was suddenly frightened. She held onto the seat of the chair to keep herself from bolting. Meanwhile the weed woman stirred a powdery white substance into a gourd filled with water. She brought it to Anna to drink.

It had a milky appearance and a pleasant herby taste. Anna drained the gourd. Immediately her lips and tongue felt numb and tingly. A great drowsiness overcame her. She allowed the women to undress her and lead her to a long table where she lay on her back on some sacking with her knees bent. Her feet were tied down, and Matilda held her shoulders.

The weed woman produced a long, slim, highly polished stick. Turning her head away Anna concentrated on the face of the man who had dismissed her from the table she had laid and the presence of her half-sister. Her stomach boiled with outrage and fear. "Help me, God," she prayed desperately. She felt sharp cramping pains in her lower abdomen. A wave of deep sorrow swept over her, and she blacked out.

The shadows outside the open door of the hut were long when she awoke. The bloody sacking beneath her made her certain she was no longer pregnant. But instead of relief she felt strangely depressed. Jeremiah and Matilda helped her into the back of the wagon, where she lay on some straw, too weak to sit up. The drive back to town over the dusty bumpy roads was a torment. At last they reached her mother's house, where she dragged herself up the stairs and fell on the bed.

In the morning she had a fever and was too ill to get out of bed. Susanna sent for the Danish doctor. He prescribed a purgative and would have bled her. But Susanna wouldn't permit it. She suspected Anna had already lost too much blood.

The infection spread rapidly, and as it spread Anna's fever rose. She felt as though she were burning up. She kicked savagely at the sheet that lay over her. She vomited again and again. Her head pounded, and unearthly noises, cracklings and shreikings, filled her ears. The ceiling spun, and when she closed her eyes she herself spun in space. Pain, a bright burning wave of pain, mounted and mounted inside her. She held on, willing it to pass. It crested, and she slid down, down into a painless, smothering abyss. But there was no rest. The pain came again and again. Then she felt her mother's hand, delicate, fluttery, and cool, smoothing her forehead, heard her crooning words of comfort. Through all the mists of fear and pain she was aware that her mother was there caring for her.

After several days of torment Anna woke from a deep sleep to see her mother sitting by the bed, her face drawn and weary.

Seeing Anna's eyes were open, Susanna smiled a tired smile and felt her forehead. "Thank de Lord. I think you get well now," she said. "This de fifth day you been sick, Anna. I feared you die."

"You took good care, Mama."

"We won de fight for you' life, Anna, but I think you lose all chance of t'be mama."

So be it, Anna thought sadly. At least the pain was gone, and she was alive.

Susanna had more to say, among other things that Christopher Hansen had left the island for good. Surprisingly he had left instructions that the deed to his house be given to Anna.

"So in spite o' wha' you think, he cared for you, my Anna. You can sell de house for good money. Or you can keep it t'rent . . . mebbe live there some day you'self."

"I never want t'live in that house, Mama!" She closed her eyes and turned her head away wearily. "I sell."

Chapter 8

FOR SEVEN YEARS the British had occupied the Danish West Indies. Now a change was about to take place. Back in 1807 Crown Prince Frederik had made the decision to side with the French in the Napoleonic wars. It turned out to be a bad decision. The English made the Danes suffer for it in many ways. Besides taking over their West Indian colonies, they bombarded Copenhagen and made off with a large part of their navy.

After the rout of his *Grande Armee* from Russia, Napoleon was further defeated at the battle of Leipzig by a coalition of northern European countries that pursued him into France. He was forced to abdicate and left the country, to return two years later and be defeated at Waterloo. That was the end. He was banished to the island of St. Helena, never to return. This was followed by the Treaty of Paris in which European countries sought to sort out territorial demands in such a way that a lasting balance of power would be established. France was reduced to her 1792 boundaries, and England agreed to return most of the colonies she'd taken over during the war to their former owners. Among these were the Danish West Indies.

The news came to the islands in the form of a formal document signed and sealed by Frederik VI, now king of Denmark, his poor mad father having died in 1808. In the document the king explained the change and told the islanders that he had appointed Lieutenant-Governor Lotharios von Oxhom to be governor-general. He also named subordinates. Copies of the document were posted and read throughout the islands.

The formalities relating to the transfer took place in Denmark in the fall of 1814. Governor-General von Oxholm was to leave for the islands immediately. The West Indians decided to postpone the celebration of the transfer until he arrived. Meanwhile, a lame duck English administration would continue to govern.

That fall Anna and her family were in no mood to celebrate. Skipper Wittrog, the father of Johannes, had taken loving care of the family for ten years. Now he was dead. Caught by a gale in a small fishing boat, his sail was blown out and he drifted aimlessly for a day and a night exposed to wind and rain before he was rescued. As a result of exposure he developed pneumonia. He was only forty-five, strong and healthy. He put up a good fight but the infection was too much for him. His lungs gradually filled with fluid and within two weeks of his mishap he was gone. He would be sorely missed.

Anna had sold the house on Strand Street, the beginning for her of a small fortune. Now that the war was over and business improving, her mother wanted to expand the store on Company Street. Anna agreed to help. Besides needles and pins they now stocked all sorts of sewing accesories and yard goods. Knitting yarn, needlepoint, and even bonnets and shawls. Susanna and Anna had good heads for business, and the store prospered. This was fortunate, for with the Skipper gone the rum shop had to be sold.

One breezy day in November Anna was alone in the store when a robust Irishman walked in. He was a good-looking man in his late thirties with a florid complexion, twinkling blue eyes, dark curly hair and a beard which showed glints of red.

"Good day t'ye, Mistress," he said. "T'is Paul Twigg, here, at your service. T'is a pleasure t'find weather the likes of this considerin' what I left behind in old Ireland."

Anna quickly put down her embroidery and slipped from the high stool behind the counter on which she'd been perched. "Good day to yourself," she said, brightly attracted by the man's jovial manner. "The weather is fine t'be sure. What can I do for you, sir?"

With an ingratiating smile he leaned over the counter toward her. "A great deal from the look o' ye . . . if ye'd a mind to. Such foine dark eyes have I seldom seen!"

The color mounted in Anna's cheeks. "Nay, sir," she said, stiffening and drawing back. "I be glad t'be o' service but I'll no stand for familiarities. Tell me what errand brings you to my mother's store."

Rebuffed, Paul Twigg studied her to see if she meant what she said. She returned his gaze unflinchingly.

"Beg pardon, Mistress. I didn't intend to affront ye. In Dublin the lasses I ken savor a bit o' blarney. Now then . . . it's this buttonless cuff that's givin' me trouble. It's no' fittin' for a prosperous merchant such as meself t'go about town with a button missin'."

"About that you're most right. Let us see if we can find one that matches."

A button was found; and Anna, sympathtic with his plight, even sewed it on for him. He thanked her and then said, "Being newly arrived I have yet to find a wench to look after me. Would ye have a suggestion, now?"

Anna thought for a moment. "No one comes to mind at this moment, sir . . ."

"Well, and I'd be grateful if ye would look around a bit, find me someone t'keep the house clean and do a bit o' cookin'."

"I'll see what I can do."

Paul Twigg doffed his hat and left the shop whistling an Irish tune.

In the weeks that followed Anna heard a good deal about the newly arrived Irish merchant. He bought a townhouse which he planned to use both as a residence and office. He contracted with a number of planters for the rum and sugar his Dublin-based firm was eager to buy. He was a gregarious sort and was scarcely settled in his house before the entertaining began. He invited chance acquaintances or business associates to enjoy his hospitality. He was not choosy as long as they were jolly sorts, enjoying a drink and a bit of song as much as he did. Sometimes the parties grew rowdy, lasting far into the night. Then his neighbors complained to the gendarmes. Mr. Twigg would be rebuked, and for a while, the singing and loud laughter would simmer down. But soon the warnings would be forgotten, and the parties would grow as boisterous as before.

He stopped by Susanna's store frequently on the pretext of buying some small item. He was an entertaining talker. When no one else required her help, Anna encouraged him for she liked his lilting Irish brogue and hearing of his life in Ireland.

One day he came into the store with an eye nearly closed and a big lump on his forehead.

"Mr. Twigg! You look bad, mon! What happen?"

"Ach! The party last night turned into a bit of a brawl. I b'leve it was a chair what hit me. Or it could be a flyin' bottle. Mistress Anna, I fear these celebrations o' mine be gettin' out o' hand. Foist thing ye know Paul Twigg'll be carried out o' town in a box. I need a good woman to add a touch of decorum, one the lads would respect. What's more t'would be foine t'have such a one see to the food what comes out of the kitchen. The swill that cook o' mine been sarvin' is like t'turn a man t'drink!"

Anna smiled. "I don't doubt, Mr. Twigg, a number of suitable women in town would be ready an' willin' t'help you entertain and see the food is prepared to your likin'. 'Course there'd be fair wages t'pay."

Ignoring her last condition he leaned over the counter. "Truth t'tell, it would be foine t'have a lass who'd be willin' t'share me bed as well. The black doxies what rally 'round the wharf suit the sailor lads well enough, but not Paul Twigg. Me tastes are somewhat more refoined."

"That be a matter mos' personal, Mr. Twigg. I could not take it upon myself to advise you."

"Ach, me proud lass, ye know well enough the one I'm after," he said with a leer, trying to grab her. Anna jerked away and drew back against the wall. Seeing a woman she knew by the open door she called out, "Good day, Mme Petersen. Pray come in and have a look. Some English prints we have just come from London."

The Danish lady stepped inside, and Mr. Twigg tipped his hat and left.

This was only one of many times Anna rebuffed him. But he was not a man to give up easily. Several weeks later he came in hanging his head with remorse after a particularly raucous party that had landed a couple of his cronies in jail. His contrite face and the misery in his voice aroused her sympathy, so that she listened receptively as he told his tale of woe, again begging for her help. Anna didn't answer at once. She turned to arranging some bolts of cloth on a high shelf to give herself time to think.

"Come, now, Mistress Anna," he begged. "Don't be turnin' yer back on me. Ye know full well I've had me eye on ye since the day I foist walked into yer shop. I'd treat ye well, believe me, like a lovin' husband. I'd give ye whatever ye fancied. This is no life for the likes of ye, behind the counter o' a small cubby of a shop doin' the work of a vinegary old maid. With yer face and figger, in the prime of yer life, ye should be makin' some lusty man happy and tastin' the joys of connubial bliss yer ownself."

Rather to Paul Twigg's surprise she came from behind the

counter and confronted him looking him squarely in the eyes. "Mr. Twigg, I take one part of your offer, that is if one of my sisters will agree to help Mama in the shop. I come t'you an' see t'your house. And I be fair good at it, havin' served another gentleman for more'n a year. I know how t'manage servants and see that you be properly served with food t'suit your taste. I play hostess at your parties if that be your wish. But I no promise t'share your bed. And I no be forced, mind you! Then there's the matter of recompense. I expect fair wage."

Anger reddened Mr. Twigg's face. "So you'd be doin' it fer the money, not as a favor to Paul Twigg, nor in gratitude for the foine life I'd be givin' ye?"

"That's right. Let it be clear between us from the start. The store pays little enough, God knows, and since my step-papa die my mama needs the money. One more thing. Let it be understood I can leave with no hard feelin's if all is no to my likin'."

For a moment Paul Twigg's jaw was slack and he stared at her baffled by the audacity of the hard terms she was proposing. Then sparks of anger showed in his blue eyes. He squared his jaw. "Then be damned to ye! Such high fallutin' ideas! Never have I heard the like. I'll find a wench more givin' than that, b'gad, or do without!" He stormed out of the store.

Two days later he was back asking what she would consider a fair wage.

Anna's life with Paul Twigg was utterly unpredictable. Much of his time was spent at the wharf haggling with captains and inspecting outward-bound cargoes. Often he dined out. Or a planter would call at the house, and if the business between them went well, he'd ask the man to stay for dinner. Anna never knew if she'd be all alone or if there'd be five or twenty—captains, merchants, planters or government people. Spur-of-the-moment entertaining kept the household in a turmoil, but Anna managed to cope capably and with good humor.

The prospect of a party buoyed the Irishman's spirits. He knew Anna would carry it off well with good food and an abundance of excellent Cruzan rum. The evenings often ended in a bit of rough and tumble, but Anna's presence tended to keep the parties from degenerating into brawls. If things got out of hand she called for help from the big black coachman who drove for Mr. Twigg. He had a way of hustling fractious guests out of the house with a minimum of hard feelings or fuss. When the parties were jolly affairs, filled with Irish song and good-natured bantering, Anna sang and laughed with the men. She sat on a lap for a moment and allowed a playful pinch now and then. But she always eluded grasping arms and roving hands. She permitted no intimacies, least of all from Paul Twigg. The day after a party was apt to find Twigg grumpy with a bad head. Anna knew what to do for that, too.

All winter the islanders waited anxiously for the arrival of Governor-General von Oxholm. He was known to have left Denmark in late November. He didn't come and didn't come. The island was rife with wild rumors, conjecture and dire prediction. Then confirmation came that the governor had been shipwrecked and forced to return to Copenhagen. It was April before he finally arrived. The official transfer of the islands was scheduled to take place on the 18th of the month. Townspeople and planters gathered around the fort to witness the ceremony.

With an Irishman's hatred of the English, Paul Twigg had started to celebrate early in the day. As he and Anna stood in the forefront of the crowd around the fort, he shouted again and again, "Here's to Frederik and be damned to George!" until Anna felt like holding her ears. Finally he threw his hat in the air, made a clumsy attempt to catch it and nearly fell. A small boy handed him his hat. He bowed elaborately, handed him a pfennig and took another swig of rum.

"Let me have the bottle, Mr. Twigg," Anna said. "You've had quite enough. One more swallow and you'll be stretched on the pavement for sure!"

"Take a nip, yerself, lass. Ye'll feel the better for it."

"Nay. I best stay sober, lest we both spend the night in jail."

His eyes travelled over her, the rum making him bold. The envious glances at Anna's face and figure from his cronies standing nearby, fired his lust. If only I could bed her, he thought. He emptied the bottle.

The governor-general made a speech. Amid the cheers of the crowd the Union Jack was lowered from the flag mast on the ramparts of the fort and the Danish Danenborg raised in its place. Then the band struck up a Danish military air.

A couple of Twigg's cronies approached recommending further

celebration in a favorite rum shop. Since he was noticeably unsteady on his feet, each took an arm. Disengaging himself with what dignity he could muster, Twigg tipped his hat to Anna and staggered off, leaving Anna to make her way home alone. The crowd dispersed. The bandsmen packed up their instruments, and it was business as usual in Christiansted.

Anna waited patiently for Twigg to come home for supper. The clock in the clock tower struck six, then seven times. After it had been dark for some hours, she arranged a cold supper on the table and went upstairs to the room under the eaves where she slept. Much later she woke to hear Twigg rumbling up the stairs to her room, where he had no business to be, his room being on the floor below. She leapt out of bed, but it was too late to bar the door. She tried her best to hold it shut, but with a mighty kick he burst it open. He cornered her, tore off her nightdress, and forced her back on the bed. She bit and scratched. She tried to get a knee up and push him away, but he was heavy, strong, and determined. In spite of her efforts to defend herself, he managed to have his way with her.

When he was spent, Anna gave a great heave and pushed him to one side. He lay on his back, his mouth half open, snoring loudly. Anna rose from the bed and looked at him with disgust. She felt her face. It was badly bruised. Her bones ached, and she felt sore inside. The foul odor that clung to her made her nauseous. She had had enough of Paul Twigg.

Hurriedly she packed. Into a large canvas bag she put her shawl, the few gowns she cared about and her toilet articles. Being careful not to make a noise she moved her dresser aside, lifted a loose floor board and removed a small sack of coins, her accumulated wages. She stepped into her housekeeper's gown and buttoned it up the front. With rapidly beating heart she tiptoed down the stairs carrying her bag and crept out the back of the house. From there she made her way to the street.

The moon was full, casting sharp, curved shadows on the walls of the buildings, shadows shaped by the many arches that bordered the street. A sudden breeze from the sea sprang up, bringing the tangy smell and taste of salt air. It was refreshing. She leaned against the wall of a building, breathing deeply until her heart had stopped racing. Then, to escape notice, she slipped quickly from shadow to shadow, at last reaching her mother's house.

She climbed the outside stair and pounded on the door. A sleepy-eyed Sophia opened it. Without a word of explanation Anna brushed past her and threw herself down on the double bed they had formerly shared. She turned her face to the wall, convinced that she hated all white men and would never trust another. Sophia slipped in beside her, filled with curiosity. But Anna pretended to be asleep.

A few weeks later, Paul Twigg shipped out of the Danish West Indies, bound for Ireland.

Chapter 9

ONE MORNING, some three years after Paul Twigg left the island, Anna and her mother were sipping their morning coffee when Anna said, "Mama, it would be good to send Johannes away to school."

Susanna looked at Anna, astonished. "Away t'school! Whatever for? Already you teach him t'read. What more Johannes need?"

"He need good education to make somethin' o' himself. He smart but he need t'know many things. In Antigua they have school like in England for boys Johannes's age. Mrs. de Pinney tell me 'bout it when she come into the shop t'buy shirts for Rodney."

"But Johannes so young!" Susanna protested. "He only fo'teen. He got no notion how hard de world be. White boy put he down when he see d'color o' he skin, an' Johannes . . ."

"Mama, it the only skin he got. All the more reason for good schoolin'. Mrs. de Pinney say the school has boys o' mixed blood—bright ones that is."

"How we pay, Anna? Fancy school cost money."

"We manage. The store doin' better. We can spare some monies from the store. Besides, I bought a bit o' land some years back. I can sell it to farmer on next property. He need more land for bigger herd."

"Aiya, it trouble me heart t'think o' him far from d'island. He mos' what I got t'live for. There be dangers at sea, storms an' pirates. Mebbe Johannes get drown or land in Spanish dungeon."

"Mama, life not safe or easy no matter what. You know that!"

Susanna finally agreed to let Johannes go. In September he boarded the school boat, an island sloop bound for Antigua. At first Susanna was inconsolable, but when yellow fever boke out in the town she was glad Johannes was away. The dreaded disease spread rapidly from town to countryside. Hundreds died. For several Sundays in a row no church bells rang, calling people to church. Everyone was too occupied with either the sick, the dying, or the dead. Susanna contracted a mild case, and Anna spent several weary weeks nursing her back to health.

In addition to disease, pirates, hurricanes, and years of drought, the islanders were plagued by a downhill slide in the sugar economy. Denmark, instead of allowing the islands to trade freely with all nations, insisted that millions of pounds of sugar be reserved for her use alone. This allotment had to be sent directly to Copenhagen in Danish bottoms. The remaining sugar sold to other nations was highly taxed. Then the worst thing that could have happened, happened. It was discovered that sugar could be made from an unlovely tuber, white with a purplish top—the sugar beet. It could be grown with less labor than cane and in the temperate climates of Europe and North America.

Still, the high-living planters did little to change their ways. The slaves suffered most. They were no longer fed and clothed as well as before. They worked just as hard but with no hope of the little extras that made life endurable. The island seethed with undercurrents of rebellion. Every now and then these bubbled to the surface, to be dealt with by the planters—fearful because they were far outnumbered—in the harshest ways imaginable.

It was late summer, 1819, the most uneasy time of the year. Every Sunday prayers of supplication were said in the churches in hopes of warding off a return of the fever or the devastation of a hurricane. The air was heavy and muggy. The tradewinds ceased. Insects were at their worst, plaguing man and beast. On many days ominous black clouds rode the horizon, making people fearful.

In the store Anna sat on her high stool fanning herself with a palmleaf fan. It was too hot even to work on her embroidery. She wished that a customer would appear, even a looker, to relieve the tedium. All at once she heard the muffled beat of drums coming from the direction of the fort. Bored and rather curious, she left the store and walked down the street toward the fort. Here she saw a small company of solders approaching. Two of them half carried, half dragged a black man wearing only a ragged pair of breeches. They were headed toward Gallows Bay. Behind them streamed a motley crowd of men and boys keyed up by the prospect of a grisly show. They laughed and jeered, shouting insults at the prisoner. The prisoner's face was gray with fear. His tongue licked his thick lips and his breeches were stained with perspiration and urine.

"What he done? What he done?" Anna asked an old woman watching the parade.

"He Joe Buckus. He spit in he master face. Bad t'ing. He hang."

Anna shivered. So a man was to die because another man had received a dollop of spittle on his face. It mattered not how dire the provocation had been. Anna imagined the final roll of drums, the bang of the falling trap door, the agonized scream of the prisoner, his feet doing a macabre dance beneath the gallows as the noose took his life.

In October a hurricane struck without warning. The day had been bright and still. The deceptive night threw a sprinkle of diamonds across the sky. Then, after the islanders were sleeping, innocent of what was to come, the night summoned sinister clouds filled with raging winds. A dirty yellow dawn faded rapidly to utter blackness. Sleepers were awakened by a shrieking wind, branches lashing the houses and metal fragments torn from tin roofs whistling through the air. Sophia and Anna leapt out of bed and rushed to the windows. They drew the hurricane shutters together and locked them.

Susanna came running from the other room. "D'store! Come, gels, we mus' save d'store. Doors mus' be barred, d'windows shut!"

Stumbling down the outside stair in the dark they held onto each other to keep from being blown away. Reaching the street they moved from door to door, latching them and dropping the heavy diagonal iron hurricane bars in place. It took all their strength to pry the heavy window shutters loose and bend them together across the openings. On the windward side of the building their bodies were plastered to the wall by the wind so that it was difficult to move.

From the sea came the thunderous roar of surf lashed into fury and beating upon the shore. By the lightening's glare the women saw a stream of people running up the street, abandoning low-lying houses in danger of being taken by the sea. Then thunder roared and black clouds, bulbous and heaving with rain burst open releasing a deluge on the hapless town. The drenched women shivered with fear and cold.

They crept back up the stair. When they unlatched the door at the top, it was blown loose from its hinges and fell into the room with a bang. The women tumbled in on top of it. Picking themselves up they managed to prop the door back in its opening. Then they pushed a heavy sea chest against it to hold it in place.

Susanna pushed the wet hair off her face and looked wildly around, seeking some form of protection against the storm. Through the open door to her room she saw the old four-poster bed. "De bed!" she shouted above the tumult of the storm. "Come! We tip it so. Then if d'roof go . . ."

The sisters helped their mother turn the bed onto its side. The three of them crouched behind it with a quilt over their heads. The roof had already started to leak. The house trembled in the storm's clutches. The old timbers creaked and groaned as they strained against their pinnings pounded by the wind. The wind's prying fingers loosened shingles from the walls and sent them flying. It whistled through the cracks. The rain pounding on the tin roof made a hideous din. In her distress Susanna prayed aloud.

Would they survive? Anna wondered. It seemed to her that at any moment the house would come tumbling down around their ears. From under the quilt she saw the cracks in the walls and around the windows glow with an incandescent light when the lightning flashed. Thunder roared like the drums of doom. Was the Lord so displeased with His island people that He had determined to be done with them once and for all?

After several hours the wind ceased, but a thick, ominous darkness still enveloped the house. All was quiet except for the rumbles of departing thunder, the wails from the street of frightened people, and the moans of the injured.

All at once there was a frantic pounding on the door. The women crept from under the quilt, dragged the chest away from the door, and peaked around it. On the stair stood Grandmother Amalie Bernard, Aunt Lucia, and her two young daughters, Frederica and Charlotte. Aunt Lucia was supporting Amalie Bernard, who had sprained her ankle.

"De roof gone!" Lucia wailed. "We come t'you in de lull."

"Come in quickly before the wind come again!" Anna urged.

Anna lit a lamp and saw by its gleam that young Charlotte's

head was bleeding. She had been hit by a bit of flying metal. Amalie Bernard had fallen in the dark and was badly bruised. Anna bound Charlotte's head with a strip of cloth. Susanna led her mother to the four-poster and helped her get settled behind it. Then the wind returned as furious as before, rampaging around the house. The lamp went out. The women huddled closer together. Charlotte seemed to lose consciousness, and Frederica began to wail with terror.

"We sing," Amalie Bernard said. "We sing hymns in praise of de Lord. He test us t'see we doubt He goodness. Come, daughters. We sing!"

And sing they did, challenging the shrieking of the hurricane with their thin, high-pitched voices. Even Charlotte roused herself and joined in.

It was late in the day before the wind abated to a mournful sigh, the thunder and lightning ceased, and the murky darkness gave way to an uncertain sunset. The women rose one by one from their cramped postions and moved stiffly out into the room. They moved the chest away from the door. A scene of utter destruction met their horrified eyes. More than half the town had been flattened. Debris—parts of houses, even large boulders washed down from the hills—was strewn about. Bodies lay in the street, rigid in death. Among them lay the injured, groaning with pain. Others sat numb with shock or weeping over the loss of a loved one. Survivors began pouring out of houses still standing to comfort those who were grieving and to aid the injured.

But it was not until the next day that the impact of the hurricane was fully known. All the ships in the harbor had either sunk or been thrown up on the shore. The sea had dashed in forty feet beyond its usual high water mark, swamping low-lying houses. Enormous waves overtook many persons who delayed running to higher ground and swept them out to sea. Over 500 homes had been destroyed.

Lucia's house was a shambles. After the roof went, nothing was to prevent the wind and rain from doing their worst. The lean-to kitchen was flattened. Furniture and bedding were soaked. Mud and rocks had been washed into the main part of the house through a breach in a wall.

Anna turned nurse. She worked in the Lutheran Church all day and into the night. Straw mattresses were put down to bed the injured. Drinking water had to be brought from the interior of the island because salt water had seeped into many of the town's cisterns turning the water brackish. Bed linens were ripped up to make bandages. The few medical supplies available were carefully doled out. Mass graves were dug in the cemetery.

Out in the countryside the suffering was not as great. The Greathouses, mostly of stone, had the strength of fortresses and could stand the hurricane's blast. The slave quarters, too, with their low roofs and shared walls, were not as vulnerable as the small wooden houses in town. As soon as roads were made passable, help from the estates flowed into town—food, clothes, and medicine.

One morning as Anna was handing out bowls of thin fish soup to her patients, a fine carriage drawn by a matched pair of bays drove up to the front of the church. A well-dressed man somewhat older than Anna stepped down and motioned to his servants to unload the hogsheads of corn meal he'd brought to help feed the famished town. He was tall and spare but well muscled. The skin drawn tightly over his aquilline nose and high cheek bones was deeply tanned from a life spent in the open. He wore a broad-brimmed planter's hat and had wavy blond hair touched with gray showing beneath it. His hazel eyes were filled with compassion when he entered the church and saw the rows of injured.

Pastor Atterday hurried forward. "Ah, good morning, Captain Knudsen. How kind of you to come! I see you've brought sorely needed supplies."

Anna looked up from spooning soup into a woman's mouth to look curiously at this newcomer. She saw a distinguished man, weathered but handsome, with the bearing of one born to position and wealth. Lowering her eyes again she wiped a few drops of soup from her patient's chin.

As Captain Knudsen was leaving he asked Pastor Atterday, "Who is she, your good-looking assistant? She has a certain presence about her one can't help but admire."

"She's a faithful member of my congregation," the pastor replied. "a fine woman of good family. Of course, she's colored."

The captain raised his eyebrows slightly. "Oh? I never would have guessed. Surely, she's mostly white."

"Aye. Her father was Jacob Heegaard."

The memory the captain took with him was of intelligent dark eyes, somewhat sad, set in an ivory oval, a shapely head held proud on a long slender neck. His concern for the needy in the church increased considerably. He found reason to stop by two or three times a week with donations of one sort or another. Before long Anna was thanking him personally, and he was inquiring of her as to the welfare of individual patients.

When the hurricane crisis was over and Anna's services were no longer needed in the church, Captain Knudsen asked leave to call on Anna at her home. She could find no good reason to refuse him, so he began regular visits. Susanna was greatly impressed, but Anna was wary. She had suffered twice at the hands of a white man and didn't want to risk another unhappy arrangement. She made discreet inquiries about town, determined to learn the worst but found no one who would speak ill of Captain and Colonial Adjutant Carl Knudsen. He was a bachelor without relatives on St. Croix, a successful planter, estate inspector, and member of the Colonial Council. He had a close friend at Court, none other than the private secretary to Prince Christian. He owned beautiful Estate Belvedere on the island's mountainous north shore.

Anna took her time. She was in no hurry to leave her mother's house. A year passed during which Hans Carl pressed his suit, taking her on outings, giving her expensive gifts and pledging his enduring affection. No mention was made of marriage. White men still felt under no obligation to legalize a relationship with a woman of color.

Little by little he wore down Anna's reservations. He was a charming and persuasive man. Besides, the prospect of living in style on Estate Belvedere had its appeal.

One bright May day he persuaded Anna to go with him to Belvedere. They took the road leading over the mountains riding comfortably in his handsome phaeton. They passed Estates Little Fountain, Betsy's Jewel, and Canaan. At the top of the ridge above Belvedere, Anna drew in her breath with pleasure, surprised at the beauty of the scene that lay before her. The mountainside fell away steeply in a series of ridges, green with waving cane all the way to the sea. The sea was a deep, deep blue ridden by white, crested waves racing close on each other's heels toward the shore. On the far horizon she saw the shadowy outlines of the other Virgin Islands, St.

Thomas and St. Johns.

Hans Carl told his driver to halt before taking the downward grade. From their vantage point he pointed out the red roof of Belvedere Greathouse nestled in a grove of coconut palms halfway to the shore.

On their way again, the horses followed a curving drive that led to the front of the greathouse. Its imposing facade stretched across the brow of the hill. Magenta and purple bougainvillea entwined its graceful arches. The interior of the house more than met Anna's expectations.

"Of course it needs a woman's touch," Hans Carl said. "The bedroom is too stark and plain. Draperies in a cheerful shade would help. I've often thought a morning room to the east would be pleasant and a terrace where we could watch the sunset while having tea. You would be mistress of all this, dear Anna, with servants to do your bidding. We'd entertain in style. I promise you'd be admired and spoken of favorably throughout the island."

It was tempting to say yes. The thought of living with a man of stature in the community, so clearly devoted to her, had its appeal. The thought of bedding with such a man, gentle yet self-assured, caused a pleasant warmth to creep through her body and made her heart beat a little faster. Still she held back, afraid to commit herself.

One evening several weeks later they returned to Belvedere. Hans Carl had a picnic basket prepared. Servants carried it, a plush robe, and firm pillows to a sheltered rocky cove on the beach and were then dismissed.

Hans Carl spread the robe on the sand and placed the pillows on its edge for Anna to lean against. He spread a damask linen cloth between them. On the cloth he arranged a picnic unlike any she'd ever imagined. From the hampers he produced silver platters of Danish ham, cheeses, and island fruits. He opened a bottle of French wine recently chilled in the root cellar. When, at last, all was arranged to his satisfaction, he let himself down on the robe beside her. "What is your heart's desire, Anna?" he asked.

In answer she turned, looking back toward the Greathouse.

"It can all be yours," he said with a smile.

After they'd eaten and finished the bottle of wine they lay back on the cushions to enjoy the brief moment of tropical splendor between sundown and dark. The hills turned to purple. The sky was pale blue. The sea danced with pink highlights caught from the disappearing sun. Anna breathed a sigh of contentment.

Hans Carl gently pulled her closer. She offered no resistance, so he undid the buttons of her bodice. She was in a euphoric state. Perhaps the wine, she thought. He kissed her breasts. She felt the fire of desire race through her body. She was ready for physical union with a man. It had been a long time.

Anna was thirty-one when she agreed to become Hans Carl's mistress. They both thought their union would be a permanent one. At first they lived at La Grande Princesse in Christiansted, where Hans Carl was the estate inspector and overseer for the Schimmelman family. This arrangement allowed time for the alterations and decorating he wished to do at Belvedere to suit Anna's taste.

When they moved in, Anna had sixteen slaves under her personal supervision. The furnishings for the house, many of them listed in Anna's name, included mahogany beds, wardrobes, and tables. There was an imposing sideboard for the dining room with a large mirror in a mahogany frame above it. There was a long inventory of carpeting, silverware, bone china, crystal and linens. Hans Carl gave her a generous allowance of rigsdollars to spend as she saw fit.

Men friends and acquaintances came to visit from all over the island as word spread of the gracious hospitality to be found at Belvedere. They sat on rocking chairs on the gallery with a view of the sea, sipping rum punches served by well-trained servants and discussing the events of the day. That year's cane crop and world sugar prices dominated their talk. If they got around to discussing social problems on the island, the rebellious or runaway slave, Anna sat stiffly erect, her embroidery lying neglected on her lap. She tried talking in private to Hans Carl about the evils of slavery, but he refused to discuss the subject with her. "The island has enough problems what with sugar pirates, the fall of the market, and that damned sugar beet. Let's not stir the pot."

That same year Sophia married Hans Peter Petersen, her cousin who had lived next door on Hill Street when she was growing up. Johannes had finished his schooling and become a lieutenant in the militia. He invested in a number of town properties and bought Aldershville, a fine estate in the hills to the west of town where he planned to raise cattle. He married a pretty brown-skinned slip of a girl with a family background similar to his, Anna Maria Elizabeth Cuming. Meanwhile, Christine's husband, Jamie Miller, had died. She was soon remarried to the son of Governor Johannes Sobotker, only to die a year later after the birth of a son. Anna keenly felt the loss of her sister.

The days at Belvedere passed swiflty for Anna, six years in all. Anna had grown exceedingly fond of the kindhearted man who brought her there. Now, in her late thirties, faint lines were beginning to show around her eyes and mouth. But her skin was still soft and supple, her eyes luminous.

Sometimes she gazed across the sea toward the other islands. In clear weather their outlines were sharp, bringing them close, though she knew they were forty miles or more distant. She wondered about them, wondered about the people who lived there. But little did she guess that her destiny lay with a man whose star was just then rising on St. Thomas, a man who was a true humanitarian, a rarity in the turbulent records of the West Indies. It was by his side that Anna would take her place in history.

Chapter 10

ACTING GOVERNOR of St. Thomas, Peter Carl Frederik von Scholten, stood on the Charlotte Amalie wharf and surveyed the damage. His adjutant, Chris Jorgensen, stood beside him. The hurricane, though not as severe as the one in 1819, had taken its toll. In places the wharf had been pounded to bits by the heavy seas, leaving large gaps in the structure. Only two ships were still afloat in the harbor and they had suffered heavy damage. Small boats had been swept ashore and smashed to kindling wood. Two of the long, narrow warehouses that stood by the wharf had lost their roofs. Only their thick masonry walls were still standing. Fishermen's shacks had been washed away, and many of the wood shingle houses of the poor were levelled to the ground.

"Appalling!" the governor exclaimed. "We must see what can be done at once to aid the homeless. I suppose most of them took refuge in the fort."

"Aye, Your Excellency . . . those that could get there."

"See to it that they have food and water and what medical assistance they need."

He glanced back up the hill toward Government House, one of the few buildings that remained unscathed. "It looks to be without damage. If I do say so, the pains I took to see that it was well built, built well enough to survive just such a catastrophe, seem to have paid off."

"Aye," Jorgensen said. "If I remember rightly there was some discussion in Copenhagen at the time about the cost. Perhaps, now . . ."

The governor laughed. "The 'discussion,' as you so kindly put it, was so heated I was forced to go to Copenhagen to justify my expenditures to parliament. My guess is the complaints originated with local contractors who resented   my   using

94

blacks, His Majesty's slaves actually, rather than Danes to do the work. Luckily for me the king has always been sympathetic to my schemes. Well, what do you make of this mess, Jorgensen? Would you say those submerged vessels can be salvaged?"

"Most of them I would judge, sir." The adjutant raised his eyes from the foundered vessels and looked out to sea. "Sir, I see a sail on the horizon. It appears to be making for the harbor."

For several minutes the men studied the approaching vessel. Finally, the governor said, "Could be the brig, *Lougen*. Hope it is. She's long overdue. Whatever ship, she's taken some damage. Her foremast is foreshortened and she's carrying only one sail. She must have had a rendezvous with our hurricane. Actually, she's lucky to have gotten off so easily."

"Is she . . . is she from Copenhagen, sir?"

"If she's the *Lougen* . . . aye, she is."

"Then, perhaps, there'll be mail."

"You expecting some, Jorgensen?"

The young officer blushed. "Yes, sir."

The governor patted his shoulder. "It's a long way from home, eh?"

"Yes, sir."

The governor turned his back on the devastated harbor. "Jorgensen, see that the boat owners get what help they need in raising their craft. The men in the garrison can lend a hand. The debris must be cleared away and the harbor made safe as soon as possible."

"Aye, aye, sir. I'll relay your orders to the commandant at once." He saluted, then strode off along Strand Street in the direction of the fort.

The governor walked briskly up the hill toward Government House. He was a driven man with many responsibilities and no time to waste gazing out to sea. In addition to being Chief Executive, he was the Royal Weigher, head of the fire department, Postmaster General and in charge of Customs.

Peter von Scholten was born in Denmark in 1784. He was only fifteen when his father, Cassimer von Scholten, was sent to St. Thomas as commandant of the island's fort. Young Peter would have liked to go along, but both his parents felt he should first complete his education. When he finally joined his father, it didn't take him long to fall in love with the islands and decide his career should center on the West Indies.

He was on St. Thomas that fateful December of 1807 when Admiral Lord Cochrane entered the harbor aboard a British man of war and demanded the surrender of the island. Commandant von Scholten decided, as did Governor Lillienschiold of St. Croix, to surrender swiftly rather than risk having his town pulverized by cannon. Von Scholten and his son were shipped to England as prisoners of war. But they were allowed to return to Denmark within the year.

In Copenhagen this extraordinarily ambitious young man set his mind to furthering his career. He married Anna Clara Thorsten, second daughter of a captain in the Danish Merchant Marine, an alliance that helped him on his way. Likable, unusually capable and energetic, he was promoted rapidly, becoming a second lieutenant, then adjutant to King Frederik.

In 1814, the year Anna was dealing with Paul Twigg, the islands became Danish once more. It didn't take von Scholten long to conceive the idea of returning to St. Thomas. He asked the king for a commission as royal weigher and was granted his request. On that day in April of 1815 when Anna fled Twigg's house, the king's royal weigher was settling into his quarters on St. Thomas. Before long he was profiting from his new position.

The governor-general had been working at his desk for several hours when a young naval officer carrying a mail pouch was ushered into his office.

"Ensign Olsen at your service, Your Excellency," he said, saluting smartly.

Von Scholten looked up from the papers he was signing. "At ease, Ensign. What can I do for you?"

"I bring mail off His Majesty's brig, *Lougen,* and Captain Varberg's compliments, sir."

"You may put the mail on my desk, Ensign, and I'll be happy to receive your captain at his convenience. You must have had a trying voyage. It's to his credit that you made port in as good order as you apparently did."

"I'll relay your good opinion to the captain, sir. He looks forward to seeing you, sir. He bears an important communication from King Frederik and wishes to present it to you in person."

Von Scholten's interest quickened. "By all means. When

would it suit him?"

"He awaits your pleasure on the gallery now, sir."

"Thank you, Ensign. I'll join him there at once." Von Scholten pushed back his chair and stretched. He always welcomed an excuse to leave his desk. He was a man of action, and desk work tired him.

It was pleasant on the gallery. The air was fresh and bracing after the storm. The sun made leafy shadows that danced on the walls. The blue water in the harbor sparkled.

Captain Varberg clicked his heels together and held out his hand.

"*Velkomen*, Captain," von Scholten said with a gracious mile clasping the outstretched hand. "Congratulations on fetching the harbor on your damaged vessel. Quite a storm out there, eh?"

"Indeed it was, Governor! We hove to for two days and took some damage to our rigging, as you perhaps observed. On a morning like this it's hard to believe the savagery the sea can muster."

"When you know these waters well, nothing comes as a surprise. They can take you from heaven to hell in short order. I understand you bear a message from our king."

"That I do, and glad I am to be able to deliver it! There were moments when I thought it would end up on the bottom of the sea along with me and my crew." He handed von Scholten a folded parchment addressed to him and bearing the king's seal. Von Scholten broke the seal and read:

WE, *Frederik the Sixth, by the Grace of God, King of Denmark, of the Vandals and Goths, Duke of Sleswick, Holstein, Storman, Ditmarsh, and Oldenburgh, MAKE KNOWN that in consideration of your exemplary service to king and country while Acting Governor of Our West Indian Island of St. Thomas, WE ARE PLEASED TO APPOINT YOU GOVERNOR-GENERAL of all Our possessions in the West Indies, St. Thomas, St. John, and St. Croix. It is Our wish that you assume the duties thereof and take full responsibility for administering these islands in Our Name, proceeding at your earliest convenience to the capital, the town of Christiansted on St. Croix. Pressing economic problems on that island demand your immediate attention.*

As further indication of Our Gratitude and Esteem it is Our decision to bestow upon you the honorary title of Chamberlain to the King . . . .

Von Scholten felt gratified that his services to "king and country" were being recognized. That he was asked to take on added responsibilities came as no surprise. He knew that Governor-General Bentsen had failed miserably in devising workable props to ease the disastrous effects of a failing world sugar market, a market that was further aggravated by the United States declaring a tariff on West Indian sugar to protect Louisiana sugar growers. Mortgages were being regularly foreclosed. The local newspaper listed some of the most famous Cruzan Estates up for auction. It was true some planters held on, surviving from crop to crop by clearing up a few obligations, paying interest only on old debts, and at the same time taking on new ones. St. Thomas, on the other hand, had a splendid harbor that attracted trade from many nations. Servicing and provisioning their vessels helped to keep its economy afloat.

Returning to his desk, von Scholten glanced at the mail which his secretary had sorted. On top of the pile was a letter addressed in the large round scrawl he recognized as belonging to Conrad, his eighteen-year-old son. He eagerly slit open the envelope and read:

My dear father, I beg that I be allowed to come out to you in the West Indies without further delay. If not, I'll be forced to go to Fredensborg where all is drill and boot-licking, not much to my taste as you can imagine. I must confess my mother is opposed to the idea but as one military man to another I believe you can understand my eagerness. I am certain I can be of service to you as I have a good head for mathematics and can converse in the English language and would even be willing to learn the Dutch creole you speak of as being useful in working with the slaves.

Von Scholten smiled. It was clever of the boy to refer to his interest in Dutch creole. He found if one took the trouble to use the tongue most familiar to the slaves the quality of understanding, and thus their performance, was vastly improved. Eventually he believed they should all learn English, the language most widely used in the islands, starting with the children. He would even be in favor of their learning to read and write, though he knew this was a revolutionary idea and would meet with much resistance. Conrad had touched on a matter dear to his heart. He read the rest of the letter:

Please, dear father, do make arrangements for me to join you. It is a desperate situation, and time is of the essence. Mother and the girls are well and send kind regards. Your obedient son...

Von Scholten continued to hold the letter in his hand. How he longed to see the boy! Of course, for now, the answer would have to be no. For once he agreed with Clara. He hated to disappoint Conrad. He knew how much he loved the islands. He remembered him at eight or nine running joyously along the beach, splashing in the clear warm water. Conrad liked to swim and fish, and was good at both. He learned to dive and was able to retrieve shells at surprising depths.

Von Scholten sighed as he thought of the day he'd boarded a ship bound for Denmark to see his family off. Up to the last moment before the ship sailed he had tried to persuade Clara to stay.

"Just because there's yellow fever on St. Croix is no reason to think it will reach us here."

"But it might, Peter. Admit it might. And Clarissa is too young and delicate for us to take the chance. The climate here has not agreed with her from the first. I fear it was a grievous mistake for me to bring the children to this uncivilized outpost in the first place. But you would have your way!"

"I'll sorely miss the children!"

"Not all that much, I dare say," she responded with some bitterness. "Your mind is filled with island affairs morning, noon, and night. You've never had much time for me or the children, and now that you've accepted another responsibilty, that of postmaster . . ."

"If you took more interest in my career and the island's problems you might be more content."

"You know very well I've had no time for the island's problems! With a child of ten months and servants that are next to useless, I've had all I could do to deal with the problems of my own household! As you know, one of the four has been ailing most of the time. Peter, my hope is that you'll give up this outlandish post and return to Copenhagen for good. With your undeniable talents we could live a life of grace and ease in Denmark. We have connections at court which would be useful in developing a worthwile social life. But never mind. We've been through all this before."

The bos'ns whistle sounded. "All ashore who's goin' ashore!" he bellowed.

Von Scholten embraced each of the children in turn. Little Clarissa clung to his neck until her mother forcibly pried her loose. Conrad turned his head away to hide his tears. Clara held her face up to receive a farewell kiss, which was dutifully planted on her cheek. Then, reluctantly, von Scholten stepped into the lighter waiting to take him ashore.

Of course, von Scholten mused further, the yellow fever scare was just an excuse. Clara was scornful of island life. She was impressed, not at all, by the exquisite beauty of the island. The exotic charm of many of its inhabitants failed to touch her. She thought the planters put on "airs," not atune to the fact that these "airs" were a sort of bravado assumed to mask the fact that they were teetering on the brink of bankruptcy. Then there were the dangers—real or imaginary—the unhealthy climate, tropical diseases, the possibility of a bloody uprising of the blacks . . .

Von Scholten had to concede she was correct in thinking the children had superior educational opportunities in Europe. But giving up his promising career in the West Indies was unthinkable. He sadly folded Conrad's letter. In another couple of years, when Conrad had finished his education, perhaps he could arrange to have him posted to one of the islands. He rang for his secretary. Many arrangements must be made in preparation for his move to St. Croix.

Von Scholten had had Government House in Charlotte Amalie elegantly refurbished when he took office. Now he would make immediate plans to give Government House in Christiansted, the former Schopen townhouse on King Street, similar treatment. He wrote to officials and friends on St. Croix telling them when he would be arriving. Ernst von Schimmelmann acknowledged his letter enthusiastically offering him a warm welcome. He asked that he might have the priviledge of hosting a reception at his Estate, La Grande Princesse, in von Scholten's honor.

The day scheduled for his departure from St. Thomas dawned bright and clear. Governor-General von Scholten boarded the schooner *Vigilant*, to make the passage between St. Thomas and St Croix. As the ship weighed anchor and took the wind in her sails, soldiers on the ramparts of the fort dipped the flag and fired a salvo of guns in his honor.

Von Scholten received the warm welcome Schimmelman had promised when he arrived in Christiansted. But it did not take the governor long to sense others were not as friendly. A certain group of planters had serious misgivings about this new man who was said to have some newfangled, excessively liberal ideas. He also had a reputation for being somewhat arrogant and overbearing, not easily swayed by the opinions of others from the course he'd set himself.

Captain Knudsen shared these misgivings. However, they did not prevent him from showing Anna the gilt-edge invitation to the reception at Schimmelmann's.

"Should we go, Anna?" he asked. He tended to prefer quiet evenings at Belvedere with Anna to social gatherings at night, especially when the distance to be travelled was considerable.

"But of course," Anna replied. "It will be a glorious affair! Aren't you curious to see this new man, this Peter von Scholten? Meeting him should be vastly entertaining. Besides, Herr von Schimmelmann would be offended if you, one of his good friends, stayed away."

"I expect you're right . . . as usual, my dear."

The evening arrived, a warm starlit one with just enough breeze to warrant the filmy white shawl Anna liked to wear over her shoulders. Her glossy dark hair, which was arranged in braids coiled over her ears, was covered by a lace snood. Her full-skirted gown of pale gold China silk was cut in a low "V" to show off her smooth throat and well-rounded bosom. A ruby and pearl broach, an extravagant gift from Hans Carl, accented the "V."

Hans Carl helped Anna into the carriage and settled beside her. She handed him the shawl, which he arranged tenderly, allowing his arm to remain across her shoulders. He had instructed their driver to take the shoreline route to spare the horses. They travelled east from Belvedere, turning inland to follow Salt River.

When they arrived at Estate Grande Princess they took their place in the procession of equipages moving slowly toward the entrance to the Greathouse. At last they reached the bottom of the staircase leading to the gallery where Ernst von Schimmelmann and the governor-general stood.

A servant held the horses while Hans Carl and Anna stepped down. Together they mounted the stone steps one by one. Blazing torches illumined the staircase and the walls of the house so that the creamy coral blocks gleamed like marble. The arches that stretched across the gallery made gracefully curved shadows on walls and floor.

The governor-general stood erect in full dress uniform. He wore a high collared scarlet jacket with golden epaulets and a chest full of medals. His forehead, heightened by beginning baldness, gleamed in the torchlight. Streaks of gray in his brown hair added to a look of distinction. In spite of his military bearing, he managed to convey an aura of wamth and graciousness to all who greeted him. He studied each face intently.

After having to pause on each step to wait for those ahead, Hans Carl and Anna finally reached the top of the staircase. Now it was Anna's turn to be presented. Her heart beat faster.

"Your Excellency," Ernst von Schimmelmann said, "May I have the honor of presenting Miss Anna Heegaard?"

Anna offered her hand, sinking into a deep curtsy. The governor-general took her hand in his and bowed low over it. "My pleasure," he said.

As Anna stood and met his gaze, an unexpected current of excitement ran through her. For a moment she stood immobile, her lips slightly parted, her eyes on his face. Then Hans Carl took her elbow, and they moved on.

"Who is that . . . that handsome creature, Ernst?" the governor-general asked in a low voice.

"She's mistress at Belvedere, Knudsen's place on the north shore."

"Not wife?"

"She's colored."

"Charming!" the governor-general murmured as he bowed to another guest.

Anna and Hans Carl crossed the gallery and entered the main hall of the greathouse, greeting acquaintances on the way. A string ensemble was playing the stately music popular for dancing in European courts at this time, the quadrille and the minuet. Scores of candles protected from the night breeze by crystal sconces threw the swaying shadows of the dancers on the light walls. The candles' gleam shone on women's faces and bare shoulders, making even the plainest attractive that night. Officers in full dress preened like peacocks. Blacks, their foreheads glistening with sweat born of anxiety as they tried earnestly to perform their duties in a manner befitting this grand occasion, were gaudy in red satin trimmed with gold. They passed champagne in small crystal goblets.

All at once, the musicians gave a fanfare and the dancing stopped. The new governor-general stood alone in the archway leading from the gallery and held up his hand for silence. The small talk ceased. He glanced around the room. Anna's blood quickened as she felt his gaze rest for an instant on her.

He raised his glass. "To the king, God bless him!" His voice was resonant and well-modulated.

"To the king!" The words were echoed around the room as all the guests raised their glasses and took a sip of wine. While everyone's attention was centered on the governor, Ernst von Schimmelmann stepped to his side. With a bow in his direction he raised his glass high. "A toast to His Excellency, the governor-general of all the Danish West Indies. To Governor von Scholten!" he cried.

"His Excellency! Hear, Hear!" The toast was drunk, followed by applause.

Anna beamed, like all the rest, on the new governor-general.

Chapter 11

IN THE AFTERNOON the sun came out from behind the clouds after two weeks of torrential rain, rain that was welcome to many because it filled rain barrels and cisterns. Water was always a problem on the island—too much during the rainy season caused flash floods that quickly ran off into the sea, and too little brought on drought conditions during the spring and summer. Rainwater caught on roofs and used to fill cisterns was the island's principle source, as the few wells that had been dug tended to be brackish.

Von Scholten was glad to see the sunbeams fingering his desk. The rains had held up the alterations he had ordered for Government House. He walked to the window. With satisfaction he saw a man on a scaffold plastering walls and heard the rat-a-tat-tat of workmen's hammers repairing the roof of the old Schopen house, which was being joined at one end to the Sobotker house to make a pleasing architectual whole. The space between the two buildings was being turned into a landscaped courtyard. The main entrance just off King Street would be reached by an imposing triple staircase of yellow ballast brick. The plastered walls of both buildings were to be painted a sunny yellow, the shutters dark green.

He took a deep breath of the rain-washed air and reluctantly returned to his desk, where he signed yet another communique to be sent to Copenhagen, fractionally reducing the pile of papers that demanded his attention. Next on the pile was a letter from a planter bewailing the slump in the sugar economy and pleading for some government help to see him through the year. Solving the economic woes of the planters was a knotty, almost hopeless problem. He put his pen down and leaned back in his chair, considering what he should say to the poor man. A knock on his door interrupted his thoughts.

"Come in," he said absently.

Chris Jorgensen, his adjutant, approached the desk. "A . . . a lady to see you, sir."

"A lady! Who is she and what does she want? As you can see, I've plenty to do."

"I can tell her to come back later or . . ."

"You didn't tell me her name."

"Why it's Heegaard, Anna Heegaard, and she refuses to state her business."

"Miss Heegaard! Well, I'll be damned! Show her in at once, Jorgensen."

Anna swept imperiously into the office, face flushed and eyes flashing with anger. "Your Excellency!" she stormed.

"Miss Heegaard!" He rose quickly. "To what do I owe the honor of your visit?" He placed a chair near his desk. "Please be seated. You seem upset and somewhat . . . somewhat overheated, if I may be so bold."

Anna sank gratefully into the proffered chair, and the governor returned to his. He smiled at her across his desk. "When you have composed yourself I'd like very much to hear what's troubling you."

Anna flushed a deeper shade. She took a deep breath and leaning forward said earnestly, "It's that pesky 'letter of freedom,' sir, that insulting bit of paper we . . . we free-colored are required to carry."

It was a pleasure to look at her, von Scholten thought. A striking woman, more West Indian looking than he had remembered. Perhaps it was the high turban of brightly colored cotton print she had wound round her head, the heightened color in her cheeks, and her flashing eyes.

He lowered his eyes, aware suddenly of his rudeness. "Yes, Miss Heegaard. Please continue."

"We should have the *same* legal rights and respect as other free people on the island. However, it doesn't work that way — not by any means. It's unjust, and that's the truth of the matter."

"Miss Heegaard," he said gravely, "this is a state of affairs that I deeply regret and hope to change during my administration. I know your complaint is well justified. But what is it that has caused you inconvenience this especially pleasant afternoon?"

"Inconvenience, indeed! It's much more serious than that, sir.

As you perhaps know, we are required by law to have this silly piece of paper with us at all times."

"I'm familiar with the so-called 'letter of freedom,' Miss Heegaard. The statute governing its use is completely obsolete. It must have been on the books for fifty years, put there when free-colored were few. It was designed to be a protection, but it has outlived its time. Governments are always slow to recognize legislation that's out of date."

Anna settled back in her chair and crossed her ankles, pleased that the man was taking her seriously. "The trouble occured yesterday afternoon, Your Excellency. My grandmother is somewhat darker than I and suffers accordingly. She's in her seventies, though remarkably spry for her age. Still, her sight and hearing somewhat fail her. She was crossing Company Street in the rain and failed to see a farm wagon come 'round the corner. To avoid hitting her the driver crashed into the curb, his horses got tangled in their harness, and a real rumpus took place. The driver blamed my grandmother for his accident, shouted abuse at her, and finally struck her, knocking her to the pavement!"

"No wonder you're upset, Madam!"

"There's more, Your Excellency. When a gendarme appeared he took the driver's part, yanked my grandmother to her feet, and demanded she produce her 'letter of freedom.' When she failed to produce it—she hasn't carried it for years—the gendarme said he'd have to detain her in the police station for questioning. And there she's been all night! I could scarce believe my ears when my mother told me of it. It's fortunate I happened to come into town for shopping."

"Yes, I agree. I am truly sorry, Miss Heegaard. You've every right to be angry. I'll send my adjutant to the police station at once with my personal apologies to your grandmother and instructions to escort her home. Was she badly injured, do you think?"

"My mother says not," Anna replied, somewhat mollified. "Mostly it was her dignity that suffered."

"I can see why. It should never have happened."

A small, satisfied smile came to rest on Anna's lips. "Thank you, sir. I'm most grateful. And when you do away with that rule entirely, my gratitude will know no bounds."

"I'll see that it's brought to the attention of the Colonial Council at the first possible moment," he assured her.

Anna rose and extended her hand. He stood and clasped it in his. Then he escorted her to the door. "It's been a pleasure to see you again, Miss Heegaard. I hope you'll not hesitate to bring any other problems that arise to my attention."

"Thank you, sir," she said and took her leave.

Intriguing woman, von Scholten thought as he returned to his desk. A pity she's attached to Knudsen.

Anna and Peter von Scholten met sometimes at social gatherings. Whenever propriety permitted he sought her out, which she found most flattering. They talked easily together of history, world politics, and social problems on the island.

"For me," he said, "the islands are my life. They challenge me. I want to make changes, radical changes that allow all men the freedom to strive for themselves and profit according to their talents and labor."

"What of slavery?"

"It must go. It must definitely go . . . and the sooner the better. There is much sentiment against slavery in all the capitals of Europe. England is talking of emancipation. But Denmark was the first nation to abolish the slave trade. Now we should go one step further and be the first to free the slaves we already possess. But freeing the slaves will make for a hard period of adjustment. Many of the planters are dead set against it."

It was heady talk. Anna felt a tingle of excitement as she listened to this crusader, with his eyes lit up, his nostrils flared, and his voice ringing strong with conviction. He found her remarkably knowledgeable and original in her thinking.

Before long Anna and von Scholten realized they were being seen together too often. People were beginning to talk. Ladies gossiped behind their fans, and some of the men, especially those unsympathetic to von Scholten, made coarse remarks about "Knudsen's wench" over their rum punches. Though a simple, trusting man, Hans Carl couldn't remain unaware of what was going on. Anna saw the pained look in his eyes after the social affairs when she neglected him in favor of the governor, and was plagued by feelings of guilt.

Loathe to wound him, Anna resolved to avoid the governor. When he asked for a dance, she was already promised. She found some excuse to move away when he approached a group of which she was a part. He seemed to accept her withdrawal rather too readily, she thought with some pique. But then she knew he had a great deal on his mind as he wrestled with the island's many woes. Also she realized he wouldn't want to antagonize as important a member of the Colonial Council as Hans Carl Knudsen.

Christmas and New Year's came and went, with occasional polite exchanges of conversation between them. Though they kept at a distance, each was acutely aware of the other's presence whenever they were under one roof. Anna missed the intimacy that they had begun to develop. Then one evening as she stood alone on the balustrade at Cane Garden while a party was in progress within, von Scholten joined her.

"Good evening, Governor," she said. "This is a surprise!"

"Anna, I've tried to stay away, but you're too attractive. I'm finding it damned difficult."

"It seemed to me you were quite successful at keeping your distance."

"Come, now. Be fair. You've been avoiding *me*."

"I didn't want to hurt Hans Carl or give those gossipy women something to talk about."

"It's no use. I can't pretend any longer. No matter what others think . . ."

"I did enjoy our conversations, Governor—hearing your views on worldly matters and island affairs."

"Anna, you're a fascinating and beautiful woman. If only you weren't committed . . ."

"You have a wife and children, I'm told."

"Aye. I married young. I was fond of my wife, and my children were a delight to me. I sorrow for them as they once were. But children grow up and become strangers."

"Especially when their father is far away and absorbed by the governing of unruly islands," Anna gently chided.

"My wife came to St. Thomas when the children were small," he continued, ignoring her rebuke. "She had some idea of making the island her home. But she found she really didn't care for island life. She worried about the children's health and education. Then came the threat of yellow fever, and she had reason to leave."

"She never came back?"

"She wasn't willing to risk it."

"Will you never see your family again?"

"When I go to Denmark . . . aye, I'll see them. But my wife

and I become less compatible as the years go by. She has her friends there, people I have no interest in, and she'll never get over her dislike of the islands. And you, Anna, are you content at Belvedere with Knudsen?"

She hesitated, looking out to sea. The stars were brilliant, and the lights on a ship, gently rising and falling, were visible on the horizon. Through the open doorway came party voices and the tinkling of a harpsichord. "Aye, I'm content."

Von Scholten turned to her, took her hands in his and looked deep into her eyes. "If ever you change your mind—"

"Are you saying you would divorce your wife and marry me?"

"Anna! That's impossible! You know it is. They wouldn't understand the divorce in Denmark, and they wouldn't understand the marrying here. Think what it would do to my reputation, how it would strike the Colonial Council!"

Without a word she turned from him, rebellion against the ancient unjust scheme of things rising strong within her. With a toss of her head left him and returned to the drawing room.

She would forget him, she decided, forget the governor and his high-minded talk. She would put him right out of her mind. He was a fraud. He pretended to be progressive but still clung to some of the old ways of thinking. She would fill her mind with other matters. She was fond of Johannes' new wife, Anna Maria, and decided to busy herself helping the young pair set up housekeeping at Aldershville.

But it was difficult sticking to her good intentions. Her thoughts strayed whenever she was off guard, and she relived the moments she and Peter von Scholten had spent together. The days at Belvedere had lost their charm, and she found herself being short-tempered with Hans Carl. For his part, Hans Carl became more determined than ever to limit their excursions from Belvedere to an absolute minimum. A month went by without her having so much as a glimpse of the governor.

It was traditional for the governor to give a ball to celebrate the king's birthday. To stay away from this event would be an affront to governor and king. This year it was the cause of great excitement for it was not only the first affair hosted by the new governor but it was to be held in the rebuilt, redecorated Government House. The dancing would take place in the new ballroom which the governor had had furnished in a style no less grand than many a royal ballroom in Europe.

The room was spacious enough to entertain several hundred people. It had a fine hardwood floor for dancing. The imported furnishings included full-length mirrors that marched the length of the room on both sides. Heavily carved gilt frames topped by the Danish crown set off the mirrors, and they were flanked by seats upholstered in fine leather, supported on the shoulders of gilt lions. Above the seats double-branched sconces held candles protected by glass shades. From the ceiling hung four matching bronze and crystal chandeliers made in London.

The ball was well underway when Anna and Hans Carl arrived from Belvedere. He left her to join some planters around the punch bowl. Anna glanced around the room and saw the governor standing alone on the edge of the dance floor. He had singled her out and was coming toward her.

She started to move away, but he overtook her and caught her hand. "Anna," he said, "Will you do me the honor of being my partner for the next dance?"

She curtsied. "Thank you, sir. How can I refuse so flattering an offer?"

They went through the dignified steps of a quadrille, forward and backward, twisting and bowing, his manner as gallant and charming as any duchess could wish. Then the violins launched into the music for a new dance, one that had just recently been introduced to the island from Vienna, a waltz. It was daringly innovative, with couples facing each other in a closed position. It was romantic and provocative. Held securely in the governor's arms, Anna whirled around the ballroom in three-four time. The candles on the walls became a blur before her eyes. She leaned back against his arm, tilted up her face, and fixed her eyes on his. He gazed down at her, his eyes serious and dark with desire. The excitement of being held close and the constant circling movement of the dance made her feel giddy. Her cheeks were burning. The music stopped. Couples stepped apart. For a moment Anna wondered if she could stand alone. She steadied herself and brushed a stray lock of hair off her damp forehead. It seemed to her that the room was revolving around her.

The governor looked at her closely. "Are you quite well? You look . . . a glass of punch would refresh you, perhaps." He headed for the punch bowl.

The air was close with the warmth of perspiring and heavily scented bodies. Anna felt the need for fresh air and space to breathe freely. She looked about the ballroom for Hans Carl. He was nowhere to be seen. In a panic she turned and fled, speeding down a back staircase leading to the courtyard. There she stood breathing heavily, her hand pressed to her breast to quiet her heart. Conflicting fears raged within her, fear that von Scholten would follow her and fear that he would not.

When he came she was standing in the shadow of an almond tree whose tiny white blossoms gave off a subtle perfume. She took a tentative step forward. He strode toward her, arms outstretched, and she came to him with a rush. He crushed her to him, kissing her hair, her forehead, and at last finding her warm receptive mouth. It was a long while before they broke apart, and then it was to stare at each other in wonder, to marvel at the intensity of their passion. It was late in their lives, yet the emotion they both felt was more compelling, more overwhelming than anything either of them had known before.

He touched her cheek gently, an amused smile playing about his lips. "Did you think to escape me?"

She tilted her head coquetishly. "You, sir, forgot the punch."

"Right you are. When I saw you leave, the only thought in my head was to follow. You don't know me well if you think a flight of stairs, even the opinion of others . . . or the hurt of that other one whom I like and respect enormously and who cares deeply for you, could defeat me. I'm a stubborn, willful man, Anna—somewhat selfish, I fear."

What was he saying? Was he saying that he loved her? His words had the sound of love. She stood silently, waiting for what would come next, her heart beating as though it would burst from her breast.

"I tried to stay away from you, but it was no good. I couldn't keep my mind on my work. I couldn't sleep at night. I was miserable. I've never felt so drawn to any other woman."

"But your wife? When you were first . . ."

"That marriage, I'm shamed to admit, was consummated for all the wrong reasons and now is completely meaningless! What do we need with marriage? I love you, Anna. I promise you my devotion needs no document to make it strong and lasting. We can be man and wife in our hearts."

This time Anna didn't turn away. She knew that if he wanted her she would become his, that she wanted to be with him always, to be his love. "Peter," she said, and the name came easily to her lips. "I'll do whatever you say. Somehow I feel that God meant us to be together. That it is our destiny."

"Anna, do you love me?"

"I do, Peter. I love you with all my heart."

He kissed her again, then led her to a nearby tamarind, where they sat on a bench under the tree's protecting umbrella. He put his arm around her and drew her close. "Anna, my dearest Anna," he said. "I know we'll be happy together, you and I, and together we can work for all the things we want for this beloved island of ours."

Her answer was to nestle closer, laying her head on his breast.

The ride back to Belvedere passed in strained silence. Hans Carl had seen her return, her hair mussed and her eyes unusually bright. The governor rejoined the party from another entrance, but no one was fooled, least of all Hans Carl.

When they reached their bedroom he took her roughly by the shoulders, a scowl contorting his usually pleasant face. "He made love to you, didn't he?' he asked hoarsely.

She nodded.

He struck her across the face with the back of his hand. She staggered back and crumpled beside the bed. Seeing her there, he was suddenly appalled by what he'd done. He sank into a chair, looking with shame at his reddened hand. Then he put his head in his hands and wept.

Anna got to her feet and went to him. "It must be awful for you, Hans Carl," she said gently. She laid her hand on his shoulder. "I'm so sorry."

"Have you ever loved me?" he asked brokenly.

"I . . . I really don't know. A different kind of love, perhaps. I came to you willingly. You always treated me with respect . . . with great kindness. We've been happy together. I'm grateful."

Hans Carl sat silently with bowed head. She sank to the floor beside him and rested her head against his knee. "You're a good man, Hans Carl. It grieves me to have hurt you."

"I wish I meant more to you. I thought when you came to me our feeling for each other would last forever. I feel a failure."

"No, no, don't say it! You have not failed. Your love has sweetened my life for seven years. We could have gone on together in harmony except that one in a thousand, a brilliant man with dreams to match my own, came into my life. He wants me to come to him, and I must go."

"You will leave me, then?"

"You wouldn't want me to stay, feeling the way I do. I pray that one day you can forgive me, forgive and forget, find happiness with another . . . one more worthy."

Anna rose wearily and began to undress.

Hans Carl gathered up his personal belongings and left the room.

Chapter 12

IN THE BRIEF half-light between dark and dawn Anna stirred. It was going to be a warm day. She pushed the sheet down to her waist and turned toward Peter, who lay quietly by her side. She thought he was asleep, but as she turned he turned, too, and put his arm over her waist. He pulled her gently toward him. "Let me make love to you," he murmured.

"Peter . . . there's that early meeting . . ."

"Let them wait."

Wanting him as much as he wanted her she snuggled closer. As she pressed her body against his she felt a strong current of desire coursing through her. It ran from her waist, along her legs. Even her toes tingled. She felt a pleasurable ache of anticipation in her breasts as her nipples hardened, and she pressed them against his bare chest.

Their mouths met. Her lips were parted slightly, welcoming him. Tongues touching lightly, he kissed her again and again. His mouth was hard and demanding on hers, his tongue thrusting, their breaths mingling. Then his kisses became gentler, more tender, and he raised her nightgown with one hand while he stroked her bare thighs with the other, his hand coming to rest, still and warm, where her legs came together.

He raised his head to look at her and unexpectedly grinned. "Can't we do without this bunch of material between us? It's certainly in the way. Besides, I like you bare. I love the feel of your skin next to mine."

She sat up and stripped off the offending gown. "You're a demanding sort," she teased. "What will you be demanding next?"

"Only that you love me and me alone."

In answer she slid down beside him, twining her legs around

his. They stayed thus, stroking and fondling each other as only those truly in tune, sensitive to each other's needs and desires, have the patience to do. At last she knew she couldn't wait much longer to have him . . . all of him. Yet the sensations she was feeling were so delicious she wanted them to go on forever.

Suddenly, he turned on his back and pulled her on top of him, his body thrusting upward to enter hers. She arched and came down on him hard and climaxed convulsively, exquisitely. Then he turned her over, entered her again, arriving at his own climax. Again she responded with a climax of her own.

Afterward they lay still in each other's arms, completely spent yet utterly content. Finally, she said, "I thank God each time we make love that he has fashioned us thus, man and woman, to find such pleasure in our loving."

"You don't think, then, that He had in mind only the reproduction of the human race?" Peter teased.

Anna gave him a playful shove. "Out! Out of my bed and get yourself dressed before your councilors descend upon us and find you naked as a fledgling bird in its nest."

"Knowing the wench I'm keeping these days I suspect they might understand . . . and be most decidedly jealous."

Peter dressed and shaved himself at the wash basin that stood in one corner of the room. Then he bent and kissed Anna lightly on the forehead. She stirred slightly but did not answer. He smiled, understanding, and left without disturbing her further.

Anna lay still, the dark mass of her hair lying in disarray on her pillow, filled with a pleasant lassitude, the aftermath of their lovemaking. Soon the light grew stronger, and with its coming she stirred again. The house was still quiet. She lay in a half dream, considering the year since she'd come to live with Peter. It held a long procession of small delights and nights of surprising passion. Their lovemaking had brought moments of ecstasy surpassing their fondest dreams. Wisdom born of maturity gave them the good sense to savor each day and night, knowing that the years allotted them were numbered.

She stretched her long legs, bending her toes upward feeling the pleasant pull on her calf muscles. Of late she was sometimes stiff in the mornings. She turned on her side and with her hand felt the slight impression made in the bed by Peter's body. She inched over and curled up in it, taking pleasure in a lingering sense of his presence.

She dozed again, to be awakened by the noise of a shutter banging. She could hear servants stirring in the house. From the street outside her window came voices in lively conversation, followed by a burst of bubbling laughter that died away as the owners of the voices moved on. Then she heard high-pitched, contentious voices as the farm women who sold vegetables on the corner of the street argued with an early customer. There was the creaking of wooden wheels belonging to a donkey cart, the driver encouraging his beast with a well chosen-mixture of curses and sweet talk. Finally, she heard the click of horse's hoofs and the swish of buggy wheels approaching the carriage entrance to neighboring Government House. Someone had arrived for the meeting of the Colonial Council.

She sat up and threw back the sheet. The air that flowed into the room smelled fresh and sweet. She slipped out of bed onto the grass matting that covered the floor and stretched her arms over her head. She felt wonderful, tingly and alive. Moving to the window she peered through the louvres of the closed shutters. Striding down the street swinging her hips came a handsome black girl with a basket of fruit on her turbaned head, full of bananas, pawpaws, mangoes, and limes. She sang out lustily as she walked, "Who buy? Who buy dese fine ripe fruits? Who buy?"

Anna adjusted the louvres to admit more light. A sunbeam shot across the room, burnishing the satiny wood of a mahogany wardrobe and setting its brasses on fire. The red roses on a porcelain pitcher burst into sudden bloom, and a pier mirror nearby tossed rainbow glints on the wall. Half dancing, she circled the room, pausing to look in the mirror and liking what she saw. She was in love, and it suited her well. She slipped on a dressing gown and rang for one of the maids to bring her breakfast.

When Anna agreed to live with Peter, he rented Judge Gjelrup's house next door to Government House as a temporary residence. Moving from the country into Christiansted was a pleasant change for Anna. She liked being near her family and the bustle of harbor and town. But the rooms in the judge's house were cramped and noisy. It distressed her that there was not enough room to unpack her possessions from Belvedere. But

Peter promised something better in the future, and she knew he'd be as good as his word.

Later that day, as Anna sat reading a book of poems Peter had given her, her brother, Johannes, was ushered into her room.

"Anna!" he blurted out. "The land next to us at Aldershville is t'be had! It's more beautiful, even, than our place . . . with a fine view of harbor an' town. I tell you it's prime for either cattle or cane. You and the governor should take a look."

Anna hugged him. "No wonder you bounce in here like boy o' ten! That's exciting news! Peter's been looking for land. This could be . . . you certain sure there's no mistake, Johannes?"

" 'Course I'm sure! I talked to Herr Grotmueller myself. The price's not bad considerin' the quality of the land. He's in debt up to his eyebrows an' must sell t'satisfy the bank."

"I wouldn't for the world drag the governor out there on a fool's errand, busy as he is. But if you're sure . . . it would be nice being neighbors, Johannes. I'll tell him about it at once. How is Anna Maria coming on?"

"These last few days she feeling better. The sickness in the morning has left her, an' she feel less dragged out."

"I'm glad to hear it. Give her m'love, Johannes, and tell her to be good to herself."

The next day she and Peter drove out in Peter's landau to inspect the property. They had to leave the carriage at the bottom of the hill because as yet there was no driveway. The hill was steep and Anna's skirts caught in the thornbush. But she and Peter were strong and healthy and enjoyed the climb.

When they reached the top of the hill she clasped her hands together in ecstasy. "Peter, the view! It's magnificent! I can see all the way across the harbor to old Fort Augusta."

"It is rather splendid," Peter agreed. "The house will be the highest on the island, and we can build a watchtower to take us even higher. Oh Anna, I think we could be proud and happy here!" He put his arms around her, and she turned her face up to be kissed.

They spent the better part of the day walking the property lines, considering the lay of the land, and deciding on the most auspicious location for the house and the way the drive should go. Peter planned on a majestic scale. The estate he visualized, in keeping with his position (he was not a modest man), would be more elaborate than any yet built on the island. It would include not only a magnificent Greathouse, a fit setting for the entertaining he and Anna would do, but many lesser buildings. There would be an overseer's house, stables, and a village for the workers.

"If we buy, the estate must have a name," Peter said. "What shall we call it?"

Anna thought for a moment, but nothing she could think of struck her fancy. "I don't know, Peter. You think of a name."

"How about Bulow's Minde? Jens Bulow was a close friend of mine when we were boys in Denmark. He died tragically, falling through the ice on the Kongens River. It was early spring, and the ice was thin. I still think of him. It would please me to name the estate in his memory."

"Do it then, Peter."

"He was a talented musician, Anna, with great promise for one so young. He played the piano like a virtuoso and composed, too. He could have been famous worldwide if he'd lived."

"Let it be Bulow's Minde then, Peter. It's a pleasant-sounding name, and would be a fine tribute to your friend."

Peter bought the property and immediately set to work drawing plans and specifications. The principal living quarters in the Greathouse would be on the second floor to provide good ventilation, security, and a view. Ample space for servants' quarters and storage would be arranged below. He drew a long, arched gallery stretching across the front of the house, reached by a "welcoming arms" staircase, and a reception hall behind it. Doors to his private rooms, including a sitting room and two bedrooms, led from the reception hall.

The Greathouse would have wings spread at an angle from the center section of the house. The right wing would hold a banquet hall designed to seat fifty people and an adjacent smaller room that could be used for music or billiards. The left wing provided space for a study of an unusual octagon shape and another informal room for intimate entertaining. He designed a private chapel, and beside it a watchtower that would command a view of town, harbor and surrounding countryside.

Anna was to have a villa for her own personal use. Connected to the right wing of the greathouse it would be as elegant, but on a smaller scale. Anna decided to call it *Hafensight*, meaning "harbor view." Peter, though full of grand ideas, was not a wealthy man. Anna was glad to help by contributing some of her own funds to the building of the estate.

The construction had been underway for some six months when, after attending an early meeting with the Colonial Council, Peter returned to their room with a fat roll of architectual drawings under his arm. Anna had not finished dressing.

"Your meeting, it is over so soon?"

"Aye, most matters were easily disposed of. In fact, there'll be time to drive out and inspect Bulow's Minde. Would you care to come?"

"Would I care to? Of course! I must check the layout of the garden before the fall rains come and see to the planting. There must be oleanders, bougainvillea, and hibiscus for color, and jasmine for scent. I will be ready in an instant. Dear Heart, help me with these buttons down the back. They're small and tedious."

The buttons were small and tedious, Peter agreed, but he enjoyed the scent of her hair and the feel of the firm smooth flesh of her back beneath his fingers. "We must decide about the furnishing of your villa, my love. You must choose paint, wallpaper, and draperies."

"Not draperies. I want the rooms to be light and airy at all times. We can hang jalousies at the windows for privacy. And of course we should provide shutters on the outside in case it comes on to blow. Peter, will you come visit me in my villa?"

"As often as you will allow, Madam," he said with an amused smile.

Anna felt sure he would. Aside from the pleasure of being together, her villa would provide an escape for him from unwelcome callers and the demands and protestations of his diverse people. She tied a blue scarf over a broad-brimmed straw hat and picked up a ruffled parasol which she twirled over her head coquettishly.

"You look bewitching, my dear," Peter said. He picked up the roll of architectual drawings, offered Anna his arm, and they went down the stairs to the street where the landau waited for them. The groom took his seat behind the horses, Peter handed Anna in, and they were off.

The horses were eager to stretch their legs. They trotted briskly up King Street past the Anglican Cathedral, the Moravian church, and took the north shore road out of town.Turquoise Bay lived up to its name, a vivid expanse of greenish blue. The reef beyond it was frosted with white foam and the sea on the other side was a deep indigo. The sky was pale in contrast, a delicate shade of orchid.

Overlooking the bay, Anna exclaimed with pleasure, "Surely 'tis a gift straight from God, such beauty!"

Touched by her delight, Peter squeezed her arm affectionately.

As they drove along he greeted people traveling the same road. Some sat astride donkeys carrying produce to town. More were on foot. The men carried hoes or machetes. Women sauntered along with bundles on their heads. Both men and women returned his greeting, calling, "Mornin' Massa Peter! Mornin', Mistress."

At Bassin Triangle the horses took Contentment Road, winding up into the hills. The road levelled off past Beeston Hill, and the horses trotted easily. But when they turned onto the new property they had to work hard to keep the carriage moving steadily along the steep, rutted lane that led to the building site. The groom applied his whip to keep them moving. Straining they climbed higher and higher. At the summit Anna eagerly stepped down from the landau to better see the view.

Poised on the brink of the hill she said, "I'll never get used to it or take it for granted. It always sets my senses to tingling."

"But gained at too much effort for the horses," Peter grumbled, coming to stand beside her. "The drive must be made smooth and widened and graded to allow a more gradual ascent so as to spare the horses. I'll go over its course with Larsen first thing. Come along, Anna. If you're impressed with this, wait till you see the view from the watchtower. The steps are yet to be finished but there's a reliable ladder."

"Lead on, Your Excellency," she said gaily, folding her parasol and depositing it in the landau. "I want to see it all, every nook and cranny!"

To approach the tower they had a steep climb over rocks. The last twelve feet required the use of the ladder. Peter held it while Anna cautiously mounted one rung, then another. Her petticoats blew in the wind and with one hand she tried vainly to make them behave.

"Forget the petticoats, Anna, and use both hands. I'm afraid you'll fall."

"I'm glad you're the only one to see this performance!" she laughed.

"So am I! I must say it's entertaining."

The parapet had yet to be built, though the loose bricks were there and arranged as they would go, so she stayed well back from the edge. Peter scrambled to the top and came to stand beside her. "Well, what d'you think of this?"

"It's splendid!" Anna said. "Besides the harbor, we can see for miles in the other direction." Looking south toward Cane Garden she could see vast fields of sugar cane, thick green mats, squares, and rectangles rippling in the wind. They covered the bottoms and tilted up against the sky.

A cursory visit to the Greathouse followed, then Peter left Anna to find his contractor. She roamed through the rooms, admiring the prospects from different window openings. She noted the fine craftmanship that had been used on the windows to line them with small imported brick or frame them in mahogany. She was pleased to see that the rooms were spacious, with high tray ceilings for coolness. Peter had told her the walls were to be painted or papered, as the case might be, in the elegant style currently used in fine European mansions. In her imagination she finished them off and placed furniture, hung paintings, and laid rugs. The four-poster would, of course, be placed in her villa.

It was in her villa that Peter found her. "Well, Madam, are you satisfied?"

"It's going to be fantastic, Peter, but such a lot remains to be done. When will it all be finished?"

"Not for years!" he teased.

"But . . . but, Peter!"

"Don't fret, my love," he said, seeing the concern in her eyes. "I'm talking about the whole plan, outbuildings and all. The Greathouse and your villa should be livable in a few months. The roofs are finished so that we're no longer at the mercy of the weather. We'll have shutters and jalousies, if that's your wish, for the windows soon. Then one fine day we'll leave town and from then on Bulow's Minde will be our home."

"I hope the time flies. We've been overlong at Judge Gjelrup's."

"It is cramped. Castle Burke mid-island is available. If you wish, we can live there while the Greathouse is completed."

"An admirable idea, Peter."

On their way home Peter and Anna stopped to visit with Johannes and Anna Maria at Aldershville. Anna was concerned about her sister-in-law. The middle months of her pregnany had gone well, but now that the date for her delivery was approaching, she was a pitiful sight. Her face was puffy and her legs were swollen. Her abdomen ballooned out enormously below her breasts. She could hardly move herself out of a chair without help.

"It won't be much longer now, little one," Anna comforted her. "Another few weeks, and you'll have the babe in your arms."

"Oh, Anna, you do think so . . . truly?"

"Of course. Take care of yourself and get plenty of sleep. Nature will take care of the rest."

Anna spoke with more confidence than she felt. She was concerned about Johannes as well. He looked desperately worried. At the door he asked, "She'll come through it all right, won't she, Anna?"

"Why not, Johannes? She's young and strong. You've arranged for a midwife to attend her no doubt."

"Old Matty's coming. She's recommended an' lives nearby. She had plenty experience, that for sure. She took care of Anna Maria's sister. But Rachel big-boned, an' babies come easy as fallin' off log."

"If Anna Maria has faith in this woman . . . . On the other hand, if you'd like to have Dr. Neilsen, Peter's physician, assist, I'm sure it can be arranged."

"Thanks, Anna. Thanks, Peter, for stoppin' by."

"Good to see you, Johannes," Peter said, patting him on the back. "We'll hope it's a boy. It's good to have a son to look after the girls."

"This over, I think a while 'fore I start another baby."

Anna smiled. "The babe will help you decide." She kissed his cheek, then started down the steps toward the waiting landau. "Send for me if you need me, Johannes. I'll come at once."

Chapter 13

LABOR BEGAN for Anna Maria on a gray September dawn. Frightened by her prolonged distress and getting little reassurance from Matty, the doom-ridden midwife, Johannes sent a servant, begging Anna to come. Anna in turn summoned Dr. Neilsen to Castle Burke. Together they travelled to Aldershville.

The doctor was glum, his chin sunk in the high collar of his starched white shirt. His black suit and cravat, attire considered appropriate for a professional man, added to his lugubrious appearance.

"Are we going to have a storm, doctor?" she asked as they drove along. She had been watching ominous clouds gathering on the southeastern horizon.

The doctor grumbled something about the parched island and the need for rain, and withdrew further into his shirt collar. He disliked obstetrical cases. They tended to be long, drawn-out, messy affairs that defeated him—babies born dead, women lost to childbed fever. He looked at his large clumsy hands, the fingernails not so clean as his shirt collar, and wondered if they could save the poor young woman who labored up on the hill at Aldershville.

Wind hustled Anna up the steps of the greathouse. She was met by an ashen-faced Johannes. "She's been at it for seven hours, Anna, the pains comin' so close and hard she scarce give time to breathe. She near exhausted and gettin' nowhere. Her screams . . . oh, it's dreadful!" He took Anna's hands in his and looked imploringly into her eyes. "Anna, don't let her die!"

Anna patted his cheek reassuringly. "Johannes, some pain is inevitable. This is Dr. Neilsen, Peter's physician. He'll know what to do."

Johannes looked hopefully at the tall, dignified gentleman beside Anna. "Thank God you've come, sir. I take you to her."

Dr. Neilsen plodded up the steps beside Johannes. "Seven hours," he muttered. "That's no time at all, young man. It could go on much longer. If anything can be done to assist your wife, I'll see to it. Then we must leave her to God's tender mercy."

Anna Maria lay on the four-poster in the couple's bedroom. Her slight body made little more than a wrinkle in the rumpled bedclothes, except for her great mound of a belly. Her small face was all one color, save for her dark lashes that made inky black lines on her waxen cheeks. A drop of blood stood on her lower lip where she had bitten it in her agony. As Anna, Johannes, and Dr. Neilsen entered the room her body arched in a strong contraction, her small impotent fists beat the bed and a scream so piercing rose from her throat it seemed impossible for it to have issued from so slight a frame. Johannes put his hands over his ears and closed his eyes.

The midwife stood idly by the window, looking out at the building storm. She was a large, uncouth woman with mottled brown skin and a grizzled head wound in a soiled white headcloth. Her eyelids drooped over her eyes, giving them a reptilian look. Seeing the doctor she came to attention. In response to a gesture on his part she raised the cover on the bed so that he could see the lower part of Anna Maria's body, the slender legs spread apart, the child-like hips and distended belly.

"She too small, doctor mon," the woman said. "Naught t'be done, poor chile. She wear sheself out, then slip away, takin' de babe wid her."

At her words Johannes sank into a chair with a groan, holding his head in his hands. "No! No!" he cried.

"I be goin' now," the midwife continued, letting the sheet fall. "No more need o' Matty. It be time of hurricane an' me shutters ajar."

She left, and Anna was relieved to see her go.

Anna bent over the four-poster and wiped the perspiration from Anna Maria's forehead and the blood from her lip. "There, there, little sister. Rest and gain strength. Dr. Neilsen is here and will try to help. Your pain will soon be over and . . . and . . ." Anna's throat closed with pity as another futile contraction contorted the tortured body. Anna Maria uttered a scream and threw her body wildly about as though to rid herself of its burden. Finally it was over. She opened her eyes to look briefly, imploringly, first at Anna, then the doctor. She closed them again as another contraction carried her into her own realm of hideous pain.

Doctor Neilsen took off his coat and hung it carefully over the back of a chair. He went to the bottom of the bed and folded the sheet away to begin his examination. He placed his hands on her belly in various positions, trying to determine the size of the child and how he lay. He measured the width of her pelvis with his hand and shook his head.

He walked over to where Johannes sat and spoke in a hushed voice. "The child is large and the space narrow. Furthermore the position is bad—legs down, I should say. I could do a Caesarean section and possibly save the child, but the mother is almost certain to die. We have no adequate way to stop the bleeding. It's your decision, Herr Wittrog."

"I won't allow it. I won't have you cut her. I'll not agree to her death. Anna, what shall we do? Help me, Anna. There must be something . . ."

"I think we should give her every chance to live. To do otherwise is forcing the hand of God."

"If that's your decision, all we can do is wait . . . wait till it's over one way or another. I'll leave you with your wife, then, Herr Wittrog. I'll be close at hand if you need me. Perhaps the servants could bring me coffee and a bite to eat. It's getting on toward noon." He started toward the door.

Anna barred his way. "Doctor, is this the best you can offer? With your education and years of experience are you so easily giving up on the life of this healthy young girl? Surely there must be some way you can help her!"

Dr. Neilsen reddened under Anna's accusing tone. He reminded himself that she was not just any frantic woman but the governor's mistress. He hesitated. "There is a possibility," he said, looking at her strong, slender hands. "Possibly with your help I could bring the babe. Would you be willing to take an active part in the delivery, willing to—to soil your hands?"

Anna's eyes flashed with scorn. "Of course! What do you take me for? I'll do anything."

"With your assistance I might be able to alter the child's position. If you can gain entrance to the birth canal you may be able to turn the child while I apply pressure from without. My hands . . ." He held up his large-boned, paw-like hands and shook his head. "You can see how impossible it would be for me!"

"How shall we proceed?" Anna asked drily.

"We'll need a basin of hot water and your highest proof rum, Herr Wittrog. Alcohol seems to be useful in preventing infection."

Johannes was on his feet in an instant, a glimmer of hope in his red-rimmed eys. He rushed to the door and spoke to the serving girl waiting there. "You hear the doctor. Quick then. Hot water and strong rum."

Looking with distaste at the bed Dr. Neilsen said, "I can do nothing in that tumble of bedclothes. That long table there. Clear it off. We must put her on it."

Anna swept the things off the table, and Johannes gently picked up his suffering little wife and laid her on it. Anna saw that she was noticeably weaker, as though she had drifted off into a far place. Even her groans had grown feeble.

"We must hurry," Anna said anxiously. "She's far gone."

"Fold back her gown," Dr. Neilsen said, "and tie her feet to the table, her knees acutely bent. Mistress Heegaard, you will attempt to insert your right hand into the birth canal after I cut her slightly to enlarge the opening."

Anna washed her hands in the hot water. She heard the wind whipping around the house and rattling the shutters. Meanwhile Dr. Neilsen took a surgical knife from his black bag, dipped it in rum, and made a short cut back from the birth canal. A trickle of blood appeared.

"Now!" he said.

Anna hesitated for only a moment. She braced herself and forced her fingers into the small opening in Anna Maria's body. The skin of the birth canal felt hot and slippery. She turned her hand this way and that pressing gently inward. Gradually the canal stretched to admit her whole hand. She closed her eyes and concentrated on her sense of touch, exploring with her fingers.

"What do you feel?" Dr. Neilsen asked.

"I feel something . . . a bit of flesh covering bone, perhaps."

"It must a leg," the doctor said. "Try and move it one way or the other . . . gently, which ever way it seems to want to go. I'll try to assist you."

At that moment a contraction caught Anna's hand in a painful squeeze. For a moment she lost all sense of touch. Then the muscles relaxed and again she felt the tiny leg. It lay across the birth canal. She pushed it gently, and it slid to one side.

At the same time Dr. Neilsen pushed hard on Anna Maria's abdomen just above the pelvic bone to change the child's position. Anna withdrew her hand as another contraction stronger than the last began.

Anna Maria opened her mouth to scream, but Anna cried, "Don't waste strength screaming and throwing yourself about, girl! Fight! Fight for your life and your babe's! Here, hold my hands. Pull on them and push. Push hard, and we'll have him out."

Staring with wide eyes at Anna, Anna Maria suddenly came back to life and hope. Pulling Anna's hands she strained with all her might. During the contraction Dr. Neilsen announced that he'd seen the baby's head. Anna Maria rested, panting like an animal. Another contraction and another heroic effort on her part brought the baby's head into clear view. Now Dr. Neilsen was able to grasp the black-haired little head in his thick, coarse fingers and draw the baby slowly from his mother's body.

All at once the wind ceased, and a soft healing rain fell on the roof overhead.

The baby was named for his father, Johannes Ludvig Wittrog. Anna became his godmother.

All summer changes had been taking place in the conduct of island affairs. The governor began appointing free-colored to government positions. He ordered the miltary commanders to allow them to earn commissions in the services. Radical measure these, and the planters grumbled about his newfangled ideas, predicting they would bring nothing but trouble to the island. Still, they respected his ability as an administrator. The common people were solidly behind him.

The governor took an even bolder step when he began holding receptions twice a week at Government House, inviting outstanding members of the community of whatever color to attend. Anna stood proudly by his side to welcome those who came to pay their respects. She was deeply moved to see that the hands that grasped hers in greeting were often darker than her own.

It was mid-January before Bulow's Minde's Greathouse and Anna's villa were sufficiently completed for the governor and his lady to move in. Moving day was an exciting one for both of them. The Christmas winds, still brisk, had cleared the sky of all trace of clouds. The air was bracing and seemed unusually pure. Most of their possessions had already been moved and carried to Bulow's Minde, where Anna and Peter would make final decisions about their arrangement. To Peter's satisfaction, the driveway was much improved. Though longer, making a broad sweep around the hill, the horses could now trot up it without strain.

The landau came to a stop at the bottom of the welcoming arms staircase. Peter handed Anna down from the carriage and offered her his arm. Together they mounted the stairs to the gallery.

Then they walked hand in hand like delighted children through the rooms of the greathouse. They moved a chair or two and adjusted some of the jalousies to let in more light.

"It needs flowers, Peter. The house must always be filled with flowers. I'll see to the choices . . . and to the arranging later. Your gardener will no doubt be willing to help."

"Tell him what you need, my love, and it shall be done."

Finding most things to their liking, they next inspected Anna's villa and were pleased with what they saw.

"Does it suit you, Anna? Is there anything more you need . . . any changes to be made?"

"The bed needs to be turned, Peter. When I wake in the morning I want to be able to see the sky. I never tire of watching the clouds move across the sky. And the chiffonier should go here where the mirror will catch a better light, though I'm not so fond of looking into it as I once was. Your chair, that planter's chair you favor, will be by the window looking toward the sea. Oh, Peter! 'Tis a charming small house! Is it . . . is it wicked to be so happy?"

Peter put his arm around her. "Not wicked, my love. We must accept gratefully what happiness comes our way, but never cease in our efforts."

She nodded her head in agreement. "I know."

Breaking away she moved to a window overlooking the cane fields. In the fields she could see a row of figures made small by distance, their motions slowed. They raised their arms, then bent their backs in one continuous well-timed motion as they cut the cane. They moved steadily along, leaving a crest of fallen stalks behind them. The overseer stood to one side with his symbolic whip. She sighed. Yes, it is wicked, she thought, to have so much when they still labor under the yoke of slavery.

That evening they dined in Anna's villa and afterwards climbed the watchtower to see the moon rise over the harbor. Storm clouds now hovered on the horizon, but the moon climbed past the clouds and shone forth boldly, making a glittering path across the dark water beyond Gallows Bay.

As they watched the wind came up, blowing strongly and ruffling the moon path. It loosened the pins in Anna's hair and blew dark wisps around her face. She reached up to repair the damage, but Peter said, "Let it fly. It's beautiful so."

Laughing she shook the rest of the pins loose and her dark hair streamed out behind her like a banner. For the first time Peter saw by the moon's bright light the streak of silver beginning at her temple. To him it added to her beauty. But at the same time it touched his heart with sadness, sadness that the years were flying by so fast. He ran his fingers tenderly along the streak, then put his arms around her and drew her to him.

From the garden below came the scent of vanilla. The oleanders were just coming into bloom.

Chapter 14

SEVERAL HUMANITARIAN CHANGES had occurred in the four years Anna and Peter had been living at Bulow's Minde. In 1832 he made a trip to Denmark. While there he persuaded the king and parliament that many of the free-colored were precisely on the same cultural and moral level as middle-class Europeans, and argued that the old colonial legal differences based on color be abolished. As a result a Royal Ordinance came from Copenhagen endorsing full equality between whites and free-colored in the sight of the law. Later in the year he persuaded the Colonial Council to vote in favor of an edict providing "Free Compulsory Education" for slave children. This sounded very grand to Anna. But getting the planters to take the necessary steps to implement it was a slow, arduous process. It would be nine years before the first public school was established on the island.

From the first Peter and Anna made a practice of entertaining both races at Bulow's Minde. They tried to set an example to others, hoping the practice would catch on. But white wives were touchy about mixing with women of color on an equal social footing.

One morning as they were strolling in the gardens after breakfast Peter asked, "Whom are we having for dinner Thursday next?"

"Let me see . . ." Anna had a list of guests on her desk, but it was lengthy and she couldn't recall all the names. "Assessor Rothe, Christopher McCutchin, the de Windts, the Pinneys, the . . ."

"There's a young man," Peter broke in, "a West Indian who has just been appointed adjutant to the Stadshauptmand, a very personable chap. His wife is said to be charming, somewhat darker than he. What would you think of including them in our dinner party?"

Anna didn't hesitate. "But of course we'll do it. Who better than we to break the old mold? It's a brave idea. I'll send the lady an invitation in my own hand. What is their name?"

"Carstensen."

The evening arrived, a clear starlit night with a welcome breeze to dissipate the heat of the day. The governor and Anna stood on the gallery at the top of the staircase to greet their guests. An undistinguished carriage pulled by indifferent horses pulled to stop below them, the first arrivals. A young military man leapt down and offered his hand to his lady. As they ascended the stairs Anna glanced curiously at the shy girl coming towards her. She was darkly beautiful with large liquid eyes and bright flowers in her closely cropped black hair. Her dress of a soft filmy material was white with a rose-colored underskirt that clung to her well-proportioned body. One hand lay lightly on her husband's arm, the other raised her skirt slightly so that she could take the steps with ease. Lieutenant Carstensens's eyes were filled with pride as he presented her. The governor greeted them both warmly. Anna gave the girl's hand an extra squeeze.

Another carriage rolled up the hill, and the Carstensens passed on into the reception hall. Major de Tully stepped down alone from his carriage. His wife was indisposed, he explained. Peter Heyliger's wife was tending a sick child. And thus it went. Before the guests sat down to dinner six places had to be removed from the table.

Anna sat at the foot of the table, her head held high. Only the high color in her cheeks hinted at the humiliation the snub had caused her. The governor, looking the length of polished mahogany between them, thought she'd never looked lovelier. But his stomach churned with anger at the white women who had chosen to let their prejudice be known in such a rude manner. He tried to make light conversation, but hard feelings around the table made it impossible. At last it was time for the table to be cleared and the gentlemen offered cigars and brandy. Anna caught Madam Carstensen's eye, and they escaped from the dining hall together. Lieutenant Carstensen, refusing to stay longer with the men, soon excused himself, also.

Alone with the other white men, von Scholten told them in no uncertain terms what he thought of their wives' behavior. At home the men passed the word along to their wives. Gradually the idea took hold that those families who wished to stay in the governor's favor had best not let their prejudices show.

William the Fourth of England, persuaded by his Prime Minister, Earl Grey, had let his people go. Slavery in the British West Indies was at an end. The year was 1833.

The news came to the governor-general of the Danish islands from his counterpart in the British islands, in the dispatch case of a young adjutant whose task it was to bring news of the outside world to Bulow's Minde as soon as it reached Christiansted. The governor was seated at his desk in his study. Anna sat on a low rocker nearby. She put her book down as the young man entered briskly, obviously excited. He presented the dispatch case to the governor, who opened it with what seemed to Anna aggravating deliberateness.

"What is it?" Anna asked impatiently.

Von Scholten was studying the topmost paper. "The slaves in the British Islands have been freed," he told her in even tones. "The workers on Tortola, Virgin Gorda, and the rest, they're free men."

Anna rose quickly from her chair and hurried to his side. Over his shoulder she read the paper he held in his hand, her face growing flushed with excitement. "What marvelous news, Peter! If that dullard on the English throne can do it, so can we. England's move will certainly strengthen your position with our planters. You must write to the king at once and tell him what you plan to do."

"And what is that, my love? Would you be pleased to tell me?"

"Don't tease, Peter! You must be as joyful as I am. It's what we've both been praying for and working toward for years. We must see that Denmark quickly follows England's lead or be shamed among nations."

"But all of a sudden! Anna, this precipitous act will throw the Caribbean into a turmoil! Having the unfree freed by one government while others remain in bondage will cause tragic unrest in this small island world of ours. "

"His Excellency is right, Mistress Heegaard," the adjutant said. "News travels faster by mouth than in dispatches. The word from Cruz Bay is that slaves are already attempting to cross the passage between St. John and Tortola to reach free

132

soil. If they can't swim they attempt the passage by hanging onto doors taken from their cabins. Some have been lost, drowned that is, or taken by sharks."

"A great pity!" the governor said. "We must send word to our man there to see what can be done to stop it. You may go, Lieutenant. I'll let you know if I have further need of your services."

After the young man left the governor began pacing the floor. As he turned on his heel, Anna stood stubbornly in his path, forcing him to face her. "So, Peter, whether everyone likes it or not, the die is cast. All Christian nations will be forced to follow England's lead. For Denmark let it begin right here on St. Croix under your guidance."

"But it should be done in an orderly manner, Anna, with an agreement among all governments in the area directly affected. More needs to be done to prepare the people, more education, a plan for their employment if they choose to leave their old masters or if their masters can no longer afford to keep them. It's only fair that the planters be considered, too. They have a huge investment in their slaves and should be compensated in some way."

"The slaves have repaid their original cost in hard labor many times over."

"In some cases. Not all. You must remember, Anna, the planters are having a hard time of it, what with drought and hurricane, and a falling sugar market."

"I have little pity for the poor planters!" Anna said bitterly. "They still live well enough! I stopped in Mama's store yesterday. Madam de Nully was buying Belgian lace to trim a petticoat."

"You don't miss much, do you, my dear?" Peter said with a wry smile. He returned to his desk and looked hurriedly through the rest of his papers, then rose to go. "I must prepare a statement to be posted in public places around the island. It's no use trying to keep this quiet. Official dispatches must be sent to St. Thomas and St. Johns. The Colonial Council will have to be reconvened to deal with foreseeable problems."

"They're small-minded men, those members of the Colonial Council! They have no consciences."

"Ah, but they do, my dear! Only sometimes their pocketbooks are more persuasive, a common human failing. I will be in touch with our king. Never fear. If he gives me the authority—" He kissed her hurriedly and was on his way.

Authority to free the slaves was not forthcoming from Copenhagen, though the governor wrote to the king and parliament, hoping they would send him directives leading in this direction.

Peter travelled extensively during the months that followed. He made regular trips to Denmark and France. He called on President Andrew Jackson of the United States. He tried to persuade the president to ease the trade tariffs on sugar so that the islanders could compete with Louisiana planters and ship more sugar, rum, and molasses north. In 1837 Victoria became Queen of England, and Peter paid his respects to her at court.

With Peter off-island much of the time, Anna immersed herself in plantation life. She made the final decisions about running the sugar operation, the feeding and fattening of animals for slaughter, the distillery. She concerned herself intimately with the welfare of the people in the slave village.

At "crop in" time everyone grew tense, Anna most of all. She dreaded the inevitable accidents associated with cutting the cane and processing it. The slaves had to work feverishly all day and sometimes by torchlight at night cutting cane, feeding it into the mill, and boiling down the juice in the factory. The cane had to be mature, but it couldn't be allowed to dry out and lose its juice.

The windmills were tricky affairs. The revolving sails were attached to gears that turned the heavy iron rollers that pressed the juice from the stalks of cane. The cane was fed into the rollers by hand. The rate with which the rollers turned was determined by the wind, and a sudden gust could speed them up, making it all too easy for a hand to be caught. Sometimes the wind blew steadily but too hard, which meant the brake crew had to sweat and strain to slow the turning of the monstrous sails. Or the wind shifted, which meant seven or eight strong men were needed in a hurry to push on the long pole, called a tail, outside the mill. It turned the entire roof on a round track to bring the sails close to the wind before the fabric was stripped away from the blades.

When the sails weren't in trouble from too much wind, the

opposite difficulty might arise. A planter with a becalmed windmill in the midst of "crop in" time became pretty desperate. Sometimes he had to resort to the old grinders turned by animal power.

In the factory were banks of "coppers," the huge iron vats in which the juice was reduced to the right thicknesss. Each had its fire box enclosed below, fed from an outside opening. The master boiler worked at the end of the row. His job, a critical one, was to decide just when the thickened syrup was ready to "strike." This was the crucial point at which the mixture would best crystallize into good grainy suger when cool. The yell of "strike" brought a whole crew of men running to ladle the boiling mass into a portable wooden trough, which carried it across the factory to long wooden cooling pans.

When Anna heard the estate bell ring during "crop in" time her heart sank, because in all likelihood it meant an accident. First-aid treatment was primitive, the most important part being an ax. It was used to sever quickly a hand or arm caught in the rollers since there was no speedy way to stop their turning. Overseers were known to say callously, "Part of a slave is better than none."

At relaxed times Anna liked to visit the slave village, where she was a welcome observer, if not a participant, in the activities of this small, self-sufficient community. Among other things she marvelled at the ingenious ways the children had of amusing themselves, making toys out of what they had at hand. They made flutes from papaya stems, beads from berries and seeds. They made rattles from the pods of the flamboyant tree and used the seeds as markers in board games. Their playing cards came from fig tree leaves etched while green, their whistles from reeds, and their box kites from the lightweight wood of the balsa tree.

In the evenings she often sat on the edge of the circle of people under a tamarind tree and listened to calypso, a sung commentary on the news of the day. Or she would listen to the village storytellers relate folk tales, some of African origin, some West Indian.

Young Johannes frequently came across the fields from Aldershville to visit "Nanan," his name for Anna. On one such evening they walked together along the stoney little path leading to the village, the intense moonlight making their way clear. Johannes held tight to her hand. It was late for him to be out, and tree limbs swaying in the breeze with the moon shining on them made creepy, jumpy shadows around them.

They rounded a curve, and down the hill they saw lights coming from a row of open doors. As they drew closer they saw that the people were gathered in a circle around a storyteller. Seeing them approach, a young girl broke from the circle and brought a three-legged stool for Anna to sit on. Johannes sat on the ground at her feet. Shy smiles of welcome shone on the faces around them. Anna smiled and nodded in return. She was pleased to see that the storyteller was old Joshi, one of the best in the village. In a smooth West Indian dialect, easy on the ear, he began, and the people grew still.

Once 'on a time a young gel wid no mama an' no papa of she own, give to ol' womon fo' stepchile. De ol' womon make gel work from de up comin' o' de sun to de down goin' o' de sun.

"Make d'turtle stew. Sweep d'floor. Scrub d'clothes," cruel ol' womon say.

Strange t'say no person in village able t'tell de gel ol' womon's name. De gel, she ask ol' womon many time, but ol' womon she just cackle like chicken in barnyard, cacklin' wid laughtah an' say, "I tell no one, but if you guess, you' work is done."

One day young gel put some o' brew ol' womon forevah puttin' in bottles in de turtle stew fo' ol' womon t'eat. By n' by de ol' womon she fall in deep sleep. De gel creep outta de house set on findin' ol' womon's name. First she go to de cow.

Please, Cow, tell me she name.
Do me a favor an' I do you d'same.
But cow say,
Wicked ol' womon talk to no one.
None know she name 'neath de moon or de sun.
De gel go 'long an' go 'long' till she come to de horse.
Horse, Horse, tell me she name.
Do me a favor an' I do you d'same.
But horse say,
Name o' ol'womon be a secret t'ing.
But ask de one down by de spring.
So gel go to de spring where she fine tantan bush, it branches whisperin' in de wind.
Please, Tantan, tell me she name.
Do me a favor an' I do you d'same.

But tantan say,
>> *I dasn't tell but look 'bout.*
>> *You fine de crab, you may fine out.*

So de gel look an' look 'round de edge o' de spring. By an' by she see hole in de sand she know belong to de crab. She sit by de hole an' wait. De sun climb up an' de sun climb down. Then come de moon an' de big fat land crab come outta o' he hole an' blink in de moonlight.

>> *Crab, Crab, tell me she name.*
>> *Do me a favor an' I do you d'same.*

Now crab he no have love fo' ol' womon 'cause she allus an' foreveah tryin' t'catch him an' put him in she pot. So de crab wink an' then he blink an' then he say,

>> *Yo' ask one who happen t'know.*
>> *She name Granny So-lo bam-bam-berio!*

De gel run home, wake ol' womon, an' tell her she name. De ol' womon plenty angry. She yell an' stomp foot, 'cause she know she no longah make gel do all she work.

So she set out with she cudgel t'fine de one who tell she name. De cow tell her it de horse. De horse say it de tantan. De tantan whisper in she ear it be de crab. So she creep 'round de edge of de spring till she see de crab sittin' by he hole, fat an' sassy in de moonlight. She sneak up behin' him an' bam, bam, she hit him with all she strength on he back with she cudgel. An' dat why all land crab t'this day have crack down de middle of de back.

The people chuckled at Joshi's nonsense tale. As Anna and Johannes walked back to the Greathouse they heard the people singing. Their voices were sweet but the words and music were sad. Except for brief interludes, their lives were made up of drudgery and danger.

Jemma, Anna's little personal maid, was horrified that her mistress sometimes walked abroad at night. "Yo' no afeared o' jumbies, Missy Anna?"

"I've never met one, Jemma. Have you?"

"Yes'm. They pops out at me all d'time where de paths go crissy-crossy. They pulls me hair if I walk in de woods after dark. Sometimes, Missy, I tell you true, I see tree walk in de moonlight. De big ol' baobab tree, he walk fo' sure. Jumbie make he do it. T'keep jumbie outside de door I puts ninety-nine seeds o' corn on de doorstep. Jumbie, he so busy lookin' fo' hundred seed he no come in house."

"That's all very interesting, Jemma. If I ever meet a jumbie I'll remember what you said."

Anna was never jumped by a jumbie, but the people's firm belief in obeah sometimes was troublesome. Jasmine was a pretty light-skinned girl Anna brought from the slave village to wait on table. One day Anna returned to her bedroom unexpectedly after the servants thought she had left for the day. She found Jasmine there. Jasmine scuttled out, the picture of guilt. Later Anna discoverd small things missing—her coral earrings, a silver-backed brush and comb, a silk scarf. Anna accused Jasmine of thieving. Jasmine denied the charge but Anna decided to remove her from temptation. She sent her back to the village, which meant once again she would work in the fields. When she dismissed Jasmine, Jasmine's pretty face turned sullen, and there was spite in her eyes.

The next evening when Jemma was turning down her bed, Anna heard a shriek. All the servants in Anna's villa, a cook and two serving maids, came running. Anna, too, hurried to the room. Jemma stood by the bed with a pillow in her hand shaking and moaning, staring fixedly at a small lavendar bag she had found under the pillow when she was arranging the bed for the night. When the other women saw it they began moaning and groaning, too.

"Obi, Missy! Obi!" Jemma wailed. "Obi evil, bring bad luck—death even!"

"Nonsense, Jemma!" Anna said. "Give it to me."

"No, Missy. I scared. I don' wanna touch no obi bag. I fetch d'poker."

Anna stepped to the bed and picked up the bag. Jemma gasped expecting that her mistress' hand would fall off or that she would feel intense pain. Anna turned the bag over in her palm and saw that it was carelessly made of coarse material. She ripped it open. It held strips of thin crackling paper, some red, some black, bound into a wad with long black hairs that she suspected were her own. It also held nail parings and other bits of indistinguishable matter. Then there was a heart, crudely carved out of soft wood. One of the long pins Anna sometimes used to pin a scarf was thrust into it.

It was all so absurd that Anna was tempted to laugh, but the serious faces around her made her think better of it. Besides, she was distressed that someone, Jasmine she guessed, wished

her ill. "Come," she said, "come with me. We'll dispose of this
. . . this foolish trash and forget it."

She carried the obeah bag to the back of the house, followed
by her trembling women. To satisfy them and allay their fear
she dealt with the obeah bag in accepted island fashion.
While the women watched from a safe distance she drew a
circle in the dirt with a twig from a tamarind tree. In the circle
she made a pile of dried grass and leaves. Then she sent the
cook for a live coal from the stove. The cook handed Anna
some tongs holding the coal. Anna placed the coal on the pile
and watched until the flames licked steadily at the debris.
Then she tossed the obeah bag into the flames. Muttering, the
women drew back further still. When nothing terrible
happened their faith in obeah was in no way shaken. Now,
however, they believed their mistress had power even
stronger than obeah.

The decade was drawing to a close when a tall, lean, bearded
man with kindly blue eyes appeared at Bulow's Minde leading
a donkey carrying saddlebags filled with books. He explained
his errand and Anna led him down to the village, where she
spoke to Amanda, a large, intelligent woman who was sitting
on her doorstep with a baby at her breast. Because the baby
was so young, his mother was excused from working in the
fields. When Anna introduced her to their visitor, her
good-natured face lit up. She rose to her feet and called in a
booming voice, "Come here, all you young'uns! Come you here
this minute!"

Children popped out of doors and scampered in from the
nearby vegetable plots where they'd been weeding. They
gathered around Amanda, eyeing the man and his donkey
curiously.

Amanda spoke again. "This here Pastor Friedrich Martin,
come all d'way from St. Thomas t'teach you you' letters an'
how t'read. Pay 'tention an' listen t'what de good mon say."

"Sit in a circle under the tree, children," Anna instructed,
"and we'll begin today's lesson."

This was the beginning of twice-a-week lessons for the
children on Estate Bulow's Minde. A Moravian minister and
teacher, Friedrich Martin visited other Estates near
Christiansted. The group of planters who were against
education for slave children argued that knowledge of the

outside world and increased ease of communication between groups of slaves would lead to more unrest, burning, murder, and violent revolt. They were not pleased with Pastor Martin.

One day when Martin was trudging along a footpath between Aldershville and Bulow's Minde, his donkey stepping daintily along behind him, he was jumped by two thugs. They beat him unmercifully and left him lying unconscious beside the path. The donkey, meanwhile, had run on to the village at Bulow's Minde. This set the people to searching for Pastor Martin. They found him and brought him back. Anna saw to his wounds. A less-dedicated man would have been discouraged, but he continued his work of teaching the children. He came to be known as the "Apostle to the Negroes."

In 1839, King Frederik VI died, and the governor lost a sympathetic friend at court. Unfortunately he died without coming to an agreement with his parliament about a plan to free the slaves. King Christian VIII, his successor, was not as agreeable to change and innovations. This setback was hard for Peter and Anna to bear.

1840 was the year of Anna's fiftieth birthday. The governor had left before Christmas on yet another trip abroad. However, before he left he promised Anna he would make every effort to return in time for her birthday. As January 25th drew near, Anna climbed the watchtower every evening to search for a ship that might be bringing him home to her. Disappointment followed disappointment. But on the 24th Peter's adjutant rode up the hill to tell her that the governor was in St. Thomas and would be returning on the *Vigilant* next day.

Anna slept well. As she walked through the garden, fresh from a pre-dawn shower, it had never seemed lovelier or the birds' song sweeter. She climbed the watchtower, and from the parapet saw the *Vigilant* hanging on her anchor out beyond Protestant Key. She had made a night crossing, and her captain was waiting only for the light to be strong enough to show him the way through the reefs. While she watched the sailors raised sail. The ship would soon be tied at the wharf.

Within the hour she was in Peter's arms. In answer to her questions he told her that with great effort he had won some slight concessions from parliament to benefit the "unfree," as he preferred to call them.

"I wonder if the people have any idea how hard you work to better their lot?" Anna said.

"The planters understand well enough what I'm trying to do. What little I've accomplished has turned them against me. I was royally snubbed on the wharf this morning, several deliberately turning their backs. Some are saying wild things. Perhaps you hadn't heard that I'm engaged in the slave trade with the French and Spanish for my own personal gain?"

"How ridiculous!"

"As ridiculous as the rumor that I'm secretly profiting from piracy. I'd laugh these foolish accusations off, but it pains me to have men I thought of as friends turn so viciously against me."

Anna took his hand and drew him along the gallery toward her villa. "Come along, Peter, to *Havensict*. You can relax there. We'll not talk of worrisome things today. It's my birthday, remember? Tomorrow will be soon enough to concern yourself with matters of government. Today, my dearest, is ours."

Chapter 15

TO THINK I sit here at fine table, me born into slavery an' held slave fo' forty year! To think I sit in de governor's own house drinkin' from fine glass an' eatin' off fancy china! It make me head swim!"

Anna assumed a severe air. "It's the rum punch, Oma. You grow tipsy."

Amalie Bernard chuckled and the others, her daughters, Lucia and Susanna, her great-grandson, Johannes, and his mother, all beamed with good humor. Granddaughters Christine and Sophia were missing from this family gathering. Both women had died young.

Amalie Bernard at eighty-seven had shrunken to gnome size, her face wrinkled as a gourd. But she was still spritely. And her mind was sharp. Young and old visited her where she lived in Lucia's town house, awed by her long memory of the past and present wisdom.

It was Sunday. Peter was in Denmark yet again. When Anna awakened she realized that unless she took action the day stretching ahead of her would be long and lonely, so she sent Samson, the groom, in the governor's coach to bring her family up from town for a visit. Luncheon—cold lobster, fruit, and white bread—was served on the sunny gallery of Anna's villa.

"To you, Oma!

Anna raised her glass. "To your continued good health and long life!"

The other ladies raised their glasses in salute to the little woman seated on a cushion at the head of the table, her head wrapped in her usual white turban, her black eyes darting about taking in all the details of her surroundings.

"There've been many changes during your lifetime, Oma, and more to come," Anna continued. "The governor works hard toward freedom for all. Day by day we draw closer to the time there'll be no more slavery."

"An' you had a hand in that loaf, Anna. Like I say long time pas', person with pow hear what you say."

"I do what I can, but the governor must decide." To young Johannes she said, "You'd like your freedom this minute, I don't doubt. Go down to the stables. You'll find your horse saddled and eager for a romp."

When he had excused himself, Susanna said, "Anna, dat driver, dat Samson, he need t'have he head turned 'round."

"Whatever d'you mean, Mama?"

"He rude, Anna. He sit on de box like a lump o' coal. He make no move t'help Oma in. He drive de horses at a gallop bouncin' us 'round like dry seeds in a pod."

"He's a new one," Anna replied. "I noticed this morning he turned sullen when I asked him to go to town and pick you up. I can't think why. He knows he's to be available to drive on Sunday mornings."

"He mutter under he breath . . . somethin' 'bout 'fetchin' up colored trash.' " Susanna flushed as she confessed the insult.

"What impudence!" Anna said hotly. "I'll have words with that one! Snobs come in all colors. A uniform with a little gold braid makes some servants think they're God's own anointed. Come. Let's go for a walk in the garden. Peter brought me a Chinese rose from Denmark last time he was there. It's doing famously."

On his return Peter told Anna that parliament had listened sympathetically to his plan for freeing the "unfree." He had had an audience with King Christian, too. But this had been disappointing. The king, a middle-aged man subject to spells of pathological melancholy, was more concerned about the growing German nationalism in Slesvig-Holstein than the plight of black slaves on three small islands thousands of miles away. Meanwhile, unfair sometimes brutal treatment of slaves was still common in the islands. On occasion Anna bought a slave to set him free, if she felt there was undue hardship.

One morning Jemma appeared with reddened eyes to tend her mistress.

"Jemma, Jemma, what ails you, girl?" Anna cried.

"Missy Anna, they aims t'sell George! They aim t'sell him off-island to Dutchmon from 'Statia." She sank to the floor at

Anna's feet and wept.

Poor Jemma! Anna thought. George, her brother, was all the family she had. They were devoted to each other. He belonged to the Lyttons, owners of nearby Beeston Hill. Anna gently lifted Jemma to her feet. "Why would the Lyttons do that, Jemma? Stop crying and tell me all about it. George, he do a bad thing?"

"No, no, Missy!" Jemma sniffed and wiped her eyes on her apron. "De Lyttons say they no can keep George. They growin' poorer every day. No money. No food. George do say they on short rations fo' weeks!"

Anna didn't doubt that the Lyttons were desperate. Times were hard for everyone. "George has a family, doesn't he, Jemma?"

"He do. Yes, he do. Cindy, de baby, an' d'boys. Law say Cindy an' baby be 'llowed t'go with George. But de boys, they nine an' ten, they stay behind. George and Cindy never see them more." Jemma began snuffling again.

Anna put her arms around Jemma, gently patting her back. "I'll look into the matter. I'll call on Mme. Lytton, and see how matters stand. Come. Fetch hot water and fill the tub. I feel stiff this morning.

"Does George do work for the Lyttons other than cutting cane?"

"Oh, yes, Missy. He blacksmith. He make all sort o' t'ings sides horse shoe. He make hinge, locks an' tools."

"That's a help. Maybe he could fend for himself in town. Lord knows we need no more mouths to feed at Bulow's Minde."

Anna bought George, Cindy, and the children from the Lyttons and set them free. He was skilled, intelligent, and enterprising. Before long he had himself set up in town as a successful blacksmith and fashioner of wrought-iron implements.

Runaway slaves had never been a serious problem on St. Croix. There was no good place to run to. Forty miles of deep blue sea separated the island from British territories and freedom. The only way was to stow away on a boat bound for the British islands or steal one. But local boats, even small ones, were kept chained and well guarded. Besides, most slaves were unable to swim and deathly afraid of the sea. Of course, they could and had run away to the caves on Ham

Bluff. Here the sea crashed on the slippery black rocks beneath the entrances to the caves, and the steep banks above were covered by an almost impenetrable growth of thornbush, making them inaccessible to all but the most determined. But the slave owners knew all about the caves. They either came after runaways with machetes, guns, and dogs, or waited until hunger drove them out of hiding and sent them "home."

Rudy, a young slave inflamed by freedom talk, habitually drove a mule-drawn wagon loaded with hogsheads of muscovado into Christiansted for shipment abroad. He figured out a scheme, risky but possible to his way of thinking, by which he hoped to jump island. He had studied the inter-island sloops tied at the wharf, many of them owned by Tortolans. These were deep-bellied craft with ballast stones in their bottoms under the floor boards to keep them steady rather than keels. Typically the open cockpits were large, taking up more than half the sloops' thirty to forty feet in length. But there were small forward decks. Under these in the forepeaks, barrels of water were stowed to slack the thirst of animals and men during a crossing. Rudy noted that the barrels didn't fit snugly into the V-shaped peaks. Could a slim young man stow away in that space? He would have to sit with his back to the stem, the barrel between his legs, hidden by cabbages, sweet potatoes, and pumpkins.

One Sunday he walked into Christiansted, a not uncommon practice, for Sunday was the day the slaves were allowed to work for themselves and sell whatever they could produce in town. His heart began to pound with excitement when he saw a sloop at the wharf with a British flag at its mast. He loitered about the wharf, keeping close watch on the sloop until darkness fell. On board were three men and two women. Rudy guessed from what talk he heard that it was a family—father, mother, son, and another son and his wife. They began cooking their evening meal over a small charcoal fire in the cockpit. The good rich smell of roast goat made Rudy's stomach growl and his mouth water. But he kept his distance. He noticed with satisfaction that the rum bottle was being passed freely from mouth to mouth.

Then he heard the old man say, "We cross tonight. A l'il nap, an' we shov' off when de moon rise. Sea mo' quiet at night." He chuckled. "Not like womon."

Before long the Tortolans were wrapped in blankets and dozing on the forward deck. Checking to see that the coast was clear, Rudy quickly and quietly climbed over the transom and lay flat in the bottom of the cockpit, surrounded by crates of chickens, bags of cornmeal, and piles of vegetable. He lay still for some minutes, scarcely breathing. Since all remained quiet, except for the snores coming from the forward deck, he began to squirm toward the forepeak. He had almost reached it when he accidentally nudged a pile of cabbages, and they toppled over hitting the deck with resounding thumps. Terrified, Rudy froze.

The old man sat up and rubbed his eyes . He walked around the deck scanning the now empty wharf and glanced into the cockpit where Rudy lay. But it was too dark for him to see the bare brown legs among the cabbages. Made careless by rum and sleepiness he lay down again beside his wife and was soon snoring. Rudy wedged himself into the space behind the water barrel.

After what seemed an eternity of sitting motionless, his back muscles aching and his legs cramped, he saw a glimmer of moonlight on the water astern. Then he heard voices and footsteps overhead. The sail rattled up the mast on its wooden hoops, and the old man gave the order to cast off. Rudy grinned in the darkness. He was freedom bound.

But it turned out that the old man was wrong about the sea. The sloop was no sooner beyond the protecting reefs surrounding the harbor than a sharp squall overtook them. The sloop began to pitch and roll. Rain and overtaking seas flooded into the open cockpit. Soon Rudy was sitting in water. He tried without much success to steady the water barrel, which was being thrown from side to side, bruising his thighs. Vegetables rolled around wildly, exposing one leg, then the other. The Tortolans, however, were too busy on deck to notice. They shouted to each other in panic-stricken voices as they tried to aid their foundering vessel. Their feet pounded heavily on the deck over Rudy's head.

The bow of the little ship rose, lifted Rudy high in the air, then descended with a bone rattling crash as a wave passed under. He was retching with seasickness and scared witless. Finally, he heard a ripping sound as the howling wind took away most of the sail. Cursing, the old man and his sons wrestled with the flapping canvas that was left.

"Get b'low!" the old man shouted to the two women. "Get

b'low 'fore you get took same way as sail!"

"I sooner be dead in d'sea then drown down dere!" the old woman protested, looking at the cargo all awash in the cockpit.

"Do wha' I say, womon!" the old man came toward her menacingly with a piece of broken spar in his hand.

The woman tumbled into the cockpit, followed by her daughter-in-law.

It was the young wife whose hand fell on Rudy's bare leg as she tried to scramble into the forepeak for protection from the pelting rain. She let out a screech heard above the howling of the wind. The two young men were upon Rudy in seconds. They pulled him out from behind the barrel, lashed his wrists together and shoved him out into the cockpit, where he lay next to a crate of half-drowned chickens.

As suddenly as it had come the squall was over. With experienced sailors' cunning the old man and his sons rigged what remained of the sail, brought the sloop about, and headed back to Christiansted.

As they sailed serenely into harbor following the moon path, the old man allowed Rudy to sit up. "Wha' yo' tryin' t'do, mon?'

"I wan' free," Rudy moaned. "Don' take me back. I be whipped near t'dyin'!"

Now, convinced that Rudy was not a pirate or intent on raping their women, the Tortolans' loyalty was torn. They had some inclination to help a black brother. On the other hand they had no choice but to return to Chistiansted with their battered vessel. There, the risk of concealment was great, and the reward for surrendering a runaway, substantial. Fear and cupidity won out. In the morning the Tortolans turned Rudy turned over to the authorities.

On the day appointed for Rudy's punishment, Governor-General von Scholten, as was required of him, stood to witness the event. Rudy's wrists were bound, stretched over his head and tied to the whipping post. He was given a hard piece of rubber to hold between his teeth. Twenty lashes were well laid on, cutting the flesh of his back to ribbons.

That evening when the governor returned at last to Bulow's Minde, Anna saw immediately that he was seriously depressed. She questioned him, and he told her about Rudy.

They agreed that though some progress had been made, much remained to be done.

Far too much power remained in the hands of owners and overseers, even though punishment of slaves was legally controlled by this time. An overseer could not carry out punishment in anger in the fields. It was supposed to be administered by the owner in the presence of witnesses. A beating administered by an owner had to be done with a cane rather than a whip, and there was a strict limitation on the number of blows. An owner could punish a slave by putting him in solitary confinement, fed only on bread and water. But this was to last no longer than twenty-four hours. Crimes considered too serious for such casual home remedies, such as becoming a runaway, were dealt with by the court.

At last the schools at Estates Little Princesse and Diamond had opened their doors to admit slave children. Anna was greatly encouraged by this first step toward organized universal education. In the beginning only children between the ages of six and nine were accepted. But Anna kept plugging away at the authorities, trying to raise the age level. In addition she visited outlying estates to see if all children eligible were being reached. If there was no way for them to get to a school she arranged to have teachers visit, as Friedrich Martin had done.

On one of Anna's visits to Bulow's Minde's slave village she stopped to visit with her friend, Amanda, and admire Amanda's little boy, Benji. Benji was playing on the doorstep with a lizard. The little creature showed no fear but ran up and down the child's arm, stopping now and then to stare up into his face.

"He tickle," Benji giggled.

Anna smiled. "He's growing fast, Amanda. He looks healthy and bright, too."

"No 'plaints 'bout Benji, Mistress Anna. He good child an' happy. But I looks at he an' ask meself, what do life bring down de road fo' him?" She paused for a moment. "Mistress, where in de states this here Massa . . . Massa-chu-setts?"

"Why that's in the northeast, I believe. Boston's state."

"There's freedom there, Joshi say. Joshi read 'bout it in de newspaper. He say lots o' white folks up there talkin' freedom for all people everywhere."

"A big order, Amanda. The people in Massachusetts and other northern states are free, but in the South—Louisianna, Missisippi, those states where they grow cotton and cane—the plantation owners have huge slave holdings. But Joshi is right. People in many places today see slavery's bad. Freedom's coming, Amanda. Before Benji's half grown, I shouldn't wonder."

In the morning Peter would be leaving for Paris. As always Anna dreaded the separation. That night he shared her bed. After lovemaking he lay sleeping peacefully, the moonlight streaming through the window laying its cool fingers on his face. Unable to sleep herself, Anna gazed at him lovingly. The years had taken their toll. His hair had receded into baldness, his temples and sideburns were touched with silver. In sleep the lines of stress across his forehead and around his eyes were softened, but she knew they were there. Ah, my dearest, she thought as she nestled her head against his shoulder, I wish I could keep you always by my side. When will these tiresome journeys end?

She smiled, thinking back to a recent wedding. Her niece, Agnes, had been married at Bulow's Minde. Half the island had been invited to the reception. It was a fine affair, the guests a mixture of white and free-colored. The food was elegant, the music toe-tapping, and Peter brought out his best French wines. Anna was only slightly ruffled when she overheard two white women whispering behind their fans.

"She's made a great to-do about her niece's marrriage for one who herself has never been wed!" said one.

"In rather poor taste, don't you think, my dear?" said the other.

Small talk, Anna thought. Without a divorce, a divorce that could only have been had by a direct petition to the king, Peter could not have married her. And if he had been legally free, there was still that old tradition that frowned on white men marrying women of color. She had suffered pangs of jealously in the early years when he visited Denmark. She knew he most assuredly visited his family there. The two of them never discussed these visits. But as the years rolled by she felt more and more sure of Peter's devotion. Now, after fifteen years of living together in harmony and love, she suspected they were more married in the eyes of God than many who were legally wed. Peter's career and position would have been jeopardized had he married her, and she knew that without that position, he would be powerless to work toward reform.

Chapter 16

AWAKENED BY an acrid, sickly-sweet odor Anna opened her eyes to the morning light. Cane burning, she thought sadly. She'd smelled it all too often of late. Throwing a robe over her shoulders she walked out onto the gallery. To the south in the direction of Cane Garden she saw a cloud of smoke pink-tinged by flames.

As Anna knew, to burn was a shackled people's way of expressing deep-seated anger and frustration. The planters kept guards armed with rifles in stone huts at the corners of the cane fields day and night to guard against arsonists, but in spite of all precautions, under cover of darkness fires were easily set, especially when the island was dry as it was now.

Anna was thankful that so far the fields at Bulow's Minde had been spared. They lay in patchwork patterns around her, pale green where the cane was newly planted, tan where the fields had been harvested. The northern hills were dried up, so dry that they looked like bulging, knobby sacks of coarse burlap piled one on top of the other.

The sugar economy was going from bad to terrible. The planters fell deeper and deeper into debt. Many gave up and went home to Denmark or England, leaving their estates in the hands of overseers or lawyers. Those who were left couldn't by the farthest stretch of their imaginations see any way of surviving if they were robbed of cheap labor. Thus resistance to freeing the slaves stiffened.

There ware hardships for everyone. But it was downright miserable being a slave. Supplies of meat, salt-fish and cornmeal ran low. Some slaves were hungry most of the time, and there were no Christmas treats, no small rewards for good behavior, no new clothes to replace the ragged garments of the year before. All this added to the people's restlessness. This was evident in the burnings, and also the beating of drums at

151

night, a form of communication strictly forbidden by the white masters.

Regardless of the masters' wishes, Anna was hearing the drums more and more regularly. Under cover of darkness drummers hid in the almost inpenetrable bush and were long gone before they could be caught in the morning. Likewise the call of the conch, traditionally the "bomba's" way of summoning laborers to the fields, was used as a signal from one village to another—a signal, perhaps, to burn? By the mid-1840s Anna heard these sounds, the beating of drums and mysterious calls of the conch almost every evening. How will it all end? she wondered.

Still many estates manged to maintain a facade of calm. Some social life continued, and island visitors came from near and far for a week or month to visit Bulow's Minde. A regular visitor was Peter's brother, Frederik. Stationed in Frederiksted, he was a major in the Danish Militia. He was a serious artist as well as a soldier. On his brother's estate he found many scenes of plantation life worth painting. He also painted portraits.

One morning at breakfast he said to his brother, "I wish you'd sit for me today. You know I've been after you for months."

"If you knew the schedule I've set for myself. . . correspondence to get onto that packet you saw in the harbor, a meeting with the Burgher Council, instructions for my overseer—"

"Anna is on my side. I spoke to her about it yesterday."

"I've had a portrait done, that one in Government House. Isn't that enough?"

"Anna and I both think it would be fine to have you in an informal pose . . . as you are at home, rather than that stiff official one in military garb. I'd really like to do it, Peter."

"Well, I think it's a lot of foolishness but clearly you two are set on it . . . formidable odds, I must say! Can I sit at my desk? Then, at least, I could be looking over my correspondence."

The major agreed. He placed his easel in position for a profile. Anna sat nearby working on her embroidery.

"The light's good," Frederik remarked as he studied his subject, arranging his paper and soft black pencils in an orderly fashion. "You may hold a letter in your hand to read but you must hold it up so that I get a clear profile."

Fleeting irritation appeared on Peter's face. Then he relaxed. He realized that having agreed to this project he had no choice but to cooperate.

The major worked for some time, the three of them silent. His preliminary outline was complete before he spoke again. "I've met an interesting young man in Frederiksted," he remarked as he was doing some broad shading. "He's a slave but a born leader if ever there was one. Naturally his goal is emancipation. But he preaches feedom without violence."

"Tell me about him," Peter said. "I'm glad to hear there's one on the island that shares my sentiments."

"He belongs to one of the Schimmelman properties, Estate La Grange. I had a talk with him last Saturday. Peter, raise your head a bit. Your face is in a shadow. Fine! Now hold it steady. I think this is going to be a . . . a rather good likeness."

"May I have a look?" Anna asked.

"Certainly. I'd be glad to have your opinion."

Anna stood by the easel, studying the drawing.

"Well . . . what d'you think?"

"It's good, Frederik. You've caught his expression admirably. Is his brow a trifle overdone, his nose too prominent?"

"Those features give his face strength, a characteristic I wish to emphasize." He continued with his shading.

Anna returned to her embroidery. "Your young man, Frederik. What does he do at La Grange?"

"He's boss in the sugar boiling shed, a tricky and responsible job, as you well know."

"What's his name . . . if we should hear of him again?"

"His followers call him Buddhoe. But his real name is Gottlieb . . . Adam Gottlieb, I believe."

Anna's needle paused in midair. Gottlieb? That strange name had a familiar sound, caused a quickening of her pulse. Why? She tried to remember. There was some poignant association from long ago. She groped for an answer. "You say he's young, Frederik. How young?"

"Mid-thirties, I should think. Peter, do you habitually sit at your desk with your legs crossed?"

Peter looked at his legs curiously. "To be quite honest with you I'd never given my legs much thought. Any objection?"

"I'm having a difficult time getting the lines right." Frederik took a soft rubber from his pocket to correct his work and redrew the offending legs. "There. That's better."

Anna's embroidery lay neglected in her lap. "Frederik, do you know ought of Adam's family," she asked. "Have they always been at La Grange?"

"No, his father, who died years ago, was from Christiansted, a first-rate groomsman, so I'm told. His grandmother was well-known about town as an outstanding cook."

Anna sat still, her heart pounding as memories of young love under the tamarind tree and on the beach near Little Princesse came back to her. She was so quiet that eventually both Peter and Frederik turned to look at her, questioningly.

She smiled self-consciously and explained, "Something I remember from long ago. Something that makes me curious to meet your young man, Frederik. I believe I knew his father."

"Astonishing!" Peter said.

"No . . . not really. After all . . . it's a very small island."

The major had returned to his duties in Frederiksted, but Anna couldn't put the young man now called Buddhoe out of her mind. She and Peter had heard nothing from Frederik for several weeks, so Anna assumed he'd forgotten her casual request for a meeting with Buddhoe. One day she screwed up her courage and suggested to Peter it might be worth their while to meet this young leader from West End and hear what he had to say. Peter agreed halfheartedly, but more pressing matters filled his days. Anna felt frustrated.

The following week Peter had to go to St. Thomas to confer with the lieutenant governor on an urgent matter. On impulse Anna made her way down to the slave village and called on her friend, Amanda. "Amanda, Major Frederik has told us about a remarkable young man out in Frederiksted called Buddhoe. You hear of him?"

"Oh yes, Missy. Every person hear 'bout Buddhoe. He big leader in de West End. He go from place t'place tellin' de workers t'get theyselves ready for d'day we set free. He say it comin' fo' sure."

"I'd like to meet this man, Amanda. I'd like to talk with him at La Grange. But no one must know. It . . . it might embarrass the governor if it were widely known. The planters, you know, put the worst possible interpretation . . ."

"How you aim t'do that, Mis' Anna?" Amanda looked doubtful.

"Would Joshi drive us?"

"What that Samson say if Joshi ask fo' d'coach? Samson mighty uppity with us here in d'village."

"No coach, Amanda. We go in the farm wagon with the mules. I'll be an old country woman and wear rude clothes. I want you to come with us."

"Joshi, he do mo's anyt'ing fo' you, you know that."

"And he's your friend, too, Amanda."

"I talk with him this night."

"Good. Let's go tomorrow evening. The governor returns the following day. Come see me before you go to your cabin tonight and tell me what Joshi says."

After dark the following evening Anna donned her oldest clothes, wrapped her hair in a turban of figured cotton, and crept out to the kitchen, where she darkened her face with charcoal. Then she made her way stealthily down to the village. Joshi had the mules hitched to the farm wagon and was waiting in front of Amanda's cabin. Anna called softly from the shadows and Amanda came to get her. She helped Anna crawl into the back of the wagon, where she made herself as comfortable as possible among a lot of old burlap bags. She was strangely exhilarated, like a child engaged in a mischievous prank. Amanda climbed up onto the seat beside Joshi.

"Joshi," Anna asked as he clucked to the mules, "are you apt to be stopped by the gendarmes, a black man driving the roads at night?"

"Don' worry, Mistress. Me an' this gel here, mus' take sick mama to de doctor in Frederiksted. I hav' special permit from Buford, de boss mon heself."

"So I'm your sick mama, Joshi?"

Joshi chuckled. "That's right, Mistress."

They drove out past Estate Anna's Hope and Strawberry to Centerline Road in silence. All three were somewhat anxious. Amanda shared the common belief that evil spirits were abroad at night. Her eyes constantly searched the shadows on either side of the road. Joshi, also a believer, was fearful lest his mules be spooked by a jumbie and the old wagon fall apart if he lost control of his team. Anna knew her behavior would be considered strange, at the very least, if she were discovered.

The road was bathed in moonlight. A night wind caused the fronds atop the palms that lined their way to do a rustling dance, throwing grotesquely moving shadows on the road. From the distant hills they heard the beating of a drum. It was answered by another far to the east. Then came the eerie, drawn-out, mournful call of the conch.

Joshi cut around Frederiksted, taking a rutted single-lane dirt road that led directly to La Grange. They drew up to the plantation village, and he halted the mules in deep shadow under a huge mango tree.

Suddenly, Amanda clutched Joshi's arm. "What that? Sumpin' movin' over there, went 'hind that tree! I swear t'goodness . . ."

Joshi peered into the shadows. Then he chuckled. "That a mon takin' a l'il leak to comfort heself 'fore he go to he cabin fo' d'night."

Amanda settled back with a sigh. This outing wasn't exactly to her liking. She was thinking fondly of her snug cabin back at Bulow's Minde.

Soft voices called their attention to a lighted doorway. Joshi handed Amanda the reins, climbed down from the wagon and entered the cabin. He spoke with someone inside, and immediately a young man stepped out into the moonlight.

Anna knew it could be no other than Buddhoe—he had the proud bearing of a leader, his head held high. She searched for traces of the boy she had loved in the man, but the man's maturity and self-assurance made it difficult. He was of medium height with broad shoulders. He was dressed in the worker's garb of coarse cotton shirt and trousers. His hair was cut rather full, and a gold earring twinkled in one ear. He had a luxuriant black moustache which set off his small white teeth to advantage when he smiled, as he did now, looking up at Anna. Then to her dismay he laughed, a low throaty laugh. "Madam, you do Buddhoe great honor goin' t' so much trouble, blackin' your face, to pay him a visit. I see, now, you come incognito. Well, perhaps 'tis best." He offered her his hand and helped her down from the wagon. Growing serious he asked, "Will you step inside and speak to my people?"

Anna shrank back. "Oh, no! I didn't come . . . uh, Buddhoe, to make a speech or be seen by anyone but you. To tell true I came because of your father."

"My father!"

"Aye."

"Very well. If you prefer to remain outside . . ." His eyes, direct and challenging, met hers. "Now what is this about my father?"

She looked away and spoke shyly. "Unless I'm very much mistaken, from what I've heard of you, your father and I were children together . . . and later on . . . I believe it was he that I loved . . . many years ago. What can you tell me of him?"

Buddhoe was unable to tell Anna a great deal about his father since he had died when Buddhoe was only seven years old. But it was enough—that his name was Obadiah, nickname of No-no, that he had grown up in a fine house in Christiansted, that he'd been in charge of the stables at Little Princesse and finally sold to a slave dealer in the West End.

"And your mother, Buddhoe?"

"She die when I born."

"Ah, I'm sorry." Anna wondered at his speech. "You have some education," she observed, looking at him again. "You speak well."

"Aye. Very young I go to the church in Frederiksted to Father O'Ryan. He teach me. Many hours I spend in study with that good mon."

They talked for an hour or more. They talked of personal concerns, of the sad conditions on the island and the interest they shared in seeing freedom come. Anna saw excitement mount in Buddhoe's eyes as they talked of freedom. But neither his words nor his eyes suggested the fanatic's love of violence. He will try to move in an orderly manner, she thought, but move he will. He will not be patient forever, and his following will be great. He has the same qualitites of leadership as my Peter. Thoughts of Peter prompted her to bring the meeting to a close. She must be getting back to Bulow's Minde.

"Come see us," she said. "I assure you the governor would like talking with you. It would be best if you came quietly, though, perhaps in the evening."

"I understand, lady. I will come. I promise."

Anna dozed on the way home. The interview, stirring old memories, had tired her. And now that the excitement of her escapade was over she felt let down and somewhat depressed by the enormity of the problems they all faced.

Buddhoe kept his word. He came to Bulow's Minde several times the following summer. He came alone on horseback, just as the quick tropical darkness spread its cloak over the island. Peter was as impressed by the young man as Anna was. The three of them held many ideas in common.

They learned, not from him but from Frederik, that Buddhoe had taken to calling himself General Bordeaux after a black folk hero who had led the slaves in the rebellion on St. Johns a hundred years earlier. It ended with many of the slaves joining hands and leaping from a high precipice into the sea. Buddhoe was heard to say, "Bordeaux jump the clock. Now the time is right to try for free."

His name was on the lips of the slaves from West End to East Point. He travelled tirelessly from estate to estate at night, gathering the slaves together in the shadows, telling them what part they must play in the strike for freedom. He calmed those whose blood was hot for vengeance, patiently explaining that to spill much blood and cause widespread destruction would be a disaster for all, white and black. At the same time he roused those who were in a lethargy of hopelessness, or hopelessly intimidated by fear of the white masters' wrath.

Anna visited her mother and grandmother whenever she drove into town. Susanna would close the store, whose hours had always been somewhat whimsical, for the time of Anna's visit. She and Anna, and sometimes Aunt Lucia, sat with Amalie Bernard, who at ninety-four was confined to her chair on the front porch of Lucia's house. Amalie Bernard still waved to passers-by and chided children if they didn't stop to speak to her. She called them back sayin, "Come here, you young rascals! Don' miss chance t'say howdy 'cause we don' know when de long night goin' t' come 'long an' snatch us."

Then word came to Anna that her mother had taken a severe chill and taken to her bed. By the time Anna reached her bedside the chill had been diagnosed as pneumonia, and Susanna was fighting for every breath. Anna did everything she could, insisted the doctor come again, and offered to purchase medicines. But he shook his head and said nothing could help, that it was only a matter of time. Anna propped her mother up with many pillows to ease her breathing and stayed by her bedside holding her hand until she died.

The spring of 1847 came, and Peter was off to Denmark again. Anna was pleased that after a brief trip he returned in a hopeful mood. Parliament at last, he told her, had reached some significant decisions favoring the freedom of the unfree in the Danish West Indies. The king promised there would be a "Royal Proclamation" of significance by the queen's birthday in mid-July, and it was widely known that the queen was freedom-minded.

"What will this proclamation contain, Peter?" Anna asked as they strolled hand in hand after dinner on the terrace above the flower gardens.

"Ah-h, on that I'm sworn to secrecy, my love. But I promise you you'll be pleased. Another couple of months and the 'Proclamation' will be read publicly."

"I should think you could give me . . . give me a hint." She felt a trifle hurt not to be privy to this information, no matter how confidential.

"Be patient, my dear. I swore to tell no one." Though his eyes were smiling, the firm lines around his mouth told her there was no use begging.

Being kept uninformed made Anna uneasy. With some misgivings she set about preparations for her part in the birthday celebration, among other things a ball at Bulow's Minde for first families, officials in the government, and military personnel of rank. The festivities would begin with a parade through the streets led by the Danish Militia and the Brand Corps of free-colored to the music of a military band. This would be followed by a grand reception at Government House, with a warm welcome to any who chose to attend. At noon the church bells would toll. Then the governor in full military regalia would read the "Royal Proclamation" from the gallery at Government House overlooking King Street, where he could be seen by all.

The birthday week arrived. Monday passed, then Tuesday. It was plain to Anna that Peter was growing increasingly anxious. "Whatever is the matter, Peter? Do you fear the proclamation will not be well received?"

"I know well enough the proclamation will not be received well by everyone, rich and poor, white and black. Such things never suit everyone," he replied testily. "But until it's read it's impossible to gauge the degree of its acceptance. It should serve as a light at the end of a dark tunnel for the unfree, and I trust it will not infuriate their owners unduly. The difficulty is, it can't be read until it arrives. As you know, tomorrow is the queen's birthday. If only King Christian would do as he says! He promised that the document would be in my hands last week!"

"You mean . . . it hasn't arrived?"

"No, it hasn't arrived. And I say it's a damned shame! Whatever can they be thinking of in Copenhagen?"

"A lot can happen mid-Atlantic, my dear. Perhaps the ship was delayed by a storm."

"In the last week several ships have made port with no word of bad weather. No, I fear they're procrastinating again . . . some fine point that displeases some ass of a lawyer who has the king's ear."

Without the proclamation the birthday celebration fell flat, though Peter and Anna put the best face on it they could. The ball was held in the queen's honor at Bulow's Minde, but no parade or reception took place in Christiansted. The fact that some of the planters took sly pleasure in Peter's disappointment added to his frustration.

The proclamation finally arrived in September and was read aloud from church pulpits the following Sunday. It was published in the newly established island newspaper, the *Avis*. Printed notices containing its text were tacked up in both towns. Each airing brought more grumbling from the islanders. Their governor had misjudged. The proclamation pleased almost no one.

Anna studied it in the privacy of her villa and sighed. It had two main provisions—that newborns among the slave population would be free at birth and that all others would receive their freedom in twelve years' time. This meant that old folks would despair of living to see the day. Young folks would feel that to have their little children free when they were still slaves was intolerable. Through recent years with increasing hardships the patience of the slaves had worn thin. As for the planters, Anna could see that they would heartily disapprove of the proclamation. Nothing was said about government control of the masses of blacks turned loose all at once on Freedom Day, even if it was far in the future. Nothing was said about government recompense for the loss of their large investments in slaves.

All in all Anna considered the proclamation a paltry bit of

legislation. It provided only half a loaf for the people when they had expected a whole one. For once she disagreed wholeheatedly with Peter and told him so. "It won't do! It won't do at all! They've endured so long! I fear it will incite them to violence that will explode all over the island."

"It was the best I could do, Anna!" Peter stormed. "The king and parliament are utterly unrealistic. In their eyes the proclamation is an act of remarkable generosity. I consider I've done well to have achieved so much. It is certainly better than nothing!"

"Is it?" The bitter disappointment Anna felt also gnawed at the hearts of some 27,000 slaves.

Chapter 17

LONG AFTER DARK Peter and Anna heard a horseman galloping up their hill. They had been sitting tensely without speaking in Peter's study, their quarrel over the royal proclamation having raised a wall of unhappy silence that after several days still stood solidly between them.

Peter stepped out onto the gallery to see who might be coming to call at such an unlikely hour. Anna followed him. By starlight they saw a rider astride a spirited white horse. He leapt from his mount at the bottom of the staircase, flipped the reins over the horse's head and boldly mounted the steps two at a time.

"Buddhoe!" Anna exclaimed.

A tragic mask sat on Buddhoe's face. "Massa Peter, what you do? My people in a turmoil talkin' fire and killin'. Twelve years, mon! That's an eternity to them! Can't you do better by your people and mine?"

"Come in and sit down, my friend," Peter said. "Anna bring something long and cool to drink. This young man must be parched after his long ride."

When Anna reentered the study she found the men deep in earnest talk.

"Freedom is coming, Buddhoe," the governor was saying. "That I promise you. It's a question of when and how to bring it about with the least suffering on all sides. If the plantation system suddenly collapses, the island will become an uncivilized jungle. It won't matter much if you're free or unfree—because you'll starve."

"That's a chance we have to take," Buddhoe said passionately. "Slavery is intolerable. It's been struck down in many places already. Twelve years is too long to wait on this island."

"What d'you propose?"

"To march for freedom. All unfree will rise up and march together. A peaceful march, God willing. But if our demands are not met . . ."

"Buddhoe, I promise I'll do what I can. I may be able to get the time reduced somewhat . . . half the time, maybe even three, two years. I'll send an urgent despatch to King Christian. I beg of you . . . just a little more time!"

Buddhoe rose without touching his drink. "I must go. Do your best for us, Massa Peter. I hope I can hold my people in check, persuade them to be patient a little longer." He turned to look at Anna, trying to read her thoughts. Her unhappy eyes told of her sympathy, that she was on his side. He knew there was no need to ask her to use her influence with the governor.

After Buddhoe left them, Anna was more distressed than ever. For comfort she clung to Peter, forgetting their differences.

He stroked her hair. "Don't upset yourself unduly, my Anna. That man paints too dramatic a picture, I should think—rather overdrawn."

"I see a confrontation coming," she said, her head against his chest. "I fear it will be a bloody thing with death and destruction on all sides."

"But both Buddhoe and I are dedicated to avoiding violence. You know that. When the leaders on both sides . . ."

After several minutes she raised her head. Her eyes were moist but she was smiling. "He did look splendid on his white horse, didn't he, Peter?"

"He did indeed, my love."

The Christmas winds lasted longer than usual in that winter of '48. They whipped the hard blue sea into frothing waves that broke savagely on the reefs. It was chilly in the slave quarters morning and evening, and for some there was no breakfast or supper. Both Anna and Peter knew that secret meetings were being held and plans formulated in the shadows surrounding the slave villages. If the other planters suspected what was going on they chose not to do anything about it. Soon it was "crop-in" time and they were so engrossed with all the activity this meant that they didn't see the bemused looks on the faces of the workers during the day or hear the drums speak at night.

Peter had tried repeatedly to persuade King Christian to

hasten the plan for freedom, but the king was not to be rushed. He was old and ill and much too preoccupied with problems at home to give much thought to the plight of planters and slaves thousands of miles away. In January, King Christian died, and Frederik the VII took his place. But the new King was as beset by troubles as the old. In May, conflict with Germany absorbed the King's entire attention. He had to concentrate on the frontier he shared with the Germans.

Denmark did not object to the people of the province of Holstein, which was adjacent to Germany, pursuing their German sympathies and becoming part of that nation. But the Holsteiners were taking advantage of a document signed in 1481. When Christian I first tried to settle forever the eternally muddled question of Slesvig-Holstein he decreed that the two duchies should remain forever undivided. His idea naturally was that Slesvig was ancient Danish territory, and that by binding the two together, Holstein would be permanently bound to Denmark. Now, the Holsteiners pointed to the old document to justify going over to Germany and taking the whole of Slesvig with them.

Despite the fact that Denmark respected Holstein's German leanings, the King and Parliament knew they could ill-afford to part with Slesvig. In opposition to the Danes, the Holsteiners, supported by Germany, mobilized an army. King Frederik had no choice but to mobilize his forces, also, and try to disperse this revolutionary force. No wonder he had little time to concern himself with the affairs of Denmark's tiny colonial outpost in the Caribbean.

On the second of July, a Sunday, Anna woke early to the song of a thrushee perched in his accustomed place on a branch outside her window. The sunlight filtering through the jalousies made pleasing geometric shadows on the wall beside her bed. She raised herself on her elbow and looked at the small clock that Peter had brought her from Paris. It was six forty-five.

She bathed and dressed with Jemma's help, then breakfasted alone. Peter was in St. Thomas and was not expected to return until late in the day. After breakfast she took a walk around the garden, noting that the bougainvillea needed trimming and that everything would profit from rain. She couldn't resist pulling a few intruding weeds, which seemed always to endure the dry weather better than her flowers.

Before ten o'clock she made her way to chapel, where a private service was customarily held for her and Peter, their guests if any, servants, and close neighbors. She sat alone on this Sunday, brooding about the island's many problems and praying solutions to some of the more pressing ones would soon be forthcoming.

At the close of the service Mme. Lytton of neighboring Beeston Hill hurried after her. Her face was pale and tense. "My dear! Have you heard the shocking news! There've been slave uprisings on the French islands, Guadeloupe and Martinique. On Guadeloupe some 180 whites were massacred, men, women, and children! My husband can tell you more. Here he comes."

"Aye, it's bad news, Mistress Anna," Lytton replied in answer to Anna's questioning eyes. He mopped his brow with a large white handkerchief before returning his planter's hat to his head. "I had it from my brother who arrived aboard a French frigate yesterday. He said the leaders had been caught and hung. Swift French justice, don't y'know. But others will soon rise up to take their place. There's a rebellious spirit abroad everywhere . . . even here. Gradual emancipation, which I understand is to begin in about three weeks, doesn't seem to satisfy them."

"You can hardly blame them," Anna said. "They've had freedom on their minds for a very long time. If it's coming, why not now?"

Lytton's eyebrows shot up. "But . . . but," he sputtered, "without their labor we'll all starve! Besides, most of them haven't the foggiest idea what freedom's all about, what it'll be like not being able to count on a roof over their heads and food in their bellies. They'll turn desperate . . . into robbers, rapists, murderers."

"As things stand now, it's only the newborn . . . hardly a threat to your safety, sir," Anna said evenly.

"It's enough. It gives them ideas. I fear some hothead will get impatient and start something disastrous to everyone, and . . ."

Mme. Lyttton grasped Anna's arm. "Anna, d'you know ought of this Buddhoe I overhear my maids whispering about? He sounds a dangerous sort."

"The rogue should be hung," Lytton blurted out, "before he—" Seeing the horrified look in Anna's eyes he paused. "Never mind. Let's not talk of unpleasant things. Mistress Anna, how about taking lunch with us today. You must get lonely with the governor gone."

Mme. Lytton's shocked look caused by her husband's invitation—after all the woman was colored and the relationship between her and the governor, irregular to say the least—gradually faded, and she recovered herself enough to add her own invitation. "Yes, yes, dear Anna. That would be lovely. Do come!"

Anna smiled wanly. "Thank you both, but I'm rather tired this morning and there's much that needs tending to on the estate. Another time, perhaps."

"Very well. Another time," Mme. Lytton conceded. "And, Anna, we do appreciate your kindness in allowing us to join you for church services. It's ever so much more convenient than going into town."

Lytton took her elbow. "Come along, Lucinda. It's damnably hot in the sun, and I'm thirsting for a rum punch."

The Lyttons drove off in a cloud of dust.

Anna was tired but too restless to relax. A strange sense of foreboding possessed her. The remainder of the day weighed heavily on her hands. She passed it as best she could by writing a few letters and reading. Toward evening she paced the gallery, watching the drive and listening for the sound of horses's hoofs. She knew Peter would come on horseback because he had allowed Frederik, who was suffering with a heavy cold, to take his coach to Frederiksted several days ago.

He came at sundown, accompanied by Captain Irminger of the brig-o'-war, *Ornen*. The Governor had been the captain's passenger from St. Thomas. Always hospitable the governor had asked the captain to dine with them and spend the night.

The governor greeted Anna warmly, and they mounted the staircase arm in arm, with the captain following. Then, remembering his missing coach, he rang for a servant, handed him a note requesting Frederik to send Samson home with the coach at once and asked the man to deliver his note in Frederiksted. Turning to Captain Irminger he said, "We'll have a rum punch, then dinner."

Anna said, "Give me a few moments warning. Whenever you gentlemen are ready, you shall have your dinner as promptly as possible."

"Thank you, my dear. There's no hurry. Captain Irminger and I have much to discuss . . . some differences of opinion."

Anna left to instruct the servants, feeling some disappointment that she would be sharing Peter with another that evening after his absence.

Dinner was indeed late. When, at the end of the meal, cigars and brandy were brought, it was nearly ten o'clock. Anna excused herself and left the men to themselves. Their differences clearly had not been resolved.

On the gallery the scents of sweet lime and jasmine were heavy about her. Though the air was balmy, a chilly breeze off the sea caused her to hold her shawl tightly about her shoulders. The countryside around her lay dark and slumbering, the gentle hills pasted in scallops against the midnight blue sky. Only toward Christiansted did she glimpse an occasional pinpoint of light.

All at once she heard the drums. They came not only from the distant hills but from villages nearby. They sounded in her ears with an urgency that swelled until the very air around her seemed to throb with their compelling sound. Conch shells spoke and were answered. Then plantation bells began to toll, an eerie sound to be heard in the dead of night. Her heart leapt. So this is it! she thought. Buddhoe has given the signal. His march for freedom will now begin!

Maintaining an outward calm she went back into the Greathouse. The men had moved to Peter's study, where they were too deep in talk to have heard what was going on outside. Anna joined them but said nothing. Peter would know soon enough. With trembling hands she took up her embroidery.

Past midnight the three of them were still there when a young militiaman burst in upon them, perspiring and covered with dust. He had been riding hard and fast.

Standing tensely at attention he saluted the governor. "Your Excellency, Major von Scholten sent me. Blacks have been pouring into Frederiksted all evening. They must be eight or nine thousand strong. They swarm about the fort crying for freedom. Buddhoe leads them."

The governor slowly rose to his feet and faced the young man. "So Buddhoe has made his move. Tell me, have they done any damage? Has anyone been hurt?"

"There's been no violence so far, but they'll not be easily dismissed. The commandant at the fort talks of firing the alarm gun. But the major hesitates to allow this without your explicit instructions."

"Quite right. It would bring the planters in from their estates to confront the blacks and would undoubtedly lead to bloodshed."

" The major awaits your instructions, sir."

Outraged Captain Irminger leapt to his feet and offered his unasked-for opinion. "Of course the alarm gun must be fired! Not only that, but those manning the fort should use whatever firepower is needed to disperse the mob. These insurrections must be nipped in the bud. Otherwise the whole island will be put to the torch. There'll be murder, rape, and all manner of atrocities!"

"Captain! Pray calm yourself," the governor said. "This young man has said there's *been* no violence. Before I give drastic orders of any sort I want to know more about what's going on. Lieutenant, what of Major Gyllich and his Brand Corps of free-colored? Has he attempted to convince the workers that they've made their desires known, persuaded them to return peacefully to their plantations while we earnestly try to work out a solution?"

"Major Gyllich has been riding about town all evening talking to the blacks and trying to keep order. He's succeeded well so far. As for getting them to disperse, their leaders, Buddhoe and the others, are much too determined to force the issue of freedom upon the attention of the planters and the government for that. It was Major Gyllich who suggested to Major von Scholten that it might be well to fire the alarm gun."

Captain Irminger, who had been pacing the floor, turned savagely on his host. "Von Scholten, how can you be so indecisive? You must act immediately, forcefully, and with conviction! You must deal with these troublemakers before they get the upper hand. I should think it hardly necessary to remind you how outnumbered we are . . . ten to one or thereabouts!"

The governor replied coldly. "And I consider it necessary to resist inflamatory acts, any act that will cause a direct confrontation and unnecessary bloodshed."

Chastened, Irminger answered, "Well, if you won't allow the fort to open fire, at least permit me to sail the *Ornen* around to Frederiksted with all possible speed. My men can be used for land action if it comes to that, and my ship can be a refuge for women and children."

"No, no, Captain, not even that at this time. I beg you to stay out of this and permit me to handle it as diplomatically as possible."

The captain continued to fume, and the young militiaman still stood at attention, while the governor weighed possible courses of action.

At length the young man said, "Major von Scholten is awaiting your instructions, sir."

"Yes, yes. Sorry to keep you waiting. Tell my brother to keep order as best he can by peaceful means. Tell him I will call my councilors together at once for an emergency meeting and after talking with them send word if it's decided more drastic action is appropriate. Ask him to keep me informed of developments. My stableboy will furnish you with a fresh horse. Oh, and young man, ask him to have a horse ready for my use, too. I may need one."

"Thank you, Excellency. I'll relay your orders." With a salute the militiaman turned on his heel and left.

Captain Irminger bowed stiffly to Anna and, giving the governor a dark look, turned to go.

"Come, Irminger, don't leave in a huff," von Scholten said. "We need more information. I must find out if there's been any disturbance in Christiansted and find out if anyone there knows what's going on in Frederiksted. I sincerely appreciate your offer of help, but for the moment I believe Major Gyllich and this Brand Corps are fully capable of protecting the planters and their families. Kindly wait below and ride into town with me. I must have a word with Anna."

"Humph!" the captain fumed and headed for the gallery and staircase leading down.

When he was gone, Peter turned to Anna. He took both her hands in his. "So it has come," he said. "May the good Lord give me wisdom this night! If ever a man had need of it . . . . You knew before I did."

Anna pressed one of his hands to her cheek. "Aye, Peter. I knew when I heard the tolling of the bells. Peter, you must stand firm against the planters. The workers must have their freedom. Their time has come."

"I had hoped to do it more gradually. Well, we'll see what my councilors have to say. I'll have to roust them out of their beds. I wish I had my coach. I must admit to being weary for the saddle. Don't expect me home, Anna, till this thing is settled. I'll try to keep you informed."

He took her in his arms, held her close to him for a moment brushing her cheek with his lips, then released her and headed for his horse waiting below.

Anna stood on the gallery listening to the horses' hoofs grow fainter and fainter. The countryside was almost quiet now—no more tolling of bells or conch calls. All she heard were drums beating in the distance. At the bottom of the hill she caught a glimpse of torches winding along the road in a procession.

When she could no longer hear the beat of horses' hoofs on the driveway she made her way to her villa. She was bone tired, yet her nerves were taut, her muscles tense. She lay on her bed fully clothed with her eyes open, not knowing what the remainder of the night might bring. Sleep, though she would have welcomed it, would not come. Her clock ticked off the seconds. Its tinkling chime marked the hours—twice, thrice, four times.

The soft gray of dawn was creeping into her room when she heard the sound of carriage wheels in the driveway. She went to investigate. She saw Peter's coach coming up the driveway. When it reached the bottom of the staircase Samson climbed down from the box and tied the horses to the hitching post. Anna hurried to meet him. "D'you have news, Samson? What goes on in Frederiksted?"

"Letter fo' de guv'ner," he mumbled holding an envelope out to her.

"The governor is at Government House," Anna said. "You'd better go there directly. What took you so long? The governor sent for you early last evening."

Hostility shone in Samson's eyes. "It mighty slow goin'. I scarse get t'rough. De people is on de march, tramp, tramp. De roads is jammed full. They is everywhere, like black rivers runnin'. They on de way to Frederiksted, Buddhoe an' freedom!" He smirked. "When we have free, Mistress, we no take orders, we giv' 'em."

"Don't be insolent, Samson! Climb right back on that coachman's seat and get started for Christiansted."

He hesitated, eyeing Anna sullenly. She steadfastly returned his gaze. Finally, with a shrug he obeyed her, slapping the reins hard across the horses' necks to get them started. She sighed. Freedom would not come easily.

After the coach was gone, Anna lingered on the gallery, distracted for the moment by the familiar, soothing sounds and sights of an awakening countryside. The sun was coming on stronger and the air was growing sultry. A cock crowed, cattle lowed, and voices drifted up from the village. Clouds, great gray domes bulging with rain, were stacked high over the eastern hills. If only the clouds would open up and let the rain fall on this parched island what a blessing it would be, Anna thought. It might even cool hot tempers. Suddenly, a keyhole opened in the clouds and a brilliant streak of yellow sunlight streamed through. The light turned the sere, brown hills to gold. Could it be a good omen? she wondered. Then, as suddenly as it had appeared, the keyhole closed, and the hills were dun-colored once more.

She turned with a little shiver and headed for her villa, where she lay down on her bed and dozed. But her sleep was of a nightmarish quality. She dreamed that she and Peter were standing on opposite sides of a wide, black swiftly flowing river. They called to each other, and she held out her hands to him, yearning for his touch. But the river was too wide. There was no way their hands could meet.

Chapter 18

Von Scholten and Irminger rode swiftly through the night headed for Christiansted. The heat was oppressive, and the dust from the road stung their nostrils. They were aware of no great commotion in the countryside but it was astir, rather like the fluttering of leaves before a storm. Lights were burning in several of the slave villages they passed, and they met knots of people carrying torches on the road all heading in the same direction.

Von Scholten stopped a young girl and leaned down from his horse to speak to her. She had no idea who he was.

"Tell me, my girl. What are you doing on the road at this time of night? Where are you going?"

"We all headin' fo' Frederiksted an' freedom, Massa."

Irminger reined his horse in sharply and said, "You'd be better off returning to your cabin and obeying your master, child."

"Not this chile," she replied with a lighthearted laugh. "For sure I'se freedom-boun'."

As the men rode on, Irminger grumbled, "Their leaders, that Buddhoe, should be strung up for putting such ideas into these innocents' heads."

"I suspect those ideas have been there for some time, Captain, long before Buddhoe."

The town of Christiansted lay calm and quiet, sleeping under a cloudy sky. The townspeople had not heard of the uprising, von Scholten concluded. The men rode directly to the fort as he knew Government House would be deserted at this hour. There they asked the sentry on duty to rouse his commander.

When the tousled, hastily dressed commandant appeared, the governor said, "Commandant, there is a general uprising of the unfree, and I need to summon my councilors for an emergency meeting. Please send some of your men to deliver this message.

Here are the names." The governor tore a page from a notebook and taking the desk pen, scribbled a dozen names on it—his councilors, the wise and the unwise, but all men who should rightfully be apprised of the situation.

With this accomplished von Scholten and Irminger again mounted their horses. The governor said to Irminger. "You may as well board your ship, Captain. Get some rest while you may. Prepare your crew to sail for Frederiksted, but wait until you hear from me to weigh anchor."

"Very well. If that's your decision."

"Be patient. I'll keep you informed of developments."

Ill-satisfied, the captain rode off in the direction of the harbor, and the governor rode to Government House. He lit a lamp and climbed the stairs to his office, where he sat at his desk with his head in his hands, thinking. They were heavy thoughts. He knew his career, possibly even his life, depended on the decisions he made within the next few hours. He tried to consider objectively, one by one, the options open to him. He was confident the slaves could be cowed into once more accepting their bonds if full miltary force was brought to bear. Though the whites were vastly outnumbered, they had firepower. Also, he could count on help from other islands. There was a tacit understanding among the French, Dutch, and Spanish governments to send aid in such an eventuality. In fact, the Spanish governor in Puerto Rico had made it plain several months ago that they were ready if called upon. On the other hand, the burning of estates and townhouses and the murder of white families was well within the blacks' capability. Destruction could be horrendous. But Anna's words kept coming back to him: "You must stand firm . . . the workers must have their freedom."

Hearing footsteps on the stairs, he rose from his desk and went to meet the first of his councilors. It proved to be Samuel Rothe. As the assessor for government affairs, it suited Rothe well to live in town. The governor was pleased to see him. He considered him a good friend and knew Rothe had long been in favor of emancipation. Rothe would act as a counterweight to those on the other side—and they would be many.

"I'm the first, Peter?"

"Aye."

"What's it all about?"

"The unfree under the leadership of that young man, Buddhoe, are on the march to Frederiksted. It's not hard to guess what's on their minds."

"Well . . . and what have you decided to do about it?"

"I've been trying to sort it out, all the pros and cons. Must we give in to their demands, or should we try to put this uprising down with vigorous military action, as it's been done in the past and on other islands? What's your view, Samuel?"

"I think you know where I stand on this issue. But let's wait and hear what the others have to say. I gather there will be others?"

"Oh, yes. I sent for as many as I thought would come."

"I don't envy you having to make this decision. No matter what you decide you'll make enemies."

"I know that, but I've got to put that thought out of my mind and try to decide what's best for the island . . . what's right and just."

They waited in the conference room, a room sparsely furnished with only a long, highly polished mahogany table surrounded by sturdy chairs, all of native wood but constructed in Denmark. Over the doorway hung the official portrait of the present governor, von Scholten himself, splendid in full military regalia.

Soon the men heard horses' hoofs in the courtyard, and members of the Colonial Council began straggling in. With them came commanders from the fort and militia. Some of the men were sleepy-eyed, with clothing haphazardly adjusted, disgruntled to have been routed from their beds. Others, mostly those from outlying estates, had been too alarmed by what was going on around them in the countryside to go to bed. They were well aware that the blacks were on the march. They had seen the roads filling with slaves and learned from their own servants that it was a general uprising. Fear for the safety of their homes and families showed in their eyes.

The men took their places around the table and began talking in agitated voices. Von Scholten called for order, and open discussions began, heated discussions doomed to get nowhere. There were those who thought with Major Falbe that the uprising should be put down immediately with severe military action. And there were those like Samuel Rothe who thought freedom for the blacks was inevitable and that now was as good a time as any for it to begin. The discussions went on and on, sometimes degenerating into violent argument.

The meeting was momentarily interrupted when Samson arrived with the governor's coach bearing the second letter from Major von Scholten. After reading it, still not satisfied about what action to take, the governor sent a rider to Frederiksted to get more information.

Meanwhile, on board the *Ornen*, Otto Irminger had gone to his cabin and poured himself a stiff drink of rum. For several minutes he paced his cabin, eyeing his bunk. But it held no attraction for him. He took his spyglass from its shelf and went up on deck. Standing by the rail he trained it on the dark hills surrounding Christiansted. His first mate came from below to join him.

"What's the unease, Captain?" the mate asked. "The watch is set, and all's well as far as I know. You should be taking your rest, sir."

"You've not been ashore, then?"

"Not I. After the crossing from St. Thomas yesterday, which you'll remember was uncommon rough, I saw to it that the men swabbed down the decks, made certain all was shipshape below, then went to my cabin. Some of the men went ashore, but they've not returned as yet."

"You heard nothing?"

"Before midnight I heard drums beating, more than usual I thought . . . oh, and I heard a bell pealing but I paid it no mind. Is anything . . ."

"The blacks are on the march, Mr. Thorsten, thirsting for blood. For certain it's a general uprising, and the governor wastes time shilly-shallying about, wanting to confer with this one and that. He refuses to let us sail for Frederiksted where the real trouble is and let us use our guns to put down this rebellion before the island is ravaged, the estates burned, and the whites murdered."

"So what do we do, Captain?"

"Round up the men who're ashore, Mr. Thorsten. The governor may yet come to his senses and order us to sail. He did instruct me to be prepared for action."

"Aye, aye, sir." the mate said and went to order a ship's boat put over the side.

Irminger remained on deck studying the island with his glass. He saw torches moving on the hill roads to the west of the town, but the town itself remained quiet.

In an hour's time a ship's boat with a collection of the seamen who had been in town came along side and was made fast. The men went below. Irminger spent the night on deck, at times pacing up and down, then again leaning on the rail trying to guess what was going on ashore, frustrated by the not- knowing and thirsting for action.

A gray dawn, shot but once with a swift shaft of sunlight, brought no word from the governor. Cursing inwardly he went below, breakfasted, bathed, and changed his clothes. Then, unable to stand the indecision longer, he had himself put ashore, went to a reading room across from Government House, and settled down to await developments. He sent a servant with a message to the governor telling him of his whereabouts. After several hours of trying to interest himself in outdated European newspapers the captain came to the conclusion that the rebellion had come to nothing after all. He felt a twinge of disappointment. He would have enjoyed a little military activity to relieve the tedium of duty in these quiet waters.

Since midnight a young militiaman had been standing rigidly on the wall guarding the gate to the Frederiksted Fort. He was frightened. Below him filling the square in front of the fort was a seething mass of hostile black faces, men and some women. They waved cane knives and stout clubs. Some had antiquated guns. An occasional stone was hurled his way. Several times he had fingered the trigger of his gun nervously with a mindless desire to blast away and rid himself of the taunting black faces below the wall, a wall none too high for comfort.

He had left Denmark, mother, father, and friends, for duty in the Danish West Indies a month ago, shortly after his seventeenth birthday. Before arriving on the island he had never seen a black face. Now to be looking down upon several thousand of them was terrifying. As they milled about restlessly, sometimes pounding on the gate to the fort with their fists shouting demands, they were so many that he was convinced they could rush the gate if they tried. He imagined them pouring into the fort. He imagined a cane knife at his throat.

He had noted several British merchantmen anchored in the roadstead off the Frederiksted beach. He saw some long boats carrying lanterns being launched from one of the ships. They approached the beach where a group of white women and children, guarded by several armed men, huddled together. The long boats were beached, and sailors helped the women and children into the boats. When the boats were safely launched, the white men elbowed their way through the mob to join the other men in the fort.

The heat was oppressive. The young militiaman was used to a northern climate where it was always cool at night. Here the heat lingered on forever. To add to his discomfort the feet of the milling crowd before him raised dust from the parched grass and brick pavement of the square. It stung his nose. A trickle of sweat ran down his brow and into his eyes.

The crowd of blacks around the fort was growing. Pressure from new arrivals coming from every direction packed the bodies ever tighter together. He had noted the field guns mounted on the water battery and by the fort gate. It would be so easy, he thought, to sweep the square in front with fire from the guns and disperse the mob. Why does the commandant delay so long? he wondered. Why wait until the number of rebellious slaves has grown to an impossible size? Again he fingered the trigger on his gun. If he and a few of his fellows were to rush out of the gates with guns and bayonets at the ready they'd make short work of this unorgananized mob, he thought with bravado he scarcely felt. His narrow chest expanded slightly.

Suddenly his attention was caught by a remarkable figure on horseback, a black man wearing a flamboyant uniform and carrying a flashing sword. In spite of his military bearing, he seemed to be calming rather than inciting the crowd as he rode among them. He spoke to them in a way that often caused the lowering of a shaking fist or a brandished club.

As the young militiaman was observing this remarkable performance and wondering who the man might be, the young militiaman's replacement arrived to take over. Relieved of duty, he climbed down from the wall, and drank long and deep from the water barrel standing in a corner of the courtyard. Standing there he heard loud voiced white men, planters he supposed, harassing the commandant of the fort.

"Fire the guns, Captain," said one, "or send out a sortie of stout fellows well armed to disperse this rabble."

"Can't be done, Mr. Carty, without orders from the governor himself. Major von Scholten is writing again for instructions."

"All this dilly-dallying is playing into the hands of the rebels. I fear the governor's too soft, too apt to coddle them. I hear he's been friendly with their leader, the one who calls himself Buddhoe, the black bastard who's out there now making a spectacle of himself."

So that must be the black rider he had observed, the young militiaman thought. Wondering at the calm courage the man displayed, the militiaman made for the small room he shared with five others and threw himself down on his cot. Here youth, exhaustion, and a sort of reassurance inspired by the black rider won out and he fell into uneasy slumber.

While he slept some 2,000 more slaves marched into Frederiksted from the northwest and north coast estates, joining another long column on the road coming in from Ham's Bluff and Mahogany Road. Chanting, they massed themselves in front of the fort. By now no one in Fredriksted was in doubt that their demand was for freedom—now!

Back at Government House in Christiansted little had changed except that, at the continued urging of his councilors, von Scholten authorized Major Falbe to take some limited military action. By eight o'clock under the major's leadership some armed soldiers were ready to march. But the governor's orders were to go no farther than center island.

At midmorning still another letter arrived from Major von Scholten, pleading with his brother to come to Fredriksted immediately, stating that the workers had set a noon deadline. The letter went on to say:

It would be quite possible to sweep the street with a couple of field guns from the water battery and the fort gate, but if the commander of the fort gives that order I fear that, in their desire for revenge, the blacks will burn down the town and destroy every white person who might fall into their hands....

In the vain hope that his councilors would authorize him to do what he knew in his heart must be done, von Scholten delayed further. But at one o'clock, when still another messenger galloped in from Frederiksted begging him to come at once, he dismissed his councilors, telling them that he would ride to Frederiksted and decide there what course to take. He called for Samson, but to his surprise learned that Samson had mysteriously disappeared. Hearing his predicament the governor's adjutant, Lieutenant Nyborg, volunteered to drive in his stead and went to see to the horses.

Before going to his coach von Scholten sent a message across the street to Captain Irminger with orders for him to sail his brig to the other end of the island. Relieved, the captain boarded his ship as quickly as possible and gave orders to hoist the sails and weigh anchor.

Assessor Rothe had lingered after the other councilors left. Now von Scholten turned to him and asked, "Samuel, will you accompany me to Frederiksted?"

Rothe studied von Scholten's face which was drawn and gray with fatigue. "On one condition: that we stop at your home. You've been up all night and you've had nothing to eat all day. You need a wash and some refreshment."

"Very well," von Scholten agreed testily. "It *is* on the way, and I need time to think, to figure out what I should say to my people. Since there's no agreement among my councilors, the decision that must be made will have to be mine alone. It will help to have you with me . . . to talk through a course of action with a friend whose judgment I respect."

"Let's get started, then, Peter. At best it will be two hours before we can reach Frederiksted."

The men hurried down the stairs to the governor's waiting coach.

Chapter 19

IT WAS A RELIEF to be awakened from her dream when Jemma brought Anna a breakfast tray.

"No person come from de village t'cook, Missy. They's gone off or they's scairt foolish an' stay inside with shutters close tight. All but Joshi. He feedin' de horses and de pigs so they no' go hungry."

"That's good of Joshi. Jemma, what d'you plan to do?

"I stay by you, Missy Anna."

Anna smiled and took the tray, but had little appetite.

The morning dragged on. The estate was strangely quiet with no servants bustling about. Anna paced her rooms, wondering what was going on in Christiansted, Frederiksted, and in between. Was Peter safe? How would he handle this crisis? At midmorning she was hopeful when she heard a carriage approaching. But when she walked out onto her gallery she saw an unfamiliar rig, not Peter's coach, coming up the hill. The horses were laboring under the lash, something Peter would never have allowed. The rig stopped at the bottom of the greathouse stairs. She went to investigate and saw that the horses were lathered as though they had been driven hard for some distance.

The driver stepped down, tied his horses, and approached the stairs. He was roughly dressed, had a red face, bristling red hair, and a mouth with a disagreeable twist to it.

"Gordon Grimes at your service, Madam," he said in a rasping voice, standing with hat in hand. "May I have a word with you?"

"The governor's not at home, sir, and I doubt that I can be of help."

"In that you're mistaken, Madam. My message is for you."

"For me? Does it . . . does it concern the governor?" Suddenly her throat felt tight. Had Peter come to harm?

Seeing her agitation he took his time in answering. He enjoyed playing on her emotions. "Aye, it concerns the governor, but it has nothing to do with his whereabouts or state of health at the moment. If you'll allow me?" He put a foot on the bottom step of the staircase.

"I have no intention, Mr. Grimes, of inviting you into the governor's residence when he's absent, but," Anna continued with resignation, "if you insist, I'll hear your message."

"Whatever you say, Madam. If you choose to refuse me the courtesy of inviting me in, I can say what I have to say right here. My message is brief and my visit need not be long."

"Then please say what you have to say and be done with it. These are trying times."

"They are indeed, and that's why I've driven all the way from the East End to warn you. It is well known that you have much influence with the governor." He smiled unpleasantly. "It's said, and I believe said true, that you have the power to bend him to suit your fancy." He cleared his throat. "Let me be plain."

"Yes, by all means."

"Concerning this uprising of the blacks. I'm warning you, Madam, that if he heeds their outrageous demand for freedom, it will be the end of his career on this island."

"That is wild conjecture on your part, Mr. Grimes. If he takes a firm stance and gives the workers their freedom he will gain many more friends than he'll lose. There are enough just men on this island, black and white, who will defend his action."

"Don't deceive yourself. Within days the leaders among the blacks will be dangling from the end of a rope. As for us planters," an angry flush suffused his face, "we are desperate men. Not one among us will thank the man who robs us of our property, our slaves, that is. It spells our ruin. And his!"

"Mr. Grimes," Anna said holding her rising anger in check, "the decision is the governor's to make. He will decide with the help of his councilors what's best for this island. His is the authority—"

"Not so, Madam!" he shouted, his face now contorted with rage. "He does *not* have the authority! If von Scholten frees the slaves it will be on his head and his alone. He has no right to do so. No right at all! The authority for such an act must come from king and parliament. He does not have that authority now, and I say he'll not get it in the foreseeable

181

future." His voice suddenly grew soft and sinister. "These are perilous times, Madam, when accidents easily occur. I swear to you that one way or another, if he sides with the blacks, you will find yourself alone on your hilltop, your home in ruins. And what will you be then? I ask you. Not the respected widow of a Virgin Islands governor. No indeed. You'll be nothing but an elderly black whore! I suggest you use your influence."

Anna clenched her fists in outrage. Her voice was icy cold and carefully controlled as she answered him. "You were quite right, Mr. Grimes, when you said your visit need not be long. I suggest you leave at once. Good day, Sir." She turned her back on him. With head held high she walked toward her villa. Not once did she deign to look back.

Once behind closed doors her dignity crumpled. She threw herself down on her bed and lay there trembling violently until she heard the odious rig depart. Then she buried her face in her pillow and wept, her tears not only for herself and the insults she'd received but because of fear for Peter's safety. The tears brought a release of sorts. Finally her trembling ceased and she lay still.

At last, shortly after one o'clock that afternoon, the governor's coach did arrive in front of the greathouse. Hearing its arrival, Anna quickly splashed her face with cold water and combed her hair. Then she went out onto the gallery to meet it. To her surprise a man other than Peter was the first to step down. As she came closer she recognized Peter's friend, Assessor Samuel Rothe. He turned to help Peter from the coach.

Anna hurried down the stairs. When she saw Peter's face she was shocked. Lines of stress and strain showed between his eyes and around his mouth. His skin was gray with fatigue.

Anna greeted Assessor Rothe, then turned to Peter. "My dear. You're so very tired," she said. "Did you get any sleep at all last night?"

"None whatsoever."

"Can you rest now?"

"No chance of that. Frederik insists I come to Frederiksted at once. The latest word is that Buddhoe will try to hold his people in check until four. He's promised I'll speak to them. That doesn't give us much time. Samuel is going with me."

Anna gave Samuel a grateful smile. "I'm glad of that."

"Anna, my own, we must have food, and I'm badly in need of a bath and fresh linen. Can you arrange for it?"

"But of course! Jemma and I will see to it. The other servants have left or refuse to budge from their cabins, but we'll manage."

Anna headed for the kitchen. The men went into the governor's study.

Jemma soon arrived with hot water so that her master could bathe and shave. Meanwhile Anna prepared a platter of cold meats, cheese, and fruit. She took it to the study, where she found Peter seated at his desk writing. She was relieved to see his color had improved and he looked refreshed. She put the platter on a table. "Peter, what are you writing?"

He rose from his desk and took both her hands in his. "I've been working on a proclamation," he said gravely. "It's only partly written. I intend to finish it on the way to Frederiksted. I believe you'll find it more to your liking than the one from King Christian. I plan to read it from the walls of the fort."

There was a triumphant look in his eyes, but the grim set of his mouth told her that whatever decision he had made had not been made lightly.

"Peter, take me with you to Frederiksted," she said imploringly.

"No, no, I can't, my love. I won't expose you to unnecessary danger. Who knows what is going on in Frederiksted? The unfree may have gone wild! The town could be in flames! The planters may have come into town hot for blood, and the sight of you might inflame them further." He smiled ruefully. "You know they think you have undue influence over me. No, Anna, you must stay here where you'll be out of harm's way."

She turned away, gravely disappointed. But she knew it was useless to beg; he was a man who seldom changed his mind.

She fixed plates of food for the men and poured a chilled fruit juice drink. They ate in haste, then dashed down the stairs to the waiting coach driven by the governor's adjutant, Lieutenant Nyborg.

With a sinking heart Anna watched them go. She stood immobile for a moment. Then, seized by a sudden impulse, she put on an old bonnet, grabbed her shawl, and ran down the winding path to the slave village and burst into Joshi's cabin.

She took hold of the old man's arms and pulled him from his chair, where he'd been sitting stoically for hours. "Joshi! I want you to drive me to Frederiksted!"

"To Frederiksted?" Joshi shook his head vigorously. "Oh, no, Missy! That no place for you!"

"Yes, Joshi. I insist! We're going to Frederiksted. The gig is light and the horse can travel fast. You know the back ways, the shortcuts. We'll get to Frederiksted before the governor."

"De gov'nor goin' to Frederiksted?"

"Yes, Joshi, yes. He will read a proclamation to the people from the fort."

"Why you so set on goin' West End, Mistress? It bad enough de gov'nor go dere. Ne tellin' what happen this day in Frederiksted. Why you want ol' Joshi take you dere?" He looked dazed.

Anna shook him a little. "Joshi, listen to me what I say. The governor will read an important proclamation. Don't you want to hear him? Don't you want to hear what he has to say to your people? Well, I do, Joshi. If you won't drive me, I'll drive myself!"

Joshi shook his head, bewildered. He didn't grasp the full import of her words. But one thing was clear. His mistress was determined to go to Frederiksted. He knew she was a lady who was not easily put off, and he couldn't let her go by herself. He picked up his wool cap, pulled it down over his ears, and headed for the stables.

As soon as they reached the main road Anna could feel the excitement in the air. She felt it in her bones, in the racing of her pulse. Soon they overtook a group of blacks marching doggedly toward West End, then, several more. The blacks carried a strange assortment of homemade weapons. Some were shouting. Some were singing. They paid little attention to the gig, so wrapped up were they in their own purpose. But one such group overflowed the road so that there was no room to pass.

Joshi slowed the gig. "Move aside dere, brother. Lemme pass t'rough."

"Why you no' marchin', ol' mon?" Joshi was challenged. "We march fo' freedom. You oughta be amarchin', too!"

"I too ol' t'march, mon. An' me ol' woman," he jerked his head toward Anna who sat with her head bowed, and pointed to his

184

brains with a waggling finger, "she gone bad in de head."

The leader of the marchers nodded sympathetically and waved them on. Then, mounting the rise at King's Hill, they saw the governor's coach just ahead. It had been halted by a crowd of blacks. Anna and Joshi could hear their excited cries. "Massa Peter! Massa Peter!"

Anna's heart sank. What if Peter saw them and was angry? What if he ordered them to turn back? "Joshi, is there another way, a way to get off the main road?"

Joshi surveyed the brown fields on either side. Spying a faint track through cane rubble he said, "We can take off over de field, Miss Anna. It be mighty rough but I t'ink we make it."

"Let's try, Joshi."

"If you say. Hold tight, Mistress."

They bumped along over the cane field, the horse stumbling now and again over the hard dry ruts left by the iron rims of cane wagons. Anna held on with both hands to keep from flying out of the gig. At last they came out onto a narrow back road near Upper Love. To their relief it was deserted. Joshi urged the horse into a trot.

They passed through Grove Place, climbed up into the hills beyond, and wound down on the other side through the rain forest on Mahogany Road. When they reached the edge of Frederiksted and found the road into town too crowded to go farther in the gig, Joshi climbed down and tethered the horse behind an outhouse.

They marched with the crowd into town, Anna keeping her shawl discreetly over the lower part of her face. The street leading to the fort was jammed. Determined to reach it with all possible haste, she elbowed her way boldly through the press of bodies.

She had expected to find a crowd, but she had not expected to find the square in front of the fort literally filled to overflowing with a surging black sea of humanity. As the pressure from behind grew too great, the bodies in front gave way, only to flow back eventually to their former positions.

The mood of the crowd was frightening. All around her Anna saw evidence of seething resentment. Men shook their fists over their heads and muttered threats. Women protested in shrill voices, heightening the sense of hysteria that was building and building. The gate to the fort was securely barred, and armed militiamen stood on its walls.

Anna saw a merchant vessel flying the Union Jack riding at
anchor. The British officers were taking aboard refugees,
mostly terrified white women and children. It was clear,
however, that the ordinary seamen sympathized with the
blacks. They sent water casks ashore to ease the thirst of those
with throats parched from shouting. On many casks the word
LIBERTY was printed in large letters.

In the midst of the crowd rode Buddhoe, an heroic figure
mounted on his white stallion, wearing his blue and scarlet
general's uniform. The afternoon sun fired the gold of his
epaulettes and glinted on the hilt of his polished sword. His
face was composed, his bearing calm in the midst of all the
turmoil. He rode expertly, seeming to be everywhere at once.
By the sheer force of his personality he strove to keep order
with now a calming gesture, now a quiet plea spoken for
patience. As he paused significantly beneath the guns of the
fort, his followers raised their voices in unison, repeating the
cry, "We want free! We want free!"

Major Gyllich, his white face conspicuous above the crowd,
shared Buddhoe's objective of keeping order. He sat his horse
on the fringes of the mob, alert for any overt sign of violence.
Suddenly, a woman threw a hatchet that barely missed his
head. The crowd surged toward him, converging on a hated
symbol of authority. The major drew his sword dramatically
and threw it to the ground. "Take my life!" he cried. "But
know that I am here as a friend, not as an enemy!"

Aware of the major's danger, Buddhoe rode to his side,
showing their common purpose. "Be patient," he shouted to his
followers. "We have set a deadline. The governor knows it. He
will come. He will hear you. He will speak to you. He is a fair
man."

Slowly the crowd drew back.

The town's aged Catholic priest, Father O'Ryan, walked
among the people, talking quietly to them. He passed close to
Anna. She overheard a man say to him, "Fader, us poor
workers can no fight de soldjers. We got no guns. But we can
burn. We can destroy wid torch an' club. That's wha' we aim
t'do if we don' get free."

"Don't be hasty, my son. Wait and hear what the governor
has to say," counseled the priest.

Behind the corner of a stone house, out of range of the guns
from the fort, Anna noticed a pile of sugar trash, dry cane

leaves from the fields. Women were busily adding to it. Anna knew that at a word from their leaders the trash would be fired and pitchforked into doors and through windows, quickly spreading fire throughout the town. Her throat grew dry with apprehension.

The crowd's patience was wearing desperately thin. As the four o'clock deadline neared the shouting increased. Groups of workers made symbolic sorties on the fort with whatever makeshift weapons they had at hand. The Danish Militia stood on the walls, their rifles at the ready. It took discipline for them to hold their fire. The abusive language and the sticks and stones hurled their way begged for retaliation.

Standing on the wall beside Captain Castonier, Commandant of the Fort, was merchant and leading citizen William Moore. He said to the captain, "My advice is to shoot to kill—or not at all." The phrase "shoot to kill" was heard by a worker standing just below him. It was repeated to those nearby, and all who heard it were infuriated. They charged up the street and broke down the door of Moore's fine townhouse. It was the first real violence, the first property to be looted.

Suddenly attention was focused on a shouting, gesticulating teenage boy who had climbed to the top of the hated whipping post. The crowd surged toward him in sympathy, took him on their shoulders, and tore the post from its foundations. Strong men carried it to the wharf, followed by a screaming mass of women. There was a heave of black arms, and the whipping post flew through the air to land with a great splash in the sea.

Next to go was the front of the police office. It was hacked to pieces with hatchets and machetes. Angry men rushed in and brought out all the records. These the crowd tore to shreds and threw to the wind.

A bustle of activity on the beach drew Anna's attention away from the bits of paper fluttering through the air. The *Ornen* had arrived and dropped anchor, and Captain Irminger's gig was being drawn up on the sand. His appearance caused more screaming, angry shouts, and fist-shaking. With incredible bravado he strode through the hostile crowd toward the fort. Anna caught her breath. Would he reach the fort unharmed? By some miracle he did, and the heavy doors were quickly opened to admit him.

But the mood of the crowd was growing uglier all the time.

Anna despaired. It seemed certain to her now that one act of violence would follow another, and before long the town would be put to the torch and blood would flow. Where was Peter? What had delayed him so long? Please God, let him come, she prayed.

All at once she felt a change. The clamoring voices were stilled. The people stood quietly, expectantly. She pressed forward to see what had made a difference. At the far end of the Strand the crowd had parted to allow a coach to pass. The Governor had arrived.

Lieutenant Nyborg was forced to drive the coach slowly as he sought to find a way through the throngs of people. The people pressed in as close as they dared, reaching out their hands in supplication, talking excitedly, spilling out their woe. Finally, the coach reached the entrance to the fort and stopped. The governor stepped down into the milling crowd. They closed ranks around him. He stood motionless, compassionate and calm. In a clear voice loud enough for all in the square to hear he asked, "My people, what is it you want?"

"Give us free! Give us free!" they shouted as one.

He nodded and smiled, showing that he understood what was in their hearts. The crowd fell back, clearing the way to the fort's entrance. He walked slowly and deliberately under the main arch through the doors opened to receive him.

Anna pressed forward to get a better view and waited breathlessly for him to reappear. She didn't have to wait long. He soon stood on the wall beside the main entrance to the fort in a commanding position. At sight of him the crowd grew silent. A sea of silent but determined black faces were turned up toward him, waiting. He wasted no time. He read the stunning words of his proclamation in a sure, ringing voice. The words left no doubt in the minds of slaves or planters as to their meaning:

"ALL UNFREE IN THE DANISH WEST INDIES ARE, FROM TODAY, FREE."

Wild cheers, stamping of feet, and joyous shouts greeted his words. The remainder of the proclamation, the part he had painstakenly composed on the road to Frederiksted, which outlined preliminary terms of emancipation and practical guidelines for all concerned, was lost in noisy celebration. The workers expressed their joy in all the ways most natural to them—singing, jumping up and down, embracing, and thumping each other on the back. They waved homemade banners, beat on tin pans, and shouted over and over the magic words, "Free! All free!"

Anna was moved to the depths of her being. Tears of joy streamed down her face. She felt joyful for the black people, her mother's people and her grandmother's, who would no longer have to labor under the yoke of slavery. She felt proud of this man, her man, who had on this day found the strength to meet the issue of slavery head on, dealing with it in a way that was right and just in spite of bitter opposition. And she felt thankful to God that at last her prayers had been answered. It was done! The people were free!

Unable to contol its exuberance, the crowd began moving away from the square while Peter was still reading. Anna was caught up by the crowd and carried along willy-nilly. She looked around frantically for Joshi but he had been swept away also. She managed, at last, to extricate herself by ducking into a doorway, where she braced herself against the frame and let the bulk of the crowd pass her by. Then, by using the protection of walls and doorways until she had left the town behind, she succeeded in making her way to the outhouse where Joshi had tied the gig.

Rather to her surprise it was still there, and the horse was calmly munching weeds, undisturbed by the historic event that had just taken place. But Joshi was nowhere to be seen. She climbed into the gig and slumped down on the seat, exhausted. She would wait awhile, and then if Joshi didn't show up she'd have to try to make her way back to Bulow's Minde on her own. It wouldn't do to have Peter return and find her gone.

Chapter 20

THE SUN had dipped below the horizon when she heard a sudden rustling in the tall weeds beside the road and Joshi's voice. "That you, Missy Anna?"

"Oh, Joshi! Thank goodness you're here! I was worried about you."

"Such a lotta commotion! I think they neber let me pass."

Anna searched his face for any sign of change. "Joshi, you heard the governor's proclamation. You're free! Aren't you glad?"

The old man scratched his grizzled head. "What free mean, Missy Anna? I don' rightly know."

"It means . . ." What did it mean to a man like Joshi, too old to make a life for himself anywhere but on the home plantation? "When you get used to the idea you'll like it fine," she said rather lamely. "Now let's go home."

"Home? Do Joshi have a home, Mistress?"

"Joshi, you'll always have a home with us . . . long as you wish."

Joshi seemed easier in his mind. He climbed into the gig, picked up the reins, and pulled the horse's head out of the weeds.

The crimson sky behind them was fading as the gig turned onto Centerline Road, leaving Frederiksted behind. They passed Whim, which had once been Christopher MacEvoy's fine estate. The Greathouse was dark and still, and seemed to be brooding. No one was about. But as they continued farther down the road, they began to see bands of ex-slaves roaming aimlessly over the countryside. Now that they had it, they were confused about what to do with their new-found freedom. Most agreed it shouldn't mean going quietly back to the estates to pick up hoe and cane knife again. Didn't freedom mean they could decide for themselves whether to work or not? A few remembered that the governor, and Buddhoe as well, had urged them to return to their homes for the time being. The governor said they could stay in their cabins and use their provisioning grounds for the next three months, that their labor in the cane fields must be paid for by the owners, but their food allowance would cease. Most were too intoxicated by the word "freedom" to have the words that followed make an impression.

Now darkness lay like a mantle over the fields. Suddenly, Anna and Joshi saw the eastern sky flare up, casting an eerie glow over the darkened landscape. A little farther and the silhouette of a Greathouse wreathed in flames came into view. Streaming away from the conflagration were torch-bearing members of an unruly mob. Yelling, hooting, laughing drunkenly, they leapt about, their excitement growing with the mounting flames. Someone had a gun and was shooting it into the air.

Anna clutched Joshi's arm, suddenly frightened. "Let's turn back, Joshi. They're so excited they scarce know what they do. Why must they burn? The governor's given them what they want."

"I dunno, Mistress. Mebbe they jus' hasta let all that feelin' come outta de barrel, all that feelin' with lid on all dere born days."

He pulled the horse to a standstill and started to turn him around in the narrow road. But it was too late. Someone in the mob had seen the gig and thought Anna and Joshi fair game. Following the leader, the mob bore down on them, blocking their way both front and back. They waved their torches under the horse's nose, laughing and cavorting around him. The horse reared and plunged again and again. Anna screamed.

"Whoa dere! Whoa, boy!" Joshi shouted, trying desperately to keep the animal under control.

His efforts were in vain. The horse bolted, jumping the ditch at the side of the road and hurtling off across an open field. The gig with Anna and Joshi in it flew after him. Anna managed to stay in by holding on with all her strength. Joshi yelled and cursed, pulling frantically on the reins, trying to slow the spooked beast. As they bumped and bolted wildy along over the rough field, the gig creaking and groaning, Anna thought it must surely fall apart at any moment. But for a time it held together. Then the right wheel caught in a deep rut and spun off. The gig tilted sideways. Joshi and Anna were thrown out, hitting the unyielding ground with a bone-crunching impact. The horse raced on into the night, dragging the rapidly disintegrating gig along behind him.

Stunned, Anna lay still. As she slowly began to regain her senses she was aware of a throbbing head and a body that ached all over. Then she thought of Joshi. Where was he? Why was he so still? She raised herself on her elbow. "Joshi," she called softly, "Are you hurt?"

There was no answer. She sat up. By the glare from the burning Greathouse she saw Joshi lying a few feet away. The torch bearers, still shouting and waving their torches, had lost interest in them and were well down the road toward Christiansted.

Anna crept over to Joshi on hands and knees, every muscle in her body crying out in protest as she dragged herself along.

"Joshi," she murmured and shook him gently. She touched his head and her fingers came away sticky, sticky with blood.

"Oh, Joshi, Joshi!" she cried out in a panic. "You're hurt. You're badly hurt!" She laid her cheek on his chest and listened. There was no heartbeat. The old man was dead.

Anna sat back, covered her face with her hands, and wept. It was all wrong for this good, gentle man, storyteller and loyal friend, to end this way, his hours as a free man cut woefully short. Why did it have to happen to him? Then she thought prayerfully, "Perhaps where you are, Joshi, you'll know a freedom more sure, more beautiful than anything here on earth." The thought brought her some measure of comfort.

Her tears spent, she became painfully aware of her cuts and bruises—and of her perilous situation. Somehow, she would have to make her way home to Bulow's Minde on foot. It was a long way. Still, if only she didn't hurt all over, it wouldn't be too difficult.

And what of Joshi? She hated to leave his unprotected body in the middle of a field. In the morning she could send someone to bring him home. Meanwhile . . .

Taking hold of his feet she tugged his body into a sort of depression at the edge of the field. She knelt beside him, folded his arms over his chest, gently closed his eyes, and covered him with cane trash. Then she gathered up her skirts, tucked them into her waistband, and started resolutely for Bulow's Minde.

The reddened sky from other Greathouses burning helped to light her way as she trudged along thinking painful thoughts about Joshi and about Peter. Peter must be home by now. He would be frantic with worry about her. When he found out where she'd been he would be angry that she had disobeyed him. She hoped that she could make him see how much it meant to her to go to Frederiksted and that then he would understand. She felt a burden of guilt about Joshi—as well as great sadness. If she hadn't insisted that he drive her to Frederiksted he would be alive at this moment. But she had to go. She *had* to. Peter proclaiming freedom for the unfree was, perhaps, the most important event of her life, the event that gave her life meaning.

She gave the burning Greathouses a wide berth and stayed mostly to the fields and groves, where she was less likely to meet unruly mobs than on the roads. As she started up the hill at La Reine she found the fallen limb of a thibbet tree, which she was able to use as a staff. Her progress was slow. She had to rest often. Footsore and bone-weary, she finally reached the drive at Bulow's Minde and dragged herself up the hill.

The Greathouse was dark. She soon discovered that Peter had not come home. What with worry about him and sorrow for Joshi, the elation she'd felt earlier in the day deserted her. With a heavy heart she made her way to her villa and fell on her bed exhausted.

Tuesday, July the fourth, was the first day of freedom in the Danish West Indies. Anna was still in bed at midmorning when Jemma came to tell her that George, her brother, had come from town with news.

"He come t'see how we farin', Missy Anna, an' t'tell what all takin' place in town."

"I'll get up," Anna said. She was still bone-weary, but didn't want to miss hearing what news George had brought. "Jemma, has the governor come home?"

"No, Mistress. He no come."

With a sigh Anna eased herself out of the four-poster. She was hideously stiff and sore. Jemma brought her dressing gown. She put it on and went out onto the gallery of her villa, where she found George.

"Mornin', Mistress Anna. I jus' come from Christiansted."

"George, we're hungry for news. Tell me what's happening."

"Yesterday, 'long 'bout sundown two bands o' workers from de country come togedder at Bassin triangle. They don' know that de gov'nor set them free. News slow gettin' to Christiansted. At Bassin a barricade be set up by de militia to keep them outta town. De soljers at de barricade young an' scairt. They see many mon comin' at them crazy with de idea o' bustin' t'rough, wantin' to reach Gov'ment House. De soljers hab a li'l ol' canon an' they fill it with gunpowder but no ball. Pouf! They shoot it off. De workers fall back scairt by de noise an' de smoke. But 'fore long they see it a trick an' come back madder 'n jack-spaniel! They shake fist, call bad name an' t'row rock an' conch shell. Then two dumbklop soljers, dere fingers jumpy on dere trigger an' scairt silly, fire for real into de crowd. They kill two persons an' hurt lots more."

"Oh, no! What a pity! I was afraid there'd be bloodshed." Anna wrung her hands in distress. "Then what, George?"

"De workers know not t'try bustin' t'rough de barricade agin, but they hell-bent on gettin' even. They get into town back ways, some here some there, an' set de town t'burnin'. What they can't burn they hack t'pieces with hatchets."

Horrified at this news and thinking of her family and Peter, Anna felt faint. She might have fallen, but George took her arm and led her to a garden bench. "You bes' sit down, Mistress. I sorry de news so bad."

"George, what of the governor? Wasn't he able to stop the destruction—calm the workers by telling them they were free men at last?"

"He no there, Mistress. He long time comin' from Frederiksted. He *do* come but mos' too late t'stop de burnin'."

"And what of my family, George? Were any of the townsfolk injured?"

"No one hurt 'mongst you' folks that I hear of. No one killed at all in de town so far I hear."

"That's a blessing," Anna said. "D'you know where the governor is now?"

"He at Gov'ment House. I hear de planters mos' awful mad with he! They want t'send out de soljers t'shoot down de people wherever they fine 'em rampagin' t'rough de countryside. De gov'nor no want that. They *do* say de planters not goin' t'accept de Freedom Proclamation. No way!"

Anna pressed her fingers to her temples. So it wasn't settled after all. "George, I'm grateful to you for coming. I'm glad no one in my family or yours has been hurt and that the governor's safe—at least for the moment. Now, you'd best get back to your family."

As George ran down the stairs to his waiting horse, Anna walked slowly back to her bedroom. She called Jemma and told her about Joshi. Then she closed the jalousies to keep out the strong light of the noonday sun and lay down again on her bed. She had a splitting headache.

Two hours later the crunch of carriage wheels on gravel again drew Anna from her bed. From her gallery she saw Peter's coach coming to a halt in front of the greathouse. The coach was accompanied by Peter's adjutant, Lieutenant Nyborg, on horseback.

Anna hurried to the top of the stairs leading down from the greathouse gallery. She saw Lieutenant Nyborg dismount and open the door of the coach. He helped an elderly man step down. Could it be . . . ? With a pang Anna realized that the elderly man was none other than Peter, her Peter, but a Peter dreadfully changed. Forgetting her own fatigue she ran down the stairs to meet him. A close look at his face only increased her distress. He looked unbelievably tired and quite ill.

He managed a weary smile. "Anna, I'm going out to reason with the newly free myself. They know I'm their friend. They'll listen to me. I must persuade them to go back to their plantations for the time being. Their rioting, looting, and burning give the planters a weapon to use against them—and me."

"Peter, I beg of you. Rest a little. You've been under a dreadful strain."

"No matter. It may already be too late to gain control, but I must do what I can. Lieutenant Nyborg, kindly go to the stables and see if you can find me a horse. We'll make more speed on horseback."

Anna put her arm under his, and they slowly mounted the staircase. When they reached the top she turned to him. "Peter, I was in Frederiksted yesterday. I heard you read your Freedom Proclamation!"

"You were there!" He looked at her in amazement.

"I had to go! You must understand! Joshi took me."

Peter saw that her eyes were wet with tears. "Why tears, Anna? Surely freeing the unfree is what you've always wanted, worked hard and prayed for! Was it not well said?"

"It was admirably said!" She threw herself into his arms.

"I'm filled with joy . . . and sorrow, both so strong that either would bring tears. I'm proud of you, proud that you said those brave words, and I rejoice in the good fortune of my mother's people. The sorrow is for us, my dearest. Already it's taken a terrible toll, placed you in grave danger. Does it mean we'll be torn apart? I have fearful premonitions. But you must rest while you can."

She left him in his study while she went to prepare cool drinks and some light food for both men. When she returned Lieutenant Nyborg was telling the governor, who was resting in a chair, that his horse was saddled and waiting. The men ate quickly. Then the lieutenant helped the governor on with his boots and gave him his hand to ease his rising from his chair.

Peter took Anna's hands in his and forced a smile. "Anna, take heart. There's no reason this can't be settled with some small compromise on both sides. Buddhoe and Major Gyllich ride together trying to calm the newly free. I will add my plea to theirs. I think the workers will listen. When they settle down on their plantations and things become somewhat normal again, the planters will see that a small wage is no price at all to pay for contented workers. It will all come right, Anna. God willing we'll have many more years together."

Anna smiled bravely back at him. "I hope you're right, Peter. If anyone can succeed with them, you can."

He took the lieutenant's arm and made his way down the stairs to his waiting horse.

Later in the day Anna walked down to the village to see how the people were faring. She found most of the cabins deserted, but Amanda sat on the doorstep of hers.

"You stay, Amanda?"

"I stay, Mistress. Benji, he in de stable waterin' de horses."

"I'm grateful, Amanda. Others will return soon. I'm sure of it. The governor has ridden out to find those that are roaming the countryside and reason with them."

"I hope they listens! Work what needs t'be done is laggin'."

From the woodworking shop came the sound of a hammer. The women knew what it meant. A coffin was being whacked together for Joshi. Sudden tears sprung to Anna's eyes.

Amanda said sorrowfully, "Jemma an' me, we wash an' dress de body . . ."

Anna bowed her head. "I wish with all my heart he was still with us, Amanda. I feel . . . I feel it's my fault that he's gone. If I hadn't insisted he drive to Frederiksted . . ."

"For true de blame no' on you' head, Missy Anna. De blame on them dat burn an' act crazy."

Amanda sniffed and wiped her eyes on her sleeve. Anna put her arms around her, and the two women clung together sorrowing.

The governor was to spend another night away from home, and yet another. He fought hard for the stand he'd taken on slavery and consistently opposed using military force in putting down the riots. Some of Bulow's Minde ex-slaves began drifting back, and Anna learned through them that like Peter, Buddhoe and Major Gyllich rode all over the island attempting to bring order out of chaos without use of arms. Surprisingly, they reported, there'd been no loss of life among the whites and little among the blacks. But there was considerable property damage, crops burned, and Greathouses put to the torch.

On the evening of the fourth day of freedom Peter returned in his coach to Bulow's Minde still accompanied by Lieutenant Nyborg. As he sank into a chair in his study Anna saw before her a broken old man. Even his speech was labored.

"They . . . they tell me I was ill last night," he said slowly. "A stroke, Dr. Knudsen said. I know I was . . . was unconscious for a short while."

"Oh, Peter! I'm so sorry!" She knelt beside him and laid her head on his knee.

He stroked her hair. "Anna, I fear I must . . . must leave the island."

She looked up astonished. Then she saw that, surprisingly, some of the old spirit and determination had come back into his eyes. "I must go to king and parliament and prove that my Freedom Proclamation is right and just, was the only course available to me. My enemies say I've exceeded my authority. My friends say to make the proclamation stand, I must have the full support of the Danish government. I must . . . I have resigned. I appointed Governor Oxholm of St. Thomas to take my place. There's an American clipper ship in the harbor. I'll board her at midnight."

Anna bowed her head, stunned by his words. Tears were streaming down her cheeks. "Peter," she said beseechingly, "must you go? Surely your enemies will come 'round."

"It's the only way, my beloved. God willing I may return one day, justified by king and parliament and be accepted by *all* the islanders as their leader."

Suddenly, there was a clamor of voices in front of the greathouse. With difficulty Peter rose and walked to the window overlooking the gallery. "There appears to be a great crowd of blacks with torches out there shouting. I wonder what—?"

Jemma came running in. "Massa! Missy!" The white of her eyes showed large with fright. "They come for de gov'nor. They bad mon, up t'no good!"

"That can't be, Jemma. Black men are my friends."

"They's no black, Massa Peter. They's blackened they face, that's all. They mean to harm you, sure!"

Brushing her tears away Anna rushed to the window. She saw an unruly crowd surrounding Peter's coach. They waved their torches, shook their fists, and shouted obscenities. She judged them to be small landowners who had lost maybe a dozen slaves. Mr. Grime's sinister words flashed through her mind. She turned to Peter and grabbed his arm. "Jemma's right. Those are white men. They're a bad lot, Peter!"

Peter moved away from the window and sank once more into a chair. "Perhaps I could reason with them."

"No! Don't go out to them, I beg of you! They hate you and what you've done. They're beyond reason!"

"You may be right. Well, I trust they'll soon tire of their sport and be off."

"I . . . I don't think they will."

She gasped. A torch had been thrust into the governor's coach and it was all ablaze. The men cheered and shouted with glee. Then several broke away from the group, cavorting around the coach and heading for the staircase. Others followed. Lieutenant Nyborg stood firmly at the top of the stairs to bar their way.

One man against so many! Anna thought with despair. She turned to face the governor. "Peter," she said taking command, "you must go! They mean to force their way in and harm you. You must go. Now!"

"But my coach, Anna," he said bewildered. "It's surrounded. How can I?"

"Go out the back way. Go down to the village. The farm wagon still stands by the stables. You'll find someone therewho'll drive you. You can go across the fields till you reach the main road, then down to the harbor, where you can board your American clipper."

She hurried to his side, desperate fear written on her face. "Dear Peter, I implore you. You must go at once!"

"So be it." He rose slowly and put his arms around her. For a moment he held her close. "Goodbye, my Anna. I will return to you if . . . if it's anyway possible. God be with you, my own dear love."

He raised both her hands to his lips and kissed them. His eyes swam with tears.

The clamoring voices were closer now, growing louder and more insistent. Reluctantly Anna pulled away. "Take care of yourself, Peter. Get well . . ."

"Yes, yes, I will. God willing."

He turned from her and headed toward the back of the Greathouse as fast as he was able.

"Jemma, go with him to the stables," Anna said. "He needs help, and I must stay and confront those ruffians. I want to give him every chance to get away."

Jemma hurried after him and took his arm.

"And . . . and Peter," Anna called.

He and Jemma paused, and Anna caught up with them. "Take my shawl. It will guard you against the night's chill." She placed it tenderly around his shoulders.

"Very well, my dear, if you insist." He smiled weakly. "I'll look like an old woman."

"No matter."

Jemma took his arm again and hurried him along.

Anna took one last look at his disappearing back, then strode resolutely out onto the gallery, where she stood straight and tall beside Lieutenant Nyborg. Her appearance was greeted by jeers.

Anna spoke quietly to the lieutenant. "He's gone. Left by the back way."

The lieutenant looked relieved. "Thank God! But you'd better look to your own safety, Mistress Heegaard. These are violent men!"

"They've no interest in me. They'll soon disperse." She held up her hand for silence. "Gentlemen. What do you want of the governor? I can speak for him."

"We want the gov'nor, not his bawd!" one of the men shouted.

"Let him stand forth if he's man enough!" came from another.

"Looks like he's hidin' b'hind his doxy's skirts!" still another suggested. This caused jeering laughter.

"He should welcome a visit from his friends, the nigger-lover," someone sneered.

"The governor's not here," Anna said in a loud, clear voice. "He left some time ago. Now, unless I can speak for him, pray begone and leave me in peace."

They didn't believe her.

"He's hidin' somewheres in there. His coach remains."

"The 'remains,' that is." There was more jeering laughter.

Several ruffians started to mount the stairs. Lieutenant Nyborg drew his side arms.

Anna spoke again. "Search the house if you'll not take my word. Surely two or three of you accompanied by the governor's adjutant can satisfy the rest. Now, if you'll excuse me. . ."

With head held high Anna descended the staircase, brushed past the men without deigning to look at them, and made her way through the mob. She walked unhesitantly toward the chapel. She paused by the chapel door, but turned from it and climbed the steps to the top of the watchtower where she could look out over the darkened town to the harbor. There she saw riding lights atop the masts of the American clipper ship.

A lively breeze chased scattered clouds across the sky. Stars were blotted out, then blinked on again. She waited. At last she heard the disgruntled mob ride off, followed soon after by Lieutenant Nyborg. The hoof beats of his horse died away in the darkness, and after that all was quiet at Bulow's Minde.

Anna watched the lights on the clipper ship for a long time. Finally, the riding lights were extinguished, and running lights were set in the peak and stern. The sails were raised, ghostly white wings spread against a now-threatening sky. Slowly the sails began to move. Then, a sudden squall overtook the ship, the sails dipped to the wind and the lights grew rapidly dim.

The squall that sent the clipper ship flying out into the open sea reached Bulow's Minde moments later. The rain wet Anna's hair, the black now amply streaked with gray. Slowly she

200

made her way down the steps and entered the lonely chapel. She knew deep in her heart that she would never see her governor-general again.

Chapter 21

BULOW'S MINDE. The name sounded as pleasing to her ears as it had years ago when she first heard it. The horse turned into the greathouse driveway, pulling her gig at a lively pace. She touched the shoulder of the young black who was driving for her. "Let the horse walk, Benji. It's hard up the hill and Ned, like some of the rest of us, isn't as young as he used to be."

"Yes'm, Missy Anna." Benji slowed the horse from a trot to a walk, and Anna settled back to savor a leisurely drive up the hill.

The day was almost spent. Shadows had deepened and grown large in the clefts of the surrounding hills. Above, clouds white and puffy, their lower edges etched in gold, swam in a pale blue sky. The golden light of late afternoon gave the Greathouse a sort of mystical glow that seemed to come from within. Her eyes, moving from the Greathouse, came to rest on her villa, which she now thought of more than ever as a haven to ease the difficult days ahead. For she had just visited Dr. Knudsen, and the news had not been good.

Benji glanced sideways at her. She was leaning against the back of the seat, obviously fatigued. He had noticed some weeks ago that the natural rose tints underlying her ivory skin had disappeared. Her skin was now the color of ashes long dead. "Are you well, Missy Anna?" he asked, much concerned.

"Not so well as I should like," Anna responded. "But I have some good days ahead of me. It's only three weeks till Christmas, Benji, and we'll celebrate as usual. We've had some fine Christmases over the years, Benji, and we'll make this a fine one, too. You like Christmas, don't you?"

"'Deed I do! Bes' day o' de year! Every person like Chris'mus, comin' to de Greathouse, dancin' an' singin', sugar cakes an sherry brandy."

It *was* a good day, Anna thought, a day when much that was unpleasant between master and servant was put aside. Even in the old slave days everyone enjoyed himself.

The drive swung around the side of the hill, then turned back on itself in a long graceful curve that rose gradually to turn once more in a grand sweep that ended at the bottom of the welcoming arms staircase. Benji drew the horse to a stop, tied him to a hitching post, and helped Anna down. She leaned heavily on his arm as he walked with her to the door of her villa.

Amanda, his mother, stepped out onto the gallery to meet them. "Missy Anna, come you in this very minute. It time you rest you'self. You plenty tired. I can tell."

It was true. She was tired, and she felt pain clutching her side beneath her ribs, but she wanted to climb the watchtower one more time—perhaps the last. "Amanda, I would like to climb the tower."

"Oh, Missy Anna!" Amanda looked stricken. She searched her mistress' face, hoping to see some sign of weakening purpose. But Anna's jaw was set with familiar firmness, and she looked back at Amanda with steadfast eyes. Seeing that her mistress was determined, Amanda said resignedly, "Then I go, too. We climb de tower togedder."

The progress along the front of the Greathouse to the base of the tower was slow. They reached the steps and took them one at a time, resting on each. At the top Anna leaned against the parapet, breathing heavily.

The air was bracing and uncommonly clear. To the north she could see the faint outline of Denmark's other West Indian possessions, the islands of St. Thomas and St. Johns. To the east she looked over the town of Christiansted to the town's harbor with Protestant Key set in its middle. Beyond was Gallows Bay, and on the far shore the ruins of old Fort Augusta.

"It was from here, Amanda, that I watched the estates burn at the time of the uprising," she mused, "Granard, Cane Garden, and the rest."

"A long time since, Missy. Ten year it be."

"It seems longer. Strange when the rest went so fast. Here, too," she added, "I always watched and waited to catch a first glimpse of a ship bringing Peter home . . . oh, so many times. He travelled a lot, you know—Europe, the United States."

"He de bes' mon dis island ever see," Amanda said. "The day

he die, all de people feel it. Our hearts grow heavy. We don' know why. Then some person say it, 'Massa Peter dead!' We know he speak true long 'fore word come from 'cross de sea. But Massa Peter, he live on in de hearts o' de people."

"I know, Amanda."

"Dey love you, too, Mistress."

"Do they?"

"'Deed they do! They know de part you play."

Anna was gazing out to sea. "There's a sail out there, now, Amanda, out beyond Long Reef."

"You' eye still good, Missy Anna. It a long way off."

"I wonder what ship . . ."

The women watched silently as the ship drew closer. It slipped behind Protestant Key, and the women waited for it to reappear.

The sun had almost left the sky. A few lights twinkled on in town. Then, slowly and majestically, just before the brief tropical twilight spent itself, the tall ship slid into view—first her long bowsprit, then her raked masts set with three rust-colored square sails. The ship rounded into the wind. The crew struck her sails, and she glided on into the harbor. "The *Vigilant*," Anna said. "There's none other like her. The shape of her hull, the set and color of her sails . . . and her rigging. I'd know her anywhere."

As she had promised Benji, Christmas was celebrated just as it had been for the past few years. It had become a Bulow's Minde tradition, one she had established after Peter left. People who had once called Bulow's Minde home came up from town to celebrate. They came decked in bright colors, the most glaring they could find. Some, who had prospered in their newfound state, even had gold coins hanging on their costumes. Anna welcomed them graciously into the Greathouse, opened especially for the occasion. This year she rested in a comfortable chair. With a brave smile on her lips she watched them dance around the reception hall, bowing and curtseying to her as they passed to show their love and respect. Her toe tapped to the rhythm of drum and cymbal.

At sundown she was forced to retreat to her villa, exhausted and in pain. Before she left she wished her friends a good night and instructed Benji to bring out the Christmas cakes and sherry brandy.

Now, a week later, she lay on her bed, the room in semi-darkness. She had asked Amanda to close the jalousies, shutting out the sun, intense at midday even in winter. Somehow the half-light seemed to ease the pain. By her bedside her small French clock, the one Peter had brought her from Paris, ticked off the seconds. She turned from side to side, trying to find a position that lessened her discomfort. It was of little use. The discomfort wouldn't go away. Finally, she drifted into a semi-conscious state in which images floated through her mind all in a jumble, unrelated and making little sense. Faces came and went, some near and dear—Peter, her mother. Others were strange to her or barely recognized. She was puzzled as to why they should intrude, now, as she lay dying.

Anna had stubbornly resisted her illness as long as possible. For more than a year after Dr. Knudsen confirmed the diagnosis of cancer, she insisted on rising in the morning and dressing as usual. She moved slowly around her rooms and took short walks in the garden.

None of the original household staff was left. When Jemma, the last to leave, married and settled in town near her brother, Amanda and Benji, now twenty-two, moved up from the village to look after Anna. Amanda brought her her meals and gave her her medicine— morphine Anna supposed—at proper intervals. It dulled the cutting edge of the pain.

The days following Christmas were hard, the pain growing ever more intense. She had been unable to take any solid food for the last three of these days. Yesterday for the first time she had truly wished for death. Her strength was gone, her body wasted. She hoped with some impatience that it would soon be over and done with.

She had never before wanted to die. Saddened as she was by Peter's departure, she found much that was worth living for. There were rewards to be had from working in her flower garden. She took pleasure in small things: a bird's song, a special sunset, the visit of a friend. She still had a deep interest in island affairs. The slaves were free men and women, the goal she and Peter had long striven for. And she found it good.

True, the first year of adjustment had been difficult for everyone. For a while the ex-slaves thought freedom meant not to work at all, liberty to do as they pleased. When they realized the planters couldn't continue to feed and house them without work being done in return, they settled down and in most cases were working as hard as before. However, there was a subtle difference. The meager wage they earned gave them a sense of dignity. A new light shone in their eyes and they carried their heads a mite higher. Now they were for hire, not bought or sold at someone else's whim.

She was lonely, of course. Sometimes she stood in her usual place on the watchtower staring out to sea. She knew in her heart her Peter wouldn't—couldn't—return to her, yet watching for him was a long-established habit. And ships did bring news. In September, the September after his departure, an important letter came from the Danish government addressed to Governor Oxholm and the Colonial Council, officially affirming emancipation. This letter was a source of satisfaction to Anna, though she thought with some bitterness of the cost it had been to them personally.

In letters from Peter, Anna learned that his health had not improved—quite the contrary. He wrote also of the humiliation he suffered at the hands of the Legal Commission investigating his behavior in handling the slave uprising. It pronounced him guilty of exceeding his authority and stripped him of his title, "Former Governor-General of the Danish West Indies." But he went on to say that in spite of his ill health, he intended to appeal the decision and take it to the highest court in the land.

Meanwhile he was suffering from lack of funds and begged Anna to sell his personal possesssions at Bulow's Minde and send him the proceeds. This she did and was able to send him 3000 rigsdaler.

A year later he sent a letter bearing good news. He said the high court had unanimously and officially declared that: "Former Governor-General Peter von Scholten was free of all blame in the uprising on St. Croix and had not exceeded his authority in acceding to the slaves' demands."

He added that he was living quietly, since his health was poor, on his country estate near Copenhagen. He sent his undying devotion. She tried to picture him in this setting. Did his Danish estate resemble Bulow's Minde? He never spoke of his wife. What of her? Did she still live?

1853 brought recompense to the planters for the loss of their slaves, though they thought, and rightly so, it amounted to only about half of the slaves' actual worth. They grumbled a lot but were secretly glad to have received anything. Rumors of irreconcilable differences between abolitionists and slave owners in the United States that some said would lead to civil war made them feel it had all gone better in the Virgin Islands.

After the summer of 1853 Anna heard nothing from Peter. Her letters were unanswered. She feared the worst, and her fears were confirmed in May of 1854 when news reached the island, three months after the event, that Peter had died while staying with his daughter near Hamburg on January 26th. He was buried without fanfare in the Copenhagen city cemetery.

When the news spread throughout the island a few callers came to offer Anna their condolences. Major Frederik came over from Frederiksted to spend a few days. Major Gyllich and Samuel Rothe stopped by. Several members of the Colonial Council came to call. These men, though they had not approved of the "Freedom Proclamation" at first, now agreed that its reading and implementation had been the only rightful course for the governor to take.

After Peter's death Anna decided to cut her responsibilities. It had become increasingly difficult for her to manage all those rolling acres of cane. On the advice of her attorney, and with a much simplified life as her objective, she sold the estate, buying back only the Greathouse, her villa, and enough land to keep a few cows, goats and chickens. Benji cared for these and for her vegetable garden. The proceeds from the sale, plus her considerable savings, were enough to support her in reasonable comfort.

During the years she lived alone, Sunday was the high point of her week. Then visitors came. Her niece Agnes, Christine's daughter, often brought along her son Benoni. Benoni was to live to tell his great-grandson of his visits to Bulow's Minde, of the impression it had made on him as a boy.

Agnes' sister, Susannah, who married Dr. Knudsen, on occasion brought Great-Aunt Lucia and Great-Grandmother Amalie Bernard to call. Amalie Bernard was so small and dried up that seeing her Anna thought she would sail like a seed pod, if a good strong sea breeze came along. When Anna bent to kiss her, the old lady's black eyes sparked withpleasure.

"When I see yo', me chile, me heart beat happy," she said.

"Me, too, Oma. It always pleasures me to have you here."

"Yo' chose de right mon in dat Peter von Scholten. He set de people free."

"But the planters were too strong, Oma. They destroyed him."

"Be dat as may be, he work live on."

Amalie Bernard lived until 1856. She was then 103 years old.

Johannes Wittrog, now nearing thirty, was a great comfort to Anna. He was studying medicine and talked of going to Denmark for further education. For the present he lived with his mother at nearby Aldershville. He was devoted to his aunt. It was to him, not long after his father's death in 1851—he was still wearing the black band of mourning—that Anna confided her final wishes.

"Lay me beside your father, Johannes. You know I've always been inordinately fond of him. I'd like a marble slab similar to his to mark my grave. Bulow's Minde will go to the girls, and it's hard to say what their husbands will elect to do with it. If your Uncle Peter were here, it'd be different. Then I'd hope we could lie side by side. Did you know that in Danish Aldershville means Old Age and Repose? I like that."

"Nanan, don't speak of your death! I can't bear it! You are well and strong. You've many years . . . much time yet to spend with us."

Anna patted his hand and smiled at him affectionately. "Of course, Johannes. Of course." Eight years had passed since then.

Amanda heard Anna moan softly. She entered the darkened room, straightened the sheet, and smoothed the pillow under Anna's head. "A taste o'chicken soup, Mistress? It giv' yo' strength."

The gnawing pain in her abdomen, like a savage beast seeking to devour her from within, made the thought of food an anathema. "A sip of water, perhaps. That's . . . that's all. Amanda, look at the clock. What does it say?"

"It be ten pas' t'ree, Mistress. Time for you' medicine. I fetch it with de water."

Seeing her mistress' pain-ridden face, Amanda felt a towering rage at fate, providence, or whatever, well up within her. How could a benevolent God let such a one as Missy Anna suffer so hideously? It shouldn't be, she told herself. It just shouldn't be!

Eased by the morphine, Anna's thoughts drifted pleasantly back to her childhood. What a carefree, joyous time it had been in Eigtved's garden! How she loved to play there, tease the lobsters and great green sea turtles in the holding pond, race around the big old silk cotton tree with the boy, No-no! She held onto No-no's impish face as long as she could. It melted into the face of Buddhoe, his gold earring twinkling on one ear. It was the night she first met him at La Grange, his face amused as he offered her his hand to climb down from the farm wagon, a country woman with blackened face in rude clothes. His amused face in turn altered to that of a stern-faced Buddhoe riding on his white stallion through the crowd around Frederiksted Fort.

What finally became of him? she wondered. She knew that without the staunch support of Major Gyllich he undoubtedly would have been shot along with nine other leaders of the rebellion. He was arrested by the militia in the major's home. But the major would not allow him to be taken alone. He insisted on riding with him to jail in Christiansted Fort. There the major shared his cell for several days to be certain he would in no way be harmed before given a proper trial. He went personally to a meeting of the Colonial Council to plead Buddhoe's cause, trying to convince the members that without Buddhoe's sane and persuasive leadership the planters would have lost lives as well as property. He pointed out that from "Freedom Day" on Buddhoe had continually ridden around the island in his company trying to convince rioters to desist and go home.

Buddhoe was interrogated over a period of weeks. His inquisitors tried to get him to say that he and the governor had conspired together. But he refused to implicate the governor in any way. Finally he was formally tried and given a relatively mild sentence: he was simply banished from the island.

The major and other friends provided him with clothing and money to start life anew. He left aboard the same ship that had played a part in the uprising, the *Ornen*. She was bound for Port o' Spain in Trinidad. Later, rumor reached the island that proud Buddhoe's new clothes and money had been taken from him and divided among the crew. In Trinidad he was put ashore penniless. Beyond this, Anna knew nothing.

She drifted off into a drugged sleep. When she woke again the pain was almost unbearable. She tried to endure unprotesting, but she couldn't prevent the tears that forced their way out from under her eyelids or stifle the low moans that escaped her lips. Her breathing was difficult.

Presently, though her eyes were closed and her mind fogged over with pain, she was aware of footsteps other than Amanda's, then low voices. She opened her eyes and saw Anna Maria and Johannes standing by her bedside with long, stricken faces.

She attempted a smile. "Dear ones . . . it will soon be over. It can't go on much longer. If I have sinned, God, I think, has . . . has punished me enough."

"Dearest Nanan, don't believe He is punishing you!" Johannes cried. "We have little understanding of His ways. But punishing you, He is not. You an angel on earth! If He could take away the pain, He would."

"And He will, Johannes, soon . . . very soon." The tiny smile she had managed lingered on her lips. "Hold my hand, Anna Maria," she murmured. "Please hold my hand."

With a sob Anna Maria sank to her knees by the bed, clasping Anna's long, slender hand in hers, the hand that had reached out to help her in her hour of labor. It felt remakably cool for so warm a day.

"Johannes."

"Yes, Nanan."

"Open the jalousies a little. I'd like a glimpse of the sky."

Johannes quickly obeyed. The sky glowed with the pale golden hue of ripe mangoes. A thrushee sitting on the limb of a flamboyant tree nearby began to sing his evening song, a long, drawn-out trill punctuated by twitters and chirpings.

Johannes turned back toward the bed. Anna's eyes were closed. She looked more peaceful now. He searched his mother's face questioningly.

"She's drifted off into a deep sleep," Anna Maria said.

They remained paiently by her bedside. But for more than an hour Anna did not stir. Finally, she gave a little shudder, her head moved fitfully from side to side, her eyelids fluttered and flew open. Then she lay still.

Anna Maria touched her forehead. "I think . . . yes I think she's left us, Johannes. Thank God her suffering is over! Call Amanda, my dear!"

When Amanda came hurrying in a few moments later she bent over Anna listening for breath, then laid her hand on Anna's chest to feel for a heartbeat. Slowly straightening up she said nothing but gently closed her mistress' eyes. It was New Year's Day, 1859.

Amanda stayed on for a while at Bulow's Minde even after the Knudsens rented it to Governor Feddersen. It was she who first told the tale, one that became a persistent legend on the island, that on moonlit nights a lovely ghost, female in form, draped in white floating garments, could be seen wandering about Bulow's Minde, hovering near the chapel, leaning against the parapets of the watchtower, or descending the staircase. Was it Anna's spirit come back to haunt the place she'd loved, waiting perhaps for her adored governor-general to return to her?

*　　*　　*

As the schooner moved away from the shore, Benoni, standing on the wharf, waved his hat. "Come back again," he yelled.

Hannah stood by the rail of the ship. "I will," she called. "I certainly will!"

Duty called, and she was on her way home to Philadelphia. But she was leaving with more than the slight tanning of her skin by the tropical sun. In her trunk lay a large bundle of papers with her small, precise handwriting covering every page. The bundle was tied together with a lavender ribbon. In between the third and fourth pages lay a pressed sprig of jasmine from the garden at Bulow's Minde.